THE CONSPIRACY

GUY ARMSTRONG,
GROUSEMATE
AUSTRALIASTRONG AND
GRABYABUM
'ARRASSMENTSTRONG
PRESENT...

THE CONSPIRACY

THE GREATEST STORY EVER
RANTED - NOW A MAJOR
MOTION BOOK

Gwumpy McBalmybong, Grabyabum
'Arrassmentstrong
The Nameless Publisher

CONTENTS

CONTENTS

AUTHOR'S NOTE
I would like to thank all the people who helped me in writing this masterpiece, especially my mother for letting me use her computer when she could have been doing something constructive with it.

I would like to dedicate this book to my bank balance.

And to anyone who, for whatever reason, is unable to unleash their inner idiot into the world.

And also to my ass.

GUY ARMSTRONG, GROUSEMATE AUSTRALIASTRONG AND GRABYABUM 'ARRASSMENTSTRONG PRESENT...

CONTENTS

CHAPTER

1

THE BIT WHERE...

THE BIT WHERE WORDSWORTH'S MOTHER IS SLIGHTLY DEAD AND MARK DOESN'T CARE THE WEENIEST PARTICLE, IN FACT, IF YOU WANT ME TO BE REALLY HONEST AND PRECISE ABOUT IT, IT'S THE BIT WHERE WORDSWORTH'S MOTHER IS SLIGHTLY DEAD AND WORDSWORTH HAS A CONSPIRACY AND MARK DOESN'T REALLY CARE THAT WORDSWORTH'S MOTHER IS DEAD BECAUSE HE'S THE BAD GUYE WITH ALL HIS CONSPIRACIES AND HE DESERVES HAVING HIS MOTHER SLIGHTLY DEAD BECAUSE HER SON'S THE BAD GUYE

"- think you're the main character of this book do you?" he inquired of Wordsworth. "Well you're not. You're the bad guye. And I'm going to push you out of your bad guye castle and do wee wees in the moat of that very same castle." "Because you've got a conspiracy" Andrew accused, poking with a smelly finger. "And you'll be pushed into the moat of your castle and my pet fish will eat you for a healthy breakfast, full of kelp and spinach." Wordsworth put his bikini on. The table. "My castle doesn't have a mote so nyeh nyeh nyeh" he said. Then he said "I don't have a conspiracy." "Yes he does" Andrew whispered conspirationalistically to Mark and Johnny. "I've seen it. I saw him playing with it in the boys' toilets." "Aha!" Johnny shouted gleefully, his smile the focal point of his entire tongue. It was even more beautiful than his back hair or his facial and bum warts. Wordsworth turned bright red at Andrew's claim of detection - he didn't like having other people see him play with his conspiracy. It was a private act of sad abducention, and he didn't like hearing talk of such confidential matters when in the company of others, particularly the friends whom he hated. They just didn't understand. "So you've seen it!" Johnny cried, marvelling at Andrew's evasive behaviour. "What does it look like?" "Well it wasn't very big" Andrew said, and all took part in the abrasion of Wordsworth's ears with their grinding laughter. "I'm not a grown man yet" Wordsworth complained. "I'm only forty-nine and three quarters point seven three two nine eight one one four, of course that's only to eight decimal places so not perfectly accurate." He felt victimised by the other three, chained to the wall of inferiority, and he had never considered himself able to rip away from the manacles of lesser worth and be their equal; only the poor git whom they tricked and played games on behind his back and right in front of, and oh, oh how passionately he hated their victorising of his victimism. "So it's pretty small, is it?" Johnny asked Wordsworth. "It's big enough." "So he does have a conspiracy" Mark inferred. "Well I'm going to shove that ski trophy of yours into your brain, then." Mark thought that was fair enough. If Wordsworth had some form of conspirational activity or stratagem taking place behind his friend's backs, or in the boys' toilets, he deserved having his ski trophy shoved into his brain. Johnny picked up the ski trophy, holding it high, so all could see. "Not very big, is it?" Mark and Andrew laughed at this, for they judged Wordsworth's phallic endowagement on this ski trophy, which was fair enough too, as he was always showing it off (his ski trophy I mean). Mark recalled shamefully the time Wordsworth had ran through the entire school making a big display of his winnings, as if such a device could replicate the high-spirited joys it had given him through his abdication - it was the only thing he had ever won, and the only thing he had to be proud of. He had bragged of it and no-one had heard nor seen hide nor hair of any other, as Wordsworth exploited his ski trophy as though it were some funny stuff or a bouncy thing that went boing boing boing. "Leave that alone please" Wordsworth begged, torn open by the knife of Johnny's torment and thrust into the vile throes of Andrew's desperation after walking through the fiery toast with bits of buttery swamp on it of Mark's abusally abusive abuse. He recalled his women's assertiveness class. "You have absolutely no right to touch what is mine. Please remove your hands from that. It's mine. I won that last year, you know." Johnny dropped the ski trophy to waist height, not letting go of it. He looked sarcastically sad. "Oh that's a shame" he said. "Better luck next time." "But I won." "I know. Just don't go crying about it. You're taking it very well. Maybe you'll win this year." Wordsworth didn't know what to think. He wondered if it was some kind of conspiracy. "What is this, some kind of conspiracy?" he asked in his best nineteen forties gangster voice. "I won it, okay? I didn't lose, I won." Mark looked at his friend reproachfully. Then he turned to Wordsworth. "There's no need to go rubbing it in our faces like that though, is there? Surely Johnny's encouragement and sympathy deserve better receivement than the receivement of abuse? Bragging on about how you won it. Johnny just wished you luck for next time. If anyone's got a conspiracy here it's you." "I don't have a conspiracy you bastard!" Wordsworth yelled. "But Andrew said he's seen it" Johnny explained gently. "What the hell kind of friend are you, anyway?" "A friend with a conspiracy?" Mark suggested. "Too damn right." "He probably hates us" Andrew said. "I do, I hate all of you, and I wish that I could never see any of you again for my whole life, or at least the rest of the book" Wordsworth said. "I hate all of you so passionately. I wish you would all die. I can't stand the sight of you. You make me sick." "What kind of friend are you?" "I'm not your friend you bastard!" Johnny moved over to Wordsdickydickworth. "Nooooooooooooooo!" shrieked Worrdswowrth as Almighty Guye Armstronge spelled his name wrong and Johnny jabbed him with a fire poker and ripped up his fifth edition Shivan Dragon. "That's what you get for being the bad guye, you bad guye" said Johnny and smashed Wordsworth's testicles in a garlic crusher. Then Guye Armstrong, who had just changed his name to Genius Aristotlestrong appeared, and peace came upon the earth. A dove flew by, and pooed on Wordsweeweeworth's head, and a bit went in his mouth.

"Our mother is dying you heartless bastard" Wordsworth told his brother when Johnny and Andrew were gone to run in the meadow and frolic in the tall grass. "Well I don't care a weeny particle" Mark said, poking his tongue out and licking Darren's skinny buttocks. Wordsworth began to begin to cry. "Don't you even care a weeny particle?" he had asked when they had both gone to bed. "No I don't care a weeny particle. The weeniest particle in the universe could not emulate my level of caring." "Care not a particle of ween, you?" "Nay, care I not a particle of finest and most splendid wcen; even ween made of solid gold I would uncare unfor. Now get out of my bed." Wordsworth had clambered reluctantly from Mark's bed where it was hot and steamy and there was a massive party with roller skating and disco lights and heaps of guys in tight pants, and into his own eiderdowned encampment of slumber. He dozed, and he dozed, his alarm set for the night's mission of utmost importance, praying that Mark was asleep. And suddenly, hours later, he was awake again, for Johnny and Andrew were vaccinating the room with their tough presence. "We're vaccinating the room with our tough presence" they said, squirting their tough presence into every nook and cranny the room had, until tough presence lay cast all over. One required a pair of rubber-textured footwear to not pollute one's leggage with the tough presence. "Get out of your bed, you naughty little boy" Johnny had commanded Wordsworth. "Yeah" Andrew had said. "We heard your alarm" Johnny said. "It woke me up." "But it hasn't dinged its little bell yet." "Well it's not a very good alarm then, is it. It was playing its whoopee cushion way too loudly. I couldn't hear myself being quiet." "That's because you were being too quiet to hear yourself be quiet while yourself was listening to you be quiet while you weren't quiet when you were quietly quiet" Wordsworth explained with a witchey-poo cackle and skinny dipped in the cauldron of slimy brimstone that he kept in bed with him and cuddled up to when he was lonely. Johnny manhandled him out of his bedding, and grabbed him by the sickle dangling collar of his bikini which he had put back on before the start of this sentence. "Me to smart be you don't" he

said cruelly. "I think I better teach you a lesson for being smart."
But Wordsworth was not scared, for he was not joking. "I warn you,
I'm not joking" he joked and he clearly as a joke wasn't joking.
Just as a joke. "Are you joking?" Mark asked him. "No I'm not.
Anyway, you should be on my side. Don't you care about her?"
Mark shuffled his feet uncomfortably, getting a bit of Johnny's
tough presence stuck to lefty. "Yes I care about her" he said. "I just
think we should wait until the doctor calls." Wordsworth glared
at him. "Traitor." "Don't you call my friend a traitor you selfish
bastard" Johnny told him. Johnny and Mark stood in front of the
window Wordsworth wanted to climb from. His and Mark's room
was on the fourth story up, and no students were allowed out until
the following weekend. Wordsworth had decided to risk a trip to
the hospital to check on his mother who was slightly dead. He
figured that the doctor in charge of her was a silly sausage, and
he was going to tell him who was boss, and squeeze his nipples,
and poke his belly button and smack his bum-bum. "You've got to
trust people, Wordsworth" Johnny continued, adopting a nice-guy
attitude that was obviously fake. "That bastard's got a conspiracy"
he whispered to Mark. "We can't trust him." "Are you guys gonna
move away from that damn window?" Wordsworth asked. "Or am
I gonna finish this sentence with a question mark?" "What's ya
question, Mark?" said Andrew, who secretly felt that his character
had not been portrayed very dramatically this far into my awesome
book. But he dared not complain lest he incur the vicious pain of
oblivion, via the mighty delete button. "I'll fiddle with his computer to distract him and you shove that ski trophy that he's always bragging about into his brain" Johnny said to Mark via Soviet
morse code message system that they had bought off the Turks
for a llama and a roll of duct tape. "Right." People got what they

deserved was Mark's motto. Johnny walked over to Wordsworth's computer and began punching it. "Alright I won't go" Wordsworth said, choking back a few tears. "I just think it's really unfair that you won't let me visit my mother-" "She's Mark's mother too, you know" Johnny interrupted. "You don't always have to be so selfish." He kept on hitting Wordsworth's computer. "You can stop hitting my computer now. I'm not going." "I'm doing this for fun" Johnny said. "I want everyone to know I'm badass. You just wait till I reset Windows to a really annoying configuration with an invalid URL and put it on a much inferior graphical user interface version 0.9 which keeps on giving those stupid options to send or not send error reports." Mark and Wordsworth tried to get Johnny out of their room and into the room he shared with Andrew but he didn't really want to go. He wanted to keep on being silly and make the page even more awesome than it was, which was just about impossible if you ask me. Wordsworth was very sad at the prospect of not visiting his mother, and he brooded about it while Johnny talked about himself and Mark read his bibble. "Come on Wordsworth" Johnny said after a few minutes. "What have you got to worry about? She's dead, right? You can't cure her." "She's only slightly dead." "No, she's dead. You can't cure dead people." "She's only *slightly* dead" Wordsworth said again. "Your mother is dead, Wordsworth" he began. "Mark has learned to accept this, haven't you Mark?" Mark smiled. "Sure have, Wordy" he said. "Because I'm a Chrysanthemum. And Chrysanthemummity's all about accepting stuff with love." "That's right" Johnny continued. "Your mother is not slightly dead. She is completely and utterly dead. That is why she does not move, talk, or breathe. She just lies there." "Well she's tired." "And she never eats anything." "She's on a diet." "And her skin's all crusty and black." "She's quite old, you know."

And she doesn't talk." "She's lost her voice." "And the doctor can't find a pulse." "The doctor's a dick." "You're a very obstinate little bastard, you know? Why the hell would you want to visit someone who's slightly dead?" "She's only slightly dead?" Mark asked, looking up from his bibble. "So there is hope after all?" "I thought she was completely dead" Wordsworth said. "No, you thought she was slightly dead" Johnny told him. "You need to listen. I said she was dead, because she probably is. I've had enough of this 'slightly dead' rubbish." "What do you mean, she probably is?" Wordsworth asked urgently, grabbing Johnny by the ensatiniac notochordialically vitelline tumefacian zykcumbofcigumsorax and trying to shake him roughly, but he only had a strength of five and failed his saving throw roll. "I thought she was completely dead" Mark said while he twirled his winkle. "Well I don't know" Johnny said, feeling rather exasperated by the brothers ridiculous 'slightly dead' nonsense; "she's either dead or she's not dead." "Well which one?" Wordsworth asked. "Well how should I know?" "Well you seem to know so much about her." "I do not. I'm no doctor. She's probably alive, actually." "So why don't we go and visit her then?" "Because she's probably just faking it. And it's the middle of the damn night." "How can she fake being alive?" "How can she fake being slightly dead?" "Who said anything about faking being slightly dead?" "You did." "No I didn't. I said she *was* slightly dead." "Well that's a pretty pessimistic attitude isn't it? She is your mother, you know. A negative attitude isn't going to get her out of her slight deadness." "I never said anything about faking stuff" Wordsworth said guiltily. "I know, that was me. I think she's been faking her whole deadness just to get attention." That's someone else saying that bit. "So if she's only faking it to get attention, why don't we go and visit her?" "Why visit her if she's dead?" They didn't go and visit Wordsworth and Mark's mother because she was still dead, but only slightly dead, according to Wordsworth. Instead they went to bed in their separate rooms, Johnny to be kept awake by Andrew's continual innocent masturbation over the thought of kissing Wordsworth, who would be kept awake by the paranoia he had developed over his dead mother, and his refusal to admit that she was dead, and the bitter ocean of denial in which his life, bereft of happiness or love, a vast chasm of emotional nothingness, a freezing chilled fiery pain, was floating. And the fact that he liked to masturbate as well.

Johnny wanted to buy a house. He had spoken to the housing and real estate man before and he was surprised at how much they cost. "Well most of our houses are pretty expensive" the housing man had told him. " . . . . around the dollar and seventy-four cents mark." "I'm not mark I'm Johnny" said Johnny. The housing man did his talky bit again: ". . . . arm around the dollar and seventy-four cents mark, Johnny." Johnny was so surprised that he ate his pubic hair. "I've only got . . . oh let me see . . ." he opened his bank book, and was shocked. "I've only got a dollar and seventy-four cents." "Well that is a shame" the housing man said. "You might have to look for something cheaper . . . around the dollar and seventy-four cents mark." Johnny thought it over. He didn't like the idea of spending only a dollar and seventy-fore cents on some crappy house - he wanted a nice place, although he couldn't really afford a whole dollar and seventy-for cents with which to buy a nicer house. "Do you think I could get a loan from the bank?" he asked the housing man. "I don't know" the housing man said. "Banks are pretty selfish when it comes to loans. How much were you wanting to borrow?" Johnny thought about it. He didn't want to be preposterously extreme in his loan - he did want to pay all of it back eventually, yet he didn't want to borrow some pathetic amount so that he'd end up with not a very nice house at all. "About a dollar and seventy-4 cents" he said. The housing man grimaced. "I don't think any bank would let you borrow that amount Johnny" he said with a shake of his beautiful head that Johnny had kissed many a time. "Don't you have any really nice houses that are going for really cheap prices?" Johnny asked. "Well these are our bargain deals that I reserve for our favourite customers. Have a look at some of these." And from a secret compartment in the wall Johnny saw him obtain folders three, which he laid gently upon the desk in front of Johnny. Johnny began to eyes and ears and mouth and nose his way through them. Then he headed, shouldered kneed and towed his pick-up truck through them, or words to that effect. Ee hee hee wizz bang. He came across a beautiful house in the country, which suited his needs perfectly. "This one, my little sugar puff" he yelled without need of exclamation mark, bashing the photo as if it were Wordsworth. "That one's a dollar and 7ty-four cents" the housing man said. "Oh goodness me no" Johnny remarked arrogantly, flicking the page aside. His finger laid upon a picture of another house, a small, quaint house with a lovely backdrop of flowers and greenery. "This is the one for me, matey" he remarked ecstatically. "Well then" the housing man said, getting up and putting a big old smile on his face. "I'll just get my dancing pants on and we'll have a look at it." Johnny was so excited that he did a fart, in fact it was the first fart in the whole book, and Johnny felt it appropriate that it should be his bum that gave it birth. After all, he is the main character. Thunderous applause rocked the stadium where the book was set, for it was a rather thunderous fart. Its succulent gas reached the epitome of musty cheesy rank gastric aroma, and Johnny was well proud of his sphincter powered methane driven gale force anal burpage. "Well there it is" the housing man said to Johnny pointing at the photo of the house. "I want it, I want it" Johnny exclaimed all happy as Larry that he was finally getting his house, and dancing around to his George Michael and Wham reunion tape. "Ooooh I'm going to put my Peter Andre poster in the hallway and my Justin Timberlake poster in the kitchen and my New Kids On The Block signed album on the roof." He was the happiest person in this part of the book. "Here you go then" said the housing man, tearing into the photo album and giving the picture to Johnny. Then that bit of the book finished really suddenly.

Johnny was an incredibly arrogant young man who really believed he was some form of God, or at least a demigod. This belief was reinforced by the fact that everything in his life went his way, and according to his PLAN, or, as he liked to call it when he was feeling technical, his CONSPIRACY. He had what every teenage boy could ever want - he was getting incredibly high marks in school (except in English, but that didn't matter, he could already speak it), his father was very rich and always on holiday, his mother stayed the hell out of his social life, and he was rather popular with the ladies. Once he even spoke to one. Johnny wasn't going to grow up and become a lawyer or other high-earning professional - he was going to be a writer, and every day after his final class he would kick Wordsworth off his computer and write his novel. His own novel that is, not Wordsworth's. It was a very good novel. A brilliant novel. It would of course sell millions of copies and he would get rich and belch smug abrasive laughter at Mr. Woodcock who had always told him that he would never amount to anything. Johnny's novel was called *102 Things To Do With A Necrophiliac* - a daring and emotional title, and yet controversial enough to kick up a fuss and make a big name for himself so he could get on Oprah and into her funky jammy-as minorities only book club. Johnny's book was better than any other book that had been written because unlike other *101 Things To Do With . . .* books his had 102 things to do. He would of course write it under a pseudonym (a word he flashed around whenever he could - when he bragged of becoming a writer and his friends whom he hated were pestering him about his pseudonym, he would simply throw back his head and laugh bwah ha ha ha haaaaa) to avoid all those annoying interviews - at least for a while. His pseudonym was Gwen Dibley. It was a good 'country boy' -ish sort of pseudonym - a simpleton's name, if one liked. It would be obvious by the name he had chosen that he didn't want to be pestered, and that he wrote practically and sensibly, for the joy of writing, purely for the love and respect of his divine art. And for the drugs, money and loose women; totally the stacks and hoes bro. He would clearly take the publishing market by storm, and his would become one of the hottest new books of the century. All of the fashionable people would buy it, and there would be whole parties with all of the greatest stars in the rich and famous business entirely indebted to Johnny and his great novel. "Well I found Number Six rather interesting" They would say to each other over wine and ball bearings and other rich person food. "Yes, but you have to admit the whole concept of the book is utterly riveting, my dear - I never would have thought of doing one hundred and *two* things with a necrophiliac." And Mr. Long Forgotten, writer of the hit *101 Things To Do With A Necrophiliac* (From which Johnny had plagiarised rather relentlessly) would be rejected publically and socially and turn to drugs for solace, go into rehab and commit suicide in a home for the elderly a few years after Johnny's publication was out, as he had realised that there really was no future for him. Johnny planned to send his manuscript in near the end of his eighteenth year - he was sixteen at the moment, right now, right absolutely *now*, no . . . hang on . . . *now*; and so he would have almost five and a quarter years to perfect it, and five minutes and a month from . . . . . oh missed it. Then! Back then or whatever. He was deadly sure that as soon as the publisher saw it, he would go absolutely crazy. "I've gone absolutely crazy" He would say to his secretary. "Quick get your clothes on. We'll publish this one. This is simply the best book I've ever seen. It's got a hundred and *two* things to do with a necrophiliac. And I'd even been considering giving up necrophilia." And Johnny would become a rising star, and be commissioned millions of dollars to write more and more books, that would each sell millions. He had already started:

102 Things To Do With A Necrophiliac
By Gwen Dibley. Not Johnny.

1. *Take your necrophiliac out to a movie. A good movie, preferably, unless you want him/her to stop seeing you.*

Johnny couldn't sleep. He wondered that night about many things as he lay awake listening to Andrew playing with his genitals and reading his filthy magazines with a torch under his eiderdown. After a while it became annoying and frustrating, not to mention painful. "Andrew, would you stop playing with my genitals and put my filthy magazines away and get out of my bed?" Johnny asked him, not really expecting anything. Andrew didn't stop until Johnny picked him up by his toenail and threw him across the room to his own bed, and told him to shut the hell up. "Shut the hell up" he commanded in his gruffest Mary Poppins voice. "But I can't sleep" Andrew complained. "Go to sleep or I'll shove Wordsworth's ski trophy into your brain you selfish git with a conspiracy" Johnny threatened. Wordsworth had a rather humble attitude to his ski trophy - he never showed it off as Johnny would have, and he preferred not to talk about it with others. It was a rather chunky piece, about half a foot tall, with a goldish coating on it, which had faded in a few places. The likeness was superb, and many commented on it. But no-one commented on it. It was shaped like a skier in mid-turn, the parallel skis jutting out from beneath it gracefully. Johnny felt ashamed and cheated that it had not been he who had won the ski trophy - he was, after all a lot better than Wordsworth, who seemed to think that skiing was about skiing and not impressing girls. Ha ha! Why would it have been called skiing if it was about skiing? That was just silly. He made a mental note to inform Wordsworth that he was a silly sausage and poke him with a chopstick and do a big mealy rolled oaty poo; yeah, a really big long muesli bar grogan in his cup of tea. Wordsworth's cup of tea I mean, not his own. Wordsworth's own I mean. I think. He longed passionately to ram his ski trophy into his stuck up head through his eye and laugh at him accusingly and say "Ha ha!" to him, just to show him who was boss, and who knew about stuff, and who had a bigger fistula, and we find ourselves on page sixteen, which is my favourite page in the book so far. Finely crafted, and aged to perfection, soaked in finest Kentucky bourbon for that smoky wood flavour, and just a bit spicy. Page sixteen sees the development of a number of storylines interacting in magnificent ways, and the personal development of some major characters. So back to the super exciting plot of the extra mega-lomaniacal suprematically powerful page seventeen, where, if you look really closely and spend a few years in libraries looking up the greats, you'll see that Andrew was the cause of Johnny's insomnia at the moment. "If you're not still and silent I'll ram Wordsworth's ski trophy into your head" Johnny told him, wielding a blazing white hot fiery toy glow in the dark car. I think I should put hyphens in that but I'm not totally sure. Oh well. But Andrew was not still and silent. Instead, he became aggressive and nasty, and called Johnny a funny thing. Johnny was taken aback by Andrew's nerve and his sheer lunacy at calling the main character a funny thing, but only for the briefest of nanoseconds. He recovered his composure reasonably instantly and barkedly barked "THaT'S ENouGh YOu NAuGHtY liTtLe bOy!" aT Andrew, who cowered in fright and fear at the accusation of being a naughty little boy, and blubbered senselessly, flustered by an overactive shift key, while the rest of the sentence was perfect, oh, so perfect, yay its perfection was salivated upon, glorified, and it had a hat with heaps of tropical fruit in it, and a V8 engine, yes it was such a loved sentence, and its merriment flowed and flowered upon a queath of exasperating exasp. He lay on the floor a quivering mess, although only for a minute or two or nine years. "I'll never

do

it again" he promised quickly, with some literary freestyle on the Tab key, space bar and return button in the midst of his sentence. "You're not the only one who's groovin' enough to be the main character." But it was too late, for Johnny had harked upon the entitiousness within his friend whom he loved whom he hated and was leaving for Wordsworth's room to thieve his precious ski trophy from him sneakily and drive it mightily into

Andrew's throbbing eyeball. "Don't drive it into me, please" pleaded Andrew's throbbing eyeball, for it was a sneaky one, and it planned on wresting the ski trophy from Johnny, but Johnny had left the desecrated temple of Andrew's carnal desire and blah blah blah

THE NEXT BIT:

Johnny was not the only one with trouble sleeping. Wordsworth and Mark, who lived across the hall, were still awake, and Mark had had enough of his brother's tomfoolery. "I've had enough of all your tomfoolery, Wordsworth" he said. That was what gave him away. "What's wrong with my tomfoolery?" Wordsworth asked. Tomfoolery was a sensitive nerve ending of a topic, and one's confidence could easily be bruised by the uncultured remarks of another. "Nothing at all" Mark assured his brother quickly, as if trying to wipe the doubt from his face and desensitize Wordsworth's tomfoolery with mere verbal patterns. "It's great tomfoolery. It's lovely. It's so much nicer than Johnny's. But I'm full." He pushed the plate to one side. "Are you sure?" Wordsworth asked him. "It's great tomfoolery." Wordsworth shovelled spoonful after heaped spoonful of steaming tomfoolery down toward the emptiness of his gullet. "No, I can't have any more" Mark said. "You can finish mine." It was at that moment that Johnny burst through the doorway into their room, and saw them sharing tomfoolery. Mark stood aghast, as he could fully predict the eventuality that was about to encircle and entwine his life with its wicked eventualnessisticallitiousnessallyism. Johnny stood aghast also, and he was absolutely still as his mind processed what was happening. He pulled his trousers down. Then he stood on his head. He pulled his teeth and gnashed his hair. Then his ear got really big and lit a ciggy. "You're eating another woman's tomfoolery" he accused Mark, who backed away, flustered easily by accusations and interrogations. "I . . . I . . . It just happened . . . it's not nice tomfoolery like yours . . . it doesn't mean anything . . ." But it was to no avail. None at all. Oh okay, maybe a bit of a veil. "You nasty liar" Johnny accused, slapping his bum with a fish slice (he slapped Mark's bum too). "You tell me mine is nicer than Wordsworth's, but you tell him his is nicer than mine. You're a nasty liar." "Yours is much nicer, I promise" Mark lied again, laying blanket upon blanket of lies upon the sleeping virgin of his existence, clouding and betraying the sweet catholic innocence of his life. "But you're lying again, Mark" Johnny accused. "You said Wordsworth's was nicer than mine. And don't bother lying to me, I've read the manuscript of this book." Mark was shocked. "Yes, I even know what happens at the end, ha ha, because I'm friends with General Armystrong and I hang out at his mansion playing pool and talking crap. Anyway, now that I've found you with another man's tomfoolery I'm going to seek vengeance upon thee" he said with a laugh and a tongue and some seriously swinging epiglotic apendagery. He reached forward to grab Mark, the evil betrayer, the traitorous gigolo, the filthsome male succubus of perverted passion to kidnap him and stuff him in a rubbish sack and into the boot of his automobile where he could finally have a game of strip tic tac toe with Mark, this page's girl next door, and make him say that only Johnny's authentic tomfoolery was the best. But before he could, Wordsworth spoke up. "You stay away from her" he told Johnny staunchly. "She'll be eating my tomfoolery from now on." He rose from his plastic Play School seat and guarded his brother, sticking his chest out into Johnny's presence. "And then we'll get married. Even though we're brother and sister. I don't care. I love her." "Well that's disgusting" Johnny accused. "And you deserve to be punished." He grabbed Wordsworth's ski trophy and shoved it into his brain. Then he shoved it into Wordsworth's brain. The infliction of Johnny's violent and savage strappado caused him great pain. Wordsworth asked God why he had been given such a nuisance of a friend, when he himself was such a good boy. "Because you're the bad guy" God said. "Without an E. And you never worship me. Now get down and kiss my black female women's rights hindu ass." Something something something description of what it did, and a whitish pus sprayed from it, and blood began to pour down the left side of his face as if it was water. And I couldn't be bothered starting that sentence properly. But that's just how us niggaz write in the hood, bitch. "Nyeeeaaaarrrgh!" Wordsworth yelled, and brought his hands up to his face, but they stopped just before they touched the protruding trophy. He wanted them to remove it, but they seemed to have a mind of their own - they of course knew that such an action would cause far too much pain, so they tensed up in front of his face. Leaving him in intense pain. It seemed ridiculous. He hoped that this was some kind of dream, or a typing error (it wasn't). The pain was incredible. He could not bring himself to do anything about it and yet he wanted so desperately for it to end. Thinking it was still just a game, Mark grabbed his younger brother and hugged him lovingly, pushing the ski trophy even further into his eye, and mushing his nose into his cheek. He was smiling, beginning to understand that it was all just one of Wordsworth's little melodramas necessary for him to get through puberty. Wordsworth really let his vocal cords go this time, and uttered a scream so loud that even Johnny who was right next to him could almost hear it. "Oh look" Mark said soothingly, "you're laughing so hard you're crying." "I'm not" Wordsworth sobbed. I'm not, I'm not, you bastard. I'm crying so hard I'm laughing." He sobbed and laughed for a few seconds. Mark began to panic, not because of the intensity of the situation, but because he's a whining little cissy bitch and secretly a fag. He worried but steeled himself so he could get Johnny to come and be the dominant male. Johnny would know what to do. "I wouldn't know what to do!" Johnny yelled stupidly from behind Wordsworth, scaring him so suddenly that he shied away, and drove his ski trophy even further into his brain and mushed his nose up even more when he bumped into Mark's mantelpiece and crushed his souvenir plate mail armor on the tea cozy with retractable quad mounted nematocystical paren-chyma. "I think this is all getting a bit silly" Mark said, adopting a staunch pose and hiking his tight black bogan white trash designer jeans up to his forehead. "You just settle down now young man" he said, taking his tongue out of Wordsworth's ear. Then Johnny dropped an anvil on Wordsworth's head. "Now that's pretty cliché" said Wordsworth, who headbutted himself in the elbow then ate his own leg hairs that had been soaking in astronauts magic happy brine from the spacesuit of a thousand farts. Then he cut off his own head and stuck it back on with Mark's Vaseline. "That's not my Vaseline" said Mark. "That's poos." Wordsworth looked dis-heartened and made a sad face. He felt like he didn't even belong in the book. "And it's only page twenty-one" he said. "What's in store for me for the rest of the book? I hope it's happy stuff." Then he banged his belly button on a fire hydrant and got his willy stuck in a revolving door. Johnny and Mark laughed even harder at this, but to Wordsworth it wasn't all that funny. His sobbing had grown loud and harsh by this time, and he was feeling very sick. His stomach felt as if it was about to bring up his tomfoolery and his eye was racked with pain. If one looked close enough, one could see his whole face had mutated into a grimace of pain with a ski trophy poking precariously out of the left eye. UNDER 16'S MT PARAPHRENIAC CARYOPSIS SKI FIELD: JUNIOR SKI TRIALS it read, WORSWORTH JOHNSON, SILLIEST HAT 1991. Andrew was looking at Wordsworth with a sort of suspicious glare, and when faced with something as weird as a ski trophy poking ridiculously from his friend's eye, he could only deduce that Wordsworth needed a hug. "Need a hug, do you Wordsworth?" he asked. Wordsworth didn't say anything. He just lay sobbing on the floor, clutching his poor head, while Johnny and Mark were laughing. "What's so funny?" Andrew asked. "Did you get the ski trophy?" He asked Johnny. "Wordsworth got the ski trophy" Johnny brayed at him, which made Mark laugh more; "laugh laugh" he laughed. The hilarity of the situation reminded Johnny of the time Wordsworth had murdered his cat. Then Wordsworth got up and ran from the room, but oh no! He had forgotten to take his willy out of the revolving door, and did a big faceplant.

A few minutes later Andrew was not having fun. "I'm not having fun" he said. That was how I figured it out. I can reed as well as right. "Your dad's a wakko!" Johnny yelled at him. Andrew began to pull his hair. Then he pulled his own hair. He waved his author-itittyive and pudgy index finger impolitely in Johnny's face. "You bastard" he almost pleaded. "You filthy heartless bastard. I love my dad. He's no wakko. You *bastard*." "Yes he is" Johnny said. "Nobody buys his food so he screams abuse at them. I can't think of a better definition of a wakko. You're probably a wakko too." "You *bastard*" Andrew insisted, and began to froth at the mouth. He pulled a considerable chunk of his hair out and rubbed it all over his face as he growled at Johnny. "Let's calm down boys" Mark said. "I don't mind taking you outside for fifteen minutes of breathing exercises to help us reach our inner selves and eat raw vegetables and calm down." But Andrew wasn't listening to Mark's new-age stuff. His breathing became deep and noisy, and he panted with his teeth stuck firmly together and his lips pulled far back toward his throat. Spittle flew from his mouth. "I am not a wakko!" he shrieked madly at Johnny and squeezed his groin until his knuckles went white. "Let go of my groin" Johnny said. "My knuckles are going white." Mark decided he was clearly a wakko. Andrew, I mean. He thought Johnny was alright. Yeah, a bit of alright for he was secretly gay and had a big girly crush on Johnny and wrote his name flowery style all over his pencil case with his twink pen.

And now on to Wordsworth, who could not believe the pain he was feeling - he had never experienced in his entire life such horror, and the decadence of his situation took him to a new level of suffering. He ran down the halls toward the main office, where he was sure the office ladies who hated him would be nice and would call him an ambulance or poke pain killers down his throat until he suffered no more. But alas! He was ambushed by a group of wandering internet nerds who prostituted him out to foreign businessmen for about ten years in return for really hard drugs like earl grey tea and marmite. He arrived at the office walking slightly funny, with blood staining his ornate clothing, the energy used to motivate himself dissipated, and with a silly hat on his head. The ski trophy interred its bounds of pain into his young body, forcing him to whimper and gnash his jaw, and even though he had tried so many times to remove such an awful protuberance from his skull, such an action was simply not possible. His arms would not obey even the slightest of his desires, disparaging his self-confidence even more every second. The office ladies were not there. A large man in his mid-twenties sat instead in the school office. He was eating potato chips at a disgustingly voracious rate, crumbs spilling down over his face. "PHONE OPERATOR" his T-shirt said. "Wow, a talking T-shirt" thought Wordsworth. He ran jerkily toward the man, and leant over through the booth. "I need an ambulance" he gasped. "I need to use the phone." "What's your name?" the man asked him indifferently, not looking up, continuing the potation of chip after crunchy chip. Wordsworth paused. He thought about the question. He wondered what the hell kind of inanely stupid question that was. Here he was, with a ski trophy sticking out of his head, calling up the emergency services, and the man there had asked him his *name?* For all this man knew there could have been a mass murder or a mad gunman or a bomb or a fire or an old lady who'd lost her hearing aid or drunk people doing karaoke, and he wanted to know Wordsworth's goddam *NAME?* Things like this made Wordsworth (who was normally a very calm, placid young man) cringe with embarrassment at the thought that he was even of the same species as people such as this inconsiderate man. This sort of apathy ate away at his sensibility till there was nothing left of it and his anger took jurisdiction over his mind and made him listen to his Jeremy Jordan records at full bore while he did the dance moves in sync in front of his mirror with his cap on backwards like a badass rebel. *How could people be so careless?* He would think when confronted with a situation such as this one. He didn't understand how some of the humans around these days didn't seem to care about things - "we only get one shot at life" he'd say and ask who he was talking to why they didn't react, why they didn't get emotional over humane things, why couldn't they *feel* life the way he could? He felt this same anger building within him the second after the telephone operator had asked him the question, the stupid *stupid* question, there could be lives at stake here and this loser wanted to know his *NAME?* Wordsworth was going to vent his hostility for such idiocy at this cretin and tell him what he should be asking. Wordsworth was going to tell him off, kick his ass, and throw him out. "My name's Wordsworth" he said. "Wordsworth Johnson." "Wordsworth, eh? Wordsworth . . . Wordsworth . . . What's your favourite colour, Wordsworth?" "Ski trophy imitation gold" "And who's your favourite singer?" "Gwen Dibley and The Fanatics" The man looked at him sternly. "So can I use the phone?" Wordsworth asked him. "I'm very badly injured." "I don't care" the man said. "Do you think I care? Well I don't. Anyway, all you teenagers think you're so funny poking ski trophies out of your brains all the time. You're just juvenile. One day one of you is going to get hurt." He kept on shovelling chips into his mouth gerundly at an alarming speed, the crumbs spreading to the lap of his pants which I'm not going to say anything about or all the women in the over-forties demographic reading this will get all hot and bothered. "I *am* hurt" Wordsworth pleaded. "That's exactly what I said. One day one of you is going to get hurt. Now look. You're hurt." "Please help me. I'm hurt." "You're not hurt. You're probably just faking it. You're just crying wolf." "I'm not faking it wolf wolf" cried Wordsworth. "I'm really hurt and I'd appreciate your help." "But I don't want to give you my help. I just want to eat my chips and abuse you." "Don't you care about other people?" "No. Don't *you* care about other people? That's what you should have said. It wasn't very caring of you to walk up to me while I'm eating my chips and looking after this place. There could be an emergency." "There *is* an emergency" Wordsworth said through his tears, hoping an italicised 'is' would get him off the hook. "I've got a ski trophy sticking out of my brain." "That's not an emergency.

You're just showing off. You're just doing it so that I'll ask you out. Anyway, if it was an emergency, I don't care." "Why not?" "Well why should I?" "Because . . . it's good to care." "Why? I think it's good for me to eat my chips." "But don't you care about other people?" "Why should I? They don't care about me." "I'm sure someone cares about you, like your mum or niacin tablets or toe fungus or someone." The man's bottom lip quivered as he turned to Wordsworth with a sad story. "Nobody cares about me. Nobody ever did care about me. I've been a loner all my life and all I ever did while I was a kid was eat chips and get laughed at because I was such a fatty and when I went to high school I never had a girlfriend and all the other teenagers despised me because I didn't fit in because all I ever did was eat chips and get laughed at and I was the most unpopular student in the whole school and so I was never invited to any trendy parties and I didn't have a date for the senior prom and then I got pregnant to a man who didn't love me and then my family was killed in a freak accident with one of the Pet Shop Boys and a silver plated tomato and I'm so fat I can't see my willy anymore and I've got a back hair diorama that says "kick me" so people keep kicking me and I don't have a rewarding job and my only dream in life is to be a Vanilla Ice impersonator doing eighties parties but I ate so many chips on the way to the job interview that I grew breasts and they wouldn't hire me because they thought I was a woman and now I've been on the Sally Jessy show thirty times in the past five minutes and I tried to kill myself but I'm so fat that when I stood on the chair to put the noose around my neck it broke the rafters and the house crashed so I tried to jump off a really high building but I couldn't fit in the lift because I'm so fat so I tried to kill myself by OD-ing on heroin but I got hooked on it and then I caught AIDS by sharing needles then I had unprotected sex then I got busted with heroin trafficking then I tried to kill myself by taking heaps of pharmaceuticals but I just got fatter so I tried to kill myself by slitting my wrists but even they were too fat so I tried to gas myself to death in my garage with my car but I didn't know how and I just blew up my house and my neighbours on both sides houses so now I'm a killer so I tried to jump off a cliff because I couldn't deal with the guilt but I just bounced right back up because I'm so fat so I tried to kill myself in a car accident but I just killed a whole lot of other people so now I'm super-duper guilt ridden and pregnant and I've got AIDS and I'm overweight and I'm a murderer and then my dog died then my cat died then my horse died then my canary died then my mouse died then my pet cow got a boil on its udder and when I squoze it some pus went in my eye and I had to get a windscreen wiper surgically fitted to my eyeball to get rid of the goo but it irritated my forehead so I got forehead cancer and I had to get my forehead removed then I was so depressed and suicidal that I failed school and my life is crap and no-one's ever showed me how to set my farts on fire, suck them back up my botty and spontaneously combust while I cast level twenty Sunfire doing 15d6 hit points damage to all enemies within a twenty foot radius barring fire salamanders, djinns, efreetis and fire elementals, both lesser and greater, which is my dream in life. Oh, my life is more tragic and painful and emotionally wrenching than watching David Campese's score against the All Blacks in Ireland in 1991. And I so wanted to be the main character of this book but I'm only on a couple of pages. And then you have the nerve to come in here wearing spotty clown pants." He began to cry. "And then you say I should care about other people when they've never cared about me. If they cared about me they wouldn't let me eat all these unhealthy chips all the time." A massive dump truck came crashing in through the office wall and poured a huge tonne of chips into his mouth through his tears. "I care about you, really I do" Wordsworth urged. He understood how the man felt at being rejected from social gatherings as a young one, and a great bond of empathy seemed to connect them. From their bumholes. "If you cared about me you'd take these chips right away from me. That's what you'd do if you cared about me." Wordsworth hesitated. Suddenly a cement mixer appeared through the hole in the wall and sent a huge blob of chips and dip into the man's mouth. Then Sally Struthers and heaps of people from *Save the Children* and *World Vision* turned up and vomited chips into his mouth. "Take the chips away, Wordsworth, please!" the man begged, grovelling on his knees as he mainlined some extra hot 'n' spicy salsa dip into a vein in his arm and ate entire packets whole without chewing or even using a bib. Wordsworth wondered if this was just some form of abusive game. But he took the chips right away from the man, with a great swipe. "Now you've taken my chips away from me you bastard!" the man cried, wringing his fists at Wordsworth passionately. Oh, yay it was so passionate, so intense, such passions didst flow, as their eyes met. "I paid a dollar and seventy-four cents for those chips!" "Here, have them back!" Wordsworth yelled, throwing the chips at him; guilt, confusion and his next line in the greatest literary marathon cliffhanger suspense thriller ever written spasming its way through his mind. But it was too late, for the man had broken down and was weeping and crying his legs off. "Have a nice day!" Wordsworth shouted to him, which just showed what a one-dimensional character he was, as it was night time. And it's like totally the cheesiest thing in the world to say. Like was he at a McDonald's or what? Like totally. So Wordsworth had to run to the hospital and use their phone to totally phone them totally, like, you know?

Wordsworth awoke in a hospital bed opposite from his father, although he wouldn't know this till much later - there were curtains (nice and happy orange curtains) pulled around his bed. He reached for the caller which would alert the nice nurses and pushed the little button. A minute or so later, a nurse walked in with a doctor. They stood in silence for a second, and then both brayed idiotic laughter at him. "What-" he began, and then realised that the ski trophy was still in his head. "Get this stupid ski trophy out of my head you bastard!" He screamed at the doctor. "I can't do that" the doctor said. "I'm not meant to be in this novel. I just wanted to see what all the fuss and controversy and great reviews are all about." The nurse did half a backflip and said "did this novel get into Oprah's book club?" "No" the doctor said because he was really up on the play. "It's a bit too serious." "I don't care." (That's what Wordsworth said, for all you who skim read like my old buddy Adrian oh where fore art thou). "Well I do. I'll get someone who is in the novel for you if you like." (That's what the doctor said) "Thanks." (That's Wordsworth again saying that bit). The nurse and the doctor left with ridiculous grins on their faces after getting Wordsworth's autograph and being politely ushered from the page by the ever clean shaven and smartly dressed Grimey Armpitpong, who didn't have body odour from staying in his room playing video games his entire life and a few minutes later a young doctor walked in. "GARY", his name badge said. "Wow, a talking name badge" said Wordsworth, reusing a joke that was a really funny one and super original and only ever used by the one and only mighty beautiful sexy genius Grappling Attachmentstrong who was really cool and radical, dude, totally, and whose books appealed to many generations and marketing demographics, and when a prospective publisher read his book they always gave him a massive advance and published it even if they didn't like it. "Yeah" said the doctor with flippant casual arrogance. "Grotty Analthong had it specially made and flown in just for this page." "Hi Gary" Wordsworth said. Gary looked at Wordsworth. Then he looked behind him. "Who's Gary?" He asked. "What is this, a conspiracy?" "I thought you were Gary." "Oh no. No no no. I'm not Gary. No no." "Could you fix up my nose and remove this ski trophy for me and put on a silly hat?" So the doctor did, and the pain was unbearable.

Johnny, Andrew and Mark didn't bother going to visit Wordsworth while he was in hospital because they totally didn't care about him at all bae, and when he arrived back at school two days later wearing an eyepatch they took him more seriously. Which was good because he was a rather serious person. "You look like a pirate" Johnny commented to him one sunny Autumn day, while they were rolling around without clothes in the long grass, discovering each other, exploring each other, laughing and playing, growing mentally and physically past the avenues of their innocence and learning of desire. "Arrr, me hearties" Wordsworth joked, but it wasn't funny. It was so n't funny that Johnny punched his friend who he hated in the eye patch with all his calf muscle hair and the transmembrane protein of a cell of leydig. "You just overdo everything, Wordsworth you little kissy doll" he had complained, slapping Wordsworth, but holding him so tight, and not letting go, ever, never, as they gazed off into the sunset and their eyes and farts met in joyous pungent aromaticity. In the elevator. "This book is supposed to achieve a distinct balance between the humorous and the overdone" Johnny said as he fired up a bunsen burner to roast Wordsworth's willy marshmallow. "It is not here for you to pillage and inject with your bad jokes and corny resuscitations of catch phrases that be worth not even a dollar and cents four and seventy. It is required by publicatory standards to reach no further than the jokes that were already plastered so superbly on the pages of yon illustrious tome. We have no need for your filth." And Wordsworth hung his head in shame, for he knew that what he had said was going to marr the success of the Almighty Greateye Arrrrrstronge by not being politically correct, for it was degrading to pirates. The ski trophy and all the other objects in Mark and Wordsworth's room that weren't too big for someone to pick up and throw found their way over to Wordsworth's side of the room as he became paranoid of further antagonism and attacks from the out of control Johnny. Hey I just discovered a cool button that makes this funny thing:

¥¨☐˜˙ßπ©∂…¬µµˇˇ¨Ô„‰¨Ôµ∫©ƒ†¨˚´∂ß≈Ωœå∑®¥¨84¡£∞§¶·‚°‡ flfi›‹Î◊Ç¨Ó^¨ÂÁfiÏ^

The four friends who hated each other had a largely uneventful time for the next four or so days - Andrew played with his army privates, Mark read his bibble, Johnny bragged about stuff, and Wordsworth worked on his story. Wordsworth liked writing stories, especially ones with a little "twist" to them. He had not shown anyone his work, and he didn't plan to, as his stories were sometimes rather strange and gruesome. Just a hobby, really. He wasn't a struggling *artiste* who lived in some crappy flat with a bunch of bogans that got stoned all the time and left the knives on and never did the dishes and kept getting bugged for rides all the time because he was the only one who had a car, until he didn't have

it any more and then *he* was the one who had to bug everyone
for rides like Almighty Greatdiamond Arcturusstrong, the most
distinguished in all the written world and master of the sci-fi/
fantasy/self-help genre. In other words he was just a little bitch.
It was a few days later that the four of them were visiting Mark
and Wordsworth's father in hospital, who was very sick. Mark and
Wordsworth's father was in a very bad situation. He was dying of
Cancer. Cancer of the face. The doctors were trying their hardest
to get it out without causing too much damage to the rest of him,
but as far as Wordsworth could tell, he would be better off if they
just left him alone - they had already removed a nostril, an ear, an
eye, a bit of lip, a bowl of porridge, a platypus and two fingers. The
fingers, the doctors explained, were for good luck. "How's it good
luck if he's still dying?" Wordsworth had asked one of the doctors.
The doctor glared at him but didn't say anything. "Don't you worry
about me sonny jim bro mate cobber bloke not arf or wot guv me
ole mugger" his father would cough out occasionally. Sometimes
he would also cough it in. These humble father and son moments
would bring tears to Wordsworth's eyes. Had Wordsworth been
less overwhelmed with grief he would have seen the situation
with more clarity and he would have thought that perhaps there
was some form of conspiracy blim-blom-bliracy going on at the
hospital - he was a skeptical one after all. God only knew what sort
of thing was happening in that place. But he wasn't about to tell
anyone. Back when Wordsworth was two years old his mother had
gone in for treatment. Fourteen years later, she had still not been
cured. Her skinny body lay there on the bed in ward one hundred
and seventy-four, silent as death, black with age. Not an ounce
of blood pulsed through her veins. Her skin hugged her bones
so that Wordsworth could see her skeleton. She reminded him of

something out of a horror movie. He was unsure of his views upon whether or not she was dead - logic told him that a body that had not moved in fourteen years could not in any way be alive, and he just had to look at her still form to realize this, and yet his emotions told him that death itself was an impossibility - it only occurred in the lives and loved ones of other people, and, of course, other people had no feelings, Wordsworth knew. No-one else existed. They simply weren't there. Only Wordsworth existed. He was an intensely passionate teenager whose emotions drove him to joyousness and hatred consistently, and others noticed this, and fed it with their abuse. He over reacted to the smallest and most trivial of things - death threats, physical abuse, nuclear testing, genocide, world wars, racism, oartism, competitions, pile-drivers, megalomaniacal despots, oppressive regimes and battery chicken farming with a dejected feeling that just ate him up. He also hated losing at scrabble. No other person could possibly understand what he was going through, no other person could have such a connection with another, no-one could *feel* what he felt, no-one could crumble psychologically as he could, no-one *thought* – *he* was the centre of everything, and none other felt such agonizing and horrible loss. What a little bitch drama queen, right? I promise I'll kill him off. And in a really cool way like a big pine tree falling on his willy or an elephant blowing him to bits with an uzi and then jumping up and down all over his cissy punk ass and mashing his bloody heap of guts and rotten intes-tinal offerings into the carpet and then a shark eats his nipples and poos them into Mark's ear for dinner and Johnny gets a letter sent home to Mom and Pop for making the carpet dirty with Wordsworth's filthsome carcass that he just left there. It'll totally kick ass. However, despite all their sympathy, Werpyderpyworth grew to loathe the doctors, who continually assured him that she was only "slightly dead" and would be better as soon as they had cured whatever it was that she had been so ruthlessly afflicted with. He blamed himself for her death, and the guilt sliced its way through him violently like a blade scouring a body of its life every time he went to see if the doctors had cured her and brought her out of the "slightly dead" state that she was in. During his night-mares, he, powerfully, would, dramatically, emphatically, superbly, envision adverbly that she had crept up to his bed, with a ghastly smile upon her once beautiful face telling him that he had better not get involved in any conspiracies, and that it was his own evil and malicious conspiracies that had killed her in the first place fourteen years ago, and led savagely to her untimely demise. Then she would ask him for a dollar and seventy-four cents - she had saved up the rest to pay for her cure, and all she needed was a dollar and seventy-four cents, just a dollar and seventy-four cents, that was all, it was a pretty pitiful amount really, all she needed, surely a strapping college-boy of a young man like him would have a dollar and seventy-four cents with which to save his mother . . . and in the dream Wordsworth would fumble in his pockets, and not find anything . . . excepts a turkey . . . clad in finest silk. "Get your hands off my finest silk" the turkey would say to him, and strut off arrogantly, with a twitch of class in its hips. "I paid a dollar and seventy-four cents for this finest silk." And Wordsworth would awake screaming of conspiracies and finest silk, and Johnny would bang on his clavicle with some plastic spouting and tell him to shut the hell up. It was on a Friday that Wordsworth first heard the news about his father. One of the school's "Office ladies" had brought him and Mark a note saying that there was some good news of their father and they had the rest of the "day" off and could go and see him in hosdibull. He and Mark decided to go down immediately and Johnny and Andrew chose to accompany them so they could get some time off school, and the rigors of not doing their homowork. Wordsworth went off to visit his mother with the vague hope that she would still be alive. Unfortunately, she was still slightly dead, but the doctors had finally found out how to cure her, and they would contact him later on. So off he went to meet his friends with his father. "I've got some good news about my cancer" his father said. The four boys had been astonished and interested and excited and hopeful and victorious and surprised and bored and pissed off all at once, and had been instantly optimistic. "Ya - boo sucks to you!" they all yelled at him in unison, throwing tomatoes and rotten eggs this way and that. "They're removing my face" Mr. Johnson said. Wordsworth felt his chest sink. "Why are they doing that?" "To get rid of the Cancer." "Well when are they doing it?" "Tonight at nine after Seinfeld." "That's just brilliant" Mark said. "Isn't it, Wordsworth?" Wordsworth was shocked. "Can I have it, please?" Andrew asked. "It'd make a really great thing to scare people with." "Sure Andrew. I'd do anything for you, you little cuddle-pie that's just oh-so inviting" Mr. Johnson said. Then a doctor walked in, and told Wordsworth to leave. "What are you removing his face with?" Johnny asked the doctor. "My new Dibleyator 2000 Facial Removal Kit" the doctor said. "It really gets rid of that stress, you know? And unlike other Facial Removal systems it folds up to fit nicely under the bed or in a cupboard or a secret compartment or under a ski trophy. And now I have much better organisms. And I've got really great abs. In just three minutes a day. Call within the next ten minutes to receive a free knife that can cut through some stuff like a pillow and a tyre." It was then that Wordsworth's father noticed his eye patch. "Why are you wearing an eye patch, Wordsworth?" He asked. "Are you playing pirate-man? The only superhero with Hardcore Pegleg Attack and the Giggling Scimitar, plus one damage versus landlubbers?" And Wordsworth told him the story of the ski trophy, and at the end of it, all were mopping up the tears they had stained the floor with. "That was a beautiful story, Wordsworth. So beautiful." The doctor spoke up. "We're performing an operation in here young lady, so you'll just have to find someone else to pester. We can do without your type trying to get hitched with one of us sexy handsome well-paid doctors. This isn't *Melrose Place*, you know. This book's about a conspiracy. Let's not get sidetracked with relationships." The doctor was a fast, hurried man who I hired to make the book more dynamic and macho. He didn't listen to other people. "But I'm not a young lady" Wordsworth said to his claim of feminism. "Oh of course" the doctor remarked sarcastically. "You're a man trapped in a woman's body. Don't give me that rubbish." And he and Wordsworth's father shared a knowing laugh that knew. "I know" the laugh said. "But why do I have to go now?" Wordsworth asked. "It's only four-seventeen." "Because we're preparing" the doctor explained. "You wouldn't want us to make a mistake, would you, and remove his pancreas as well, would you, eh, would you, eh, eh, eh, would you, eh, eh, would you, would you, eh, would you? No of course you wouldn't. So give your father a kiss, a fighting kiss, a soft yet angry kiss, a kiss so severe and passionate, a kiss that lingers for *years* afterwards . . . a man's kiss." The doctor put on his favourite operating pajamas, got his plastic *Toyworld* scalpel ready and spoke his next line in my multi-million ultra-high budget Hollywood blockbuster farty book. "I'll have my bimbo secretary with the call you tomorrow. Now get out." So Wordsworth got out. He and his friends mucked around the hospital until they realised that no matter what they did the nurses were too busy to notice them, so they went back to their dorm. Of course, what the doctor had said about Wordsworth's gender had left him confused. Having no parents living with him to teach him about the ways of boys and girls, he had learned all he had learned from watching other teenagers. It left him so confused, and he wondered if *girls* had a pee-pee and *boys* had a thingy, and if he was really a girl who *thought* she was a boy, and the butt of a big joke. So he was just a dumbass really, even though he was into Star Trek and played Magic and Runequest and went to sci-fi conventions, and had big mathsy conversations about uncertainty principles and quantum critical mass and oriental love balls with Mr. Woodcock, the boys maths teacher.

Mr. Woodcock was a borderline schizophrenic, whose life was in the state of being constantly worth living and not worth living at the same time. Twelve o'clock, to be precise. Ha ha! So we were at the bit where Johnny is holding the stash of money, drugs and naked people over the cliff and he says to Mark: "Don't move or I'll drop it into the shark, alligator, crocodile, camian, piranha, stone-fish, box jellyfish, electric eel, sea serpent, Janet Jackson album infested cup of tea. Oh yeah and I'll shoot you too." He raised the bazooka with egg popper attatchment to Mark's bum freckle. Mark looked into the cup of tea. "It looks like there's icthyosaurs in there too" he said noting sharp teeth and claws. "That's the Janet Jackson album" said Johnny. Mark poked at the thing, and it promptly bit his arm off and spat it out. "Told you so." Then all of a sudden Andrew and Wordsworth drove up around the side of the cliff precariously, their Ferrari horse and cart hybrid cybercar totally Macgyver styling it right on the edge of the precipice of the chasm of the drop of the cliff of the halfpipe of the tea saucer of the footpath. Wordsworth jumped out of the car with a madness and Andrew fell asleep at the wheel, cuddling his teddy and sucking what he thought was his thumb. Wordsworth ripped open his T - shirt to expose his long pendulous breasts that dangled to his knees, and his knipples made of gold. "Get away from the loot!" he yelled at Johnny and rugby tackled him into the cup of tea where Johnny was eaten and chopped up by the Janet Jackson album and all its evil bits and willies. "Noooooooooooo" screamed Johnny really melodramatically for it was no way for the main character to die at the end of the book but Wordsworth did his bad guye laugh - "nyah ha ha" and ran off with the loot and left Johnny for - hang on! That bit isn't supposed to go there! That doesn't happen till the end! Ooops! Actually I'll probably change that ending. "Nah, keep it, keep it, it's great" Wordsworth just told me. So I think I'll DEFINITELY change it now. We were up to Mr. Woodcock and him being completely mental. Weeeeeeee mental mental mental silly bum to a carrot cake. Mental mental boompittywoompitty mental. Me's glad me's not mental. So Mr. Woodcock is the boys maths teacher. The students made life hell for Mr. Woodcock, which was good and bad. It was good because it gave him another reason with which he could guiltishly justify the harshness and purposeful difficulty he inflicted upon them, and it was bad because he cared so much about what they thought of him. He was a very gifted man when it came to maths - he had a natural aptitude for figures and diagrams, yet he was a shocking teacher - instructing the younger generation in parts of the course in haphazard ways, moving from one subject to another each week - a week on quadratics, another on cosine, sine and tangent functions, a few days instructing them to learn some things on graphs, one millisecond on algebra, three weeks and a minute on fractions, ever confusing, and ever destructive to the students' comprehension of senior high school mathematics, and never giving them what was required for them to know to pass the relevant tests that ensued at the end of the school year. His enjoyment at watching the students cram an entire years' worth of mathematical study into a few weeks before their exams made him smile, and he contemplated their defeat with a venomous indifference and a shallowed innocence that hid his true feelings of frustration. He laughed as they wracked their hormonally - charged brains and struggled with polynomials, antiderivatives, calculus, rectal sphinctal propulsion, statistics, acoustic guitar levitation and begged him for advice, apologising strongly for all the times they had wronged him. Like when Johnny had set fire to his wheelchair and pushed him out the window into a truck full of cowpat, ripping off *Back to the Future* but way funnier and more originally. And the time Wordsworth and Andrew had catapulted a cow through the blackboard with a diagram on it that had taken Mr. Woodcock the entire lesson to draw. And this other time when Johnny found the ark of the covenant and opened it up and Mr. Woodcocks face melted without an apostrophe. Yeah, *that* one pissed him off. Mr. Woodcock could always justify his revenge. He laughed as he heard that no-one could go to Johnny's party as they were all studying for their mathy exams. Not even Johnny was at Johnny's party, he was in the library. He giggled with un-adulterated glee as he saw them cast dismal looks of failure across their ugly and conceitful faces that had been ravaged by acne, and did certainly not need the additional stress of mathing. He gloated and sniggered as he saw them holding their heads in their hands as they removed themselves from the examination rooms with whispers of conspiracies and unfairness, and he laughed hardest when he saw that their parents had, in fact, killed and eaten them for failing. He laughed and he laughed and he laughed. Once he laughed so hard that he did a poo in his pants. Not a sloppy poo, but a muesli bar look-a-like that he quickly flung out the window to disguise his explosion inducing humour triggered pooey bum bum. He liked the end of the year because the students were about to fail and the holidays were coming and he could spend some quality time at home doing something enjoyable and away from the job he hated. He could finish his two times tables. He had nearly figured out two times five. At the same time he loathed the end of the year, for it meant less time until the beginning of the next year and he would have to stay home bored for weeks on end waiting for something enjoyable to do - and that was the job that he loved. I told you he was mental. See how deep and rugged I make my characters? Yeah I know you love it, slut. Bend over and take it. Mr. Woodcock was a suspicious paranoid one and his mistrust grew and grew until it totally ruled him - he was forever suspicious and dubiously attempting to wheedle out a more sinister and cynical truth in any request asked of him, and determine its consequences and the nature of whomever had requisitioned him for any form of small favor. "Would you pass me a banana, please Mr. Woodcock?" Mr. Tracheotomy, a physical education teacher had asked him once during lunch time in the staff room. Mr. Woodcock didn't like Mr. Tracheotomy. He thought it was better for people in general to know what vitamins and minerals did for the human body than it was for them to know how to graph a trig function backwards in six dimensions and with one's left hand under the opposite leg while at the same time juggling a scientific calculator, a lifesize cardboard cutout of a McLaren F1 racing car and a cauldron in the shape of a bit of paper while you figure the zigglyboge unction metaphysicationalistically corfopronic parallelepiped up the Starship Enterprize's bum. He thought physical education and health and saving people's lives was important. He thought press ups had some form of interuniversal jurisdiction and superiority over sine curves. He thought it was better to know how to give CPR and start someone's heart than it was to know how to derive the base formula from a polynomial expansion while trajectoring the complement angles in a two-sided triangle. He thought it more appropriate that they understand their bodies, the maintenance required for standard longevity therein, and the knack of defeating sicknesses than understand a set of rigorously precise hyperbolic curves and their uncannily fascinating relation to Pythagoras' lingerie hypothemule algebimbazigwemar with the abstract conceptualizings of Socrates' equation to infinity. Mr. Woodcock suspected him of being part of a conspiracy. "And for what purpose, Mr. Tracheotomy, would you have assigned me to give unto your wholesome self such a fruitial form of matter, praytell? And in what way would the eventual downfall register with myself, hmm? Perchance you could instruct me in what beneficial circumstance that would manifest itself in my reality if I partake in this act you so request? Surely a physically enhanced specimen such as yourself would receive most enjoyment from the meandering of getting it on your own? And for what reason should I employ myself in such an action?" "Because I'll punch you in the face if you don't." That was another reason Mr. Woodcock didn't like Mr. Tracheotomy, and suspected him of being part of a conspiracy: he liked threatening Mr. Woodcock with physical abuse. "I'm gonna tell my mum on you" said Mr. Woodcock, as he poked his tongue out at his assailant, and wriggled it around like a boy playing guitar with his diddle in the shower. "Now gimme your lunch money or I'll

give you a Chinese burn" Mr. Tracheotomy threatened with a gloat
and an insane cackle, for he was really a witch and his coven were
about to meet at their clubhouse and dance around to Steps and S
Club 7. Sure enough, Mr. Tracheotomy had been given his banana,
and on that day he had strolled off not without casting a look back
over his muscular shoulders, and muttering something about Mr.
Woodcock's conspiracy.

The plot thins . . .

Mr. Tracheotomy felt that Mr. Woodcock was a prat, because
he felt it was more important to know stuff about maths more
than it was to know stuff about whether the Abflex was best or
just doing sit-ups. He suspected Mr. Woodcock of being part of a
conspiracy. He regarded his fellow estudiate with condescension
and arrogance, and he longed for the day when Mr. Woodcock
would wheel his way in front of a car and get killed, or fall out of
his wheeled chairlet and down the stairs and have a heart attack,
or choke on some high - cholesterol food, or perhaps even get Re-
petitive Strain Injury from using his failing big red pen so much,
all so Mr. Tracheotomy could either advise him to see a doctor or
laugh at him because he was about to die. He pictured, in his more
angered daydreams, the day Mr. Woodcock WOOD wheel his way
in front of a car and Mr. Tracheotomy could keep laughing at him
as he died and bringing him back to life so he could keep laughing
at him. "Those polynomials aren't much use to you now, are they?"
he would repeat again and again as he brought Mr. Woodcock back
to lifey life with the pumpy pump of his handy hands and the
airy air from his lungy lungs and laughed his laughy laugh. That
would teach his adversary to be part of a conspiracy. He would

breathe new life into a graceful Mr. Woodcock... and when their eyes met, locked together with passion... they knew, they would be... together... forever. "You don't think Woodcock's part of some . . . well . . ." Mr. Tracheotomy whispered once to Mr. Jenkins, head of the Colouring In Department and one of the chemistry teachers. "Some . . . er . . . conspiracy?" Mr. Jenkins clutched his test tube till it really hurt and the blood stopped and turned suddenly to face his friend, ignoring his Iodine. "What makes you say that?" He asked shrewdly. "Well he's always -" "Yes I know what you mean" Mr. Jenkins said. "I know exactly what you mean." "How? You interrupted me in mid-sentence? I didn't get to tell you what I mean." "Well I still know what you mean. I'm very clever, you know. Us chemistry types have far more brain cells than you physical education lot, you know." "So tell me what I mean then" Mr. Tracheotomy challenged. He was sick of being abused just because he knew about press ups and stretching instead of test tubes and chemicals and concoctions and compounds and crap. "Well he's always -" "Yes I know what I mean, you don't have to tell me, I know what I mean." The two had left each other after such nonsensical conversing, both suspecting the other of involvement in some form of conspiracy, and it was all Mr. Woodcock's fault. Everything that went wrong in the teacher's lives at school was Mr. Woodcock's fault, he was the one they picked on and to whom they grumbled when the coffee had melted and the Kenyan tea had run out, it was always he who had stolen the final biscuit from the inviting tin, and it was always he who set the students pestering complaints off with his ridiculous difficulty and tests that jumped evasively from subject to difficult subject. The other teachers and school staff laughed at him to his face and behind his back and on his left and upside down and would never cease their incessant guffawing at the fact that he knew all about the mathematics they had failed as children and regarded as intellectual and unnecessarily unfashionable. He was not popular as far as teachers went, which was saying something. He was almost as unpopular as an English teacher. Actually, Mr. Woodcock found arithmetic relatively easy - it simply oozed logic and simplicity to him. His job would have been exceedingly boring had he not manipulated the innocent students with his surprise tests and the ferocity with which he instructed. His blackboard was cluttered with his jagged, unreadable writings, that so many of the teenagers complained about, and no sooner had it been lain down it was wiped off with a piece of old tea towel, to make way for new embafflementisticism. He could not quite comprehend the apathy and slowness that the students learned what he showed them, not to mention the way some teachers taught their maths - reconstructing the same diagrams week after week, day after day, to younger ones who would not and could not absorb such logical yet intricate patterns into their mental systems and brain gloop. He rushed them through everything, not repeating himself as other teachers did and taking time with individuals, instead he hurried and abused them and annoyed their attempts to learn, writing equations upside down and back to front on the blackboard and cutting the blackboard into bits and making them eat it and yelling at them when they couldn't have eyes in their stomachs. He would always pull his wheelchair up on one wheel and do big jumps off their desks and if any girls in the class had ski-jump boobs he would totally do 540 Impossibles and Judo Madonnas off them. Sometimes he wrote the equations in Japanese, even though he didn't know how. His only problem was Johnny. And now it's time for the next bit.

"Is that Wordsworth Johnson?" "Where?" "Just there, the one with the small conspiracy." I don't know. I'm Wordsworth Johnson." "So you're Wordsworth Johnson, then." "Speaking." "Ah, good. Now it's about your father. We've got his face right here, and he's just dandy. Now do you want us to mail his face to that Andrew chappie then?" "Yes please." "All right. That's just fine. Your mother's in a bit of a fix though. We've been researching what she's got, and it's not Wordsworth's disease." Wordsworth breathed a sigh of relief at this. He did not want to be responsible for his mother's death. "So I didn't kill her." The doctor went on. Then he went off. "After months of science stuff, and forking out heaps of cash we discovered a cure for Wordsworth's disease, and so we gave it to your mother. And it didn't work. So she's still . . . you know . . . a bit dead. But don't you worry. She's just a *bit* dead. Just a little bit." "So why didn't this cure work?" Wordsworth asked. "Well it's your mother's fault. Firstly, she didn't tell us that it wasn't Wordsworth's disease. She showed all the symptoms of Wordsworth's disease, then goes and dies on us when we give her the damn cure. She's hardly a cooperative patient. Secondly, she wasted all of our cure. Now nobody else can get any. That's hardly fair is it? No, I don't think so. There's a lot of people suffering from Wordsworth's disease out there, and your mother's just being plain selfish. I thought she was our friend. Friendship's about sharing, you know. So obviously she was tricking us - maybe she's got some kind of conspiracy. But don't worry, we'll still cure her." "So what's she got now?" Wordsworth asked. He loved his mother very very much, and he would have swapped places with her if such power was under his command. But I won't let him near the keyboard to change the ever exciting plot of my super-selling mega-thriller spooky-suspense cliffhanger-legal thrill-er hyphenatey novel so he'll just have to keep suffering slowly nyah nyah like when I beat Phil and Aaron at Magic with my undead deck. "Well now we think she's got Anthony's disease. The symptoms are similar to those of Wordsworth's disease, and we're suing the old bag as soon as possible." Wordsworth was astounded at such harshness and cruelty coming from a doctor - a man who was trained to save lives, not sue them. "We're suing her for fooling all of the science people down here who worked on that cure - it cost us heaps of money, as I said before. We're suing the intestines out of her. And that cure thing used up lots of resources. And it used up a lot of our time - we could have been working on curing a really superior disease like Johnny's disease or Mark's disease, or Andrew's or even the uncommon cold for Goodness Sake. But no, your silly mother has to make us cure her silly inferior dweeby never-has-been-fashionable and never-will-be-fashionable Wordsworth's disease, then make us look like idiots when we find out that she doesn't have it at all. She's made a mockery out of the entire medical profession, and we're a bit sick of it. And she's been in the same bed for fourteen years - she's used up heaps of hospital space, you see. And she doesn't even eat the dinners that we cook for her. She hasn't eaten a thing in fourteen years. That's how selfish she is. It's a wonder she's still alive." Wordsworth was confused. "I thought she was dead." "Oh dude she is. She's totally dead, man, we're gonna get her. Because she tricked us. So that's why we're suing her. For heaps. A million at least. Put my kids through university. Whatever that is. Ha ha ha. Buy me a jacuzi. Whatever that is. Serve her right. Teach her what's cool in hospitals. Whatever *they* is. Now on a more positive front, your father's just dandy. Except for one thing - he's got cancer of the forearms, so we're going to remove them. We'll send them to that Andrew chappie. He seems like a nice guy. So that's that then." Wordsworth thought that the doctor was crazy so he stuck the phone up his bum. Totally crazy. "How can I get money to pay for a lawyer and court fees and all that?" he asked. "Become a hospital" the doctor said, and hung up. Then he hung ten.

Johnny smashed smashed smashed s!m!a!s!h!e!d Wordsworth in the nuts with a woman and a porpoise with a purpose. His purpose was to smash Wordsworth in the nuts. "Good thing you smashed me in the nuts and not in the testicles" said Wordsworth, grabbing a walnut from the bag of nuts and eating it. Then Johnny smashed him in the testicles and electrocuted his nipples with a dump truck battery, set his hair on fire and circumcised him. They were in a pub on the twelve and a three quarterth and a halfth and an atomth floor of their alcove in the stairway to heaven. No they weren't. Yes they were. No, but *really* they were in maths class. Ha ha, what did you think of that ginormous plot twist eh? Did it surprise you and sneak its cunning little way past your defenses? Mr. Woodcock, the boys legless maths teacher sat atop his wheeled throne, the king of the pimpled ones, morose, mighty, grand. Nah, just joking, he was pretty lame. His nappies flapped in the breeze and made strange coughing noises. He gazed over the scumbag students whom he hated; fed, and preyed on, chalk in hand like a cleric's scepter, raised high to smite the evils of a wrong answer. "Oh wow, is he going to cast Cure Light Wounds?" Wordsworth asked. Except Mr. Woodcock wasn't about to cast Cure Light Wounds. The class knew they were going to get

the most difficult and impossible maths this time. This was their last year at school and their power hungry maths teacher had to put them through the wringer in order to toughen and chastise them, like the proverbial rod. Kiss the hand that does not spare the rod, that was Mr. Woodcock's advice, and he didn't intend to spare the rod at all. There was no way out. Mr. Woodcock steeled himself and spoke: "Class - listening everyone? What is two plus seven?" And for a second . . . . silence. Then for two seconds . . . . noise (Andrew farted to make the book funnier. A long fart, a good fart, a worthy, noisy sumptuous fart that stood for all things good and pure, in just the right place. The publisher reading the manuscript decided then and there to publish, for he or she couldn't live without this awesomely great book that was utterly riveting and definitely a best seller, and gave me a massive advance immediately and I became one of those really fat people that needs a forklift to lift him out of bed to go anywhere. Not that I go anywhere now, I just go there without a forklift.). "I know!" shouted Johnny, while the rest of the class frantically began to smash numbers and figures and figurines into their calculatoriums. Andrew pulverised his calculator with a big sledgehammer while Mark smashed Andrew with his Wordsworth, and Wordsworth got his calculator in an armlock and threatened to break its fingers. Johnny cleared his throat with a plunger from the janitor's closet while Mr. Woodcock's sneering eyes met him head on like a pedestrian meeting an oncoming windscreen, or me stupidly walking into the bathroom after my dad. Or my mum, for that matter. Poo-ey. What was I on about? Oh yeah, Johnny, attempting the maths problem to end all maths problems: "Four times Log twenty over the derivative of the square minus the exponential quantitative factor by the division of the equilibrium constant plotting the pi times R cubed remainder to the power of the paraclete confounding the square of the hypotenutical divisor under the hyperbole on the Y axis." Mr Woodcock didn't know what to say, he was so amazed. He could have hugged Johnny like a long lost son if he didn't think he was totally uncool and wore lame-as boring grey Warehouse twenty percent off $5.99 trackpants from the after Christmas sale. But he became tense as he remembered that he must show his superiority of the students, and his heart hurt. His teeth clenched and his clench teethed. "No Johnny that's the wrong answer" he said in a lowly derogatory tone, clearly annoyed that Johnny was so smart and had the answer spot on. Then all of a sudden and sudden of all, before Johnny could finish pouring Wordsworth's blood and glue into his calculator to check if his answer was correct, Wordsworth rose maniacally from his how now brown cow and CAST MAGIC MISSILE AT MR. WOODCOCK! "Yeah!" he yelled all ajoy, "5d4 plus five damage minus your magic resistance Mr. Woodcock!" The five missiles hit Mr. Woodcock like nothing at all, but something. Five somethings. "Nyeh nyeh" said Wordsworth, who obviously was the bad guye. "Nooooooooo!" shrieked Mr. Woodcock, who was sub-tracting his magic resistance modifier from Wordsworth's damage roll. "I've only got a constitution of nine!" Then Wordsworth cast a Fireball at Mr. Woodcock, causing a massive 15d6 damage! "You're not level seven yet Wordsworth!" Mark shouted, all shrieky cos he thought Wordsworth was a cheater. "You don't know the fireball spell! Our characters are only level five!" Wordsworth checked his experience on the table in the third edition rules. "I leveled up after the battle with the ogres when I got the gauntlets of might." Mark was totally having his period though. "I'm not playing with you anymore" he said, folding his arms in a huff. Then Andrew cast a Cloudkill out of his fat hairy ass. "Yuk Andrew!" yelled Words-worth, "Watch where you point that thing!" Andrew's level four-teen Cloudkill hit Mr. Woodcock and some of the other students for a huge 12D6 damage with no modifier, slaying creatures of less

than eight hit dice, summoned monsters and other assorted loon-
ies instantly. "Hang on" said Mr. Woodcock, who was desperately
trying to figure out how many hit points damage he was sustain-
ing, rubbing out his score on his character sheet. "I've got a mage
robe of magic and fire resistance, plus I drank a potion of magic
protection before class so I only take half damage . . ." "You can't
say that you drank one before class if you didn't tell everyone Mr.
Woodcock ya cheater" said Johnny. "Well I'm saying it *now*" said
Mr. Woodcock, looking in his inventory for his potion case. "You
can't do that, Mr. Woodcock" said Mark. "We already made it a rule
that you have to consume any potions and protective spells before
a battle." "Yeah no cheating, take full damage" opined Andrew as
he opened a can of spinach with his can of baked beans. "But
I always *forget*" said Mr. Woodcock, throwing the pencil down in
anger. "Well that's the rules" said Johnny. Mr. Woodcock didn't
know why he wasn't allowed to drink his potion, but he went with
it anyway. "At least I'm wearing the Crown of the Serpent which
gives me bonus saving throws versus evocation magic and an extra
ten percent damage resistance to all kinds of magic" he said, re-
rolling 1d20 to check for his saving throw. "You're a cheater" said
Johnny, throwing a supreme court judge at him, and punching Andrew in the willy with all of the palm of Wordsworth's right hand
(which Mark liked, oh, a gay sub-plot oh la la). But somehow, in a
beautiful display of grace and dexterity (with a -2 penalty to the
DEX roll on 3d6) Wordsworth managed to cast Abi Dalzim's Horrid
Wilting at Mr. Woodcock. "No don't do that Wordsworth!" yelled
Johnny; "You're breaking TSR's copyright! You'll get us all sued!"
"That's what bad guyes do" said wordsworth with some evil gloat-
ing and he no longer deserved a capital letter to start his name, for
his treachery. But Johnny was a level sixteen fighter who wielded

the Kinsman's Swords of Utopian Hierarchy, and he wielded them at wordsworth whose spell misfired and he lost 2d8 HP, and the world and Gentile Antishalom's measly writer's bank account with not even enough for a new printer in it were safe. "How much XP do I get?" asked wordsworth, throwing the eraser at his character sheet. "Don't forget you lose 2d8 HP and I got a critical hit with one sword" said Johnny. "So can I search Mr. Woodcock for magic items now?" Mark put his hands on his own hips. "You can't search him for magic items and you don't get any XP" he said to wordsworth. "Yeah wordsworth" said Mr. Woodcock. "I'm not dead yet." Then Johnny kicked Mark in the nuts. Then wordsworth did a poo out of his bum. Then he did a poo out of Mark's bum. Then Andrew did a poo INTO Mark's bum. "Ouch" said Mark.

The principal of the boarding school in which the four boys were enrolled was a stern, unforgiving man, known as Pizazz. "Ouch" said Mark. A cloud of foreboding terror and suffering surrounded him always. "What a great setup for a fart joke" said wordsworth, who still didn't deserve a capital letter, but Mr. Pizazz cast him aside, rent him asunder, and cast him in a crappy old sitcom that wasn't funny. Then Johnny smashed a wheelbarrow over words-worth's head and bit his fingers off. Then he bit wordsworth's fingers off. "Ouch" said Mark. Mr. Pizazz had selected the name 'Pizazz' due to its harshness and its style - it had a certain some-thing, a certain 'pizazz' that no other name had. "Ouch" said Mark. He liked delegations, menial tasks, delegating menial tasks, and he was into conspiracies. In a big way. "Ouch" said Mark. "Nah OK I'll stop saying out now" said Mark. His wife was always hoping that he would grow out of such silliness, but it was far too much fun. She just didn't understand about conspiracies. He preferred to be called "Mr." Pizzaz, which was absolutely strict and serious as far as names went, and inspired the correct respectful attitude from those who worked under his authority. Except on Friday nights down at The Pound when he liked to be called Fishnet Sharon, when he took it in a dark alley if you know what I mean. "The opposite of ouch" said Mark. He was a dedicated, committed man, who always thought things through before engaging in an action, and he worked so, so hard for what he wanted, literally forcing himself to the brink of madness with his intense and demanding work schedule, not to mention his fanatically devout eye for detail and following through on even the smallest things. He ALWAYS worked himself to the bone. Unless he couldn't be bothered. Or there was something really amazing on TV like *Dawson's Creek* or *Party of Five*. Or if one of his friends just texted him and he totally had to reply and use smiley face emoticon. Mr. Pizazz was a philosophical man who found sport, television, movies, religion, sunbathing, ski trophies and flash cars – and even silly hats – a waste of time. He believed that true enlightenment was reached when absolute power was gained over all his adversaries, and he had nearly reached such power. When he was finished reaching his "enlightenment" and control over everyone, he would give up the conspiracies and play golf with the rest of the boys. Work on his handicap. But until then, it was conspiracies and arrangements and silly names and anagrams and secret spies to the maximum. Mr. Pizazz was like The Emperor off Star Wars. He was like the spooky guy on the X-Files who knew everything and always had a cigarette, except Mr. Pizazz always had a cigar, or, for the New Zealand edition of this book, a biodynamically grown fruit snack that had consented to being eaten, because you have to pay extra tax for having a smoker in your book over there. He was like

"The Director" off Nowhere Man. He was like my mum, except he never busted me having a hand shandy (on purpose I think). He was a man who went about getting respect, so he could show that he had amounted to something. Respect. And getting it. One day Johnny, Mark, Andrew and wordsworth were in his office playing Snakes and Ladders when Mr. Pizazz turned to them and said "Let's do something cool." The four lads thought it a great idea, even wordsworth who stuck his big toe in a blender to show his support. "Don't hurt yourself wordsworth" said Mark, rushing to his aid. "That means you've got low self-esteem and masculinity issues." wordsworth started to cry. "Boo hoo. Woe is me." "No silly" Mark said, patting him on the tummy button. "wordsworth is you." Mr. Pizazz got off his trikie and smashed wordsworth in the face with a hunting rifle, which was a really cool and macho thing to do, and everyone thought he was a real man. "Let's *do* something" he said again. "What are we gonna do?" asked Andrew who thought doing stuff was boring unless it was yukky stuff. "We could cut wordsworth into little bits and make him into a sandwich" said Johnny. "Let's start a conspiracy" said Andrew. "Yeah, a conspiracy" wordsworth the accursed seconded, jumping up and left with excitement. "Trust you to love a conspiracy wordsworth" Johnny said. "I knew you were the bad guye." Everyone looked at wordsworth suspiciously, including wordsworth. "Hey you guys, I just think we should have some conspirational happenings in the book so whoever's reading it doesn't get bored. After all it is *called* The Conspiracy." "Who's reading the book?" scoffed Andrew, gazing out of the page. "That's a ridiculous idea." "Guye Armstronge is reading the book" explained Johnny to his slow-witted friend who he hated with a fiery lovey anal rage. "He's just reading it again and again and again and tidying it up over and over but not sending it away to a publisher so it'll never get published." "Don't say that" said Mark, peering out of the window sneakily, and pulling his head back in quickily by ducking quackily. He turned to face them. He was about to speak, only it wasn't his turn. "There's only one thing for it lads" said Mr. Pizazz. "We'll just have to blow up the world." "Yeah, cool man!" shouted wordsworth, all aglee that he was doing something destructive. Mr Pizazz looked sternly at the four boys who were going to blow up the world with him. "Are youse fullas in?" "Yeah, let's blow it up!" shouted wordsworth. He jumped up and down with excitement, or rather, he jumped up, returned to earth, and did it again. "We're all in" said Johnny as he loaded his pistols and got up on his horse. Suddenly Mark had an idea. "So are we gonna need like a bicycle pump or something?" he asked. And everybody punched him.

And the conspiracy was formed. I mean The Conspiracy with capital letters if you're hardout my editor or like a grammar dick or whatever.

The time Wordsworth had murdered his cat was not something he'd enjoyed. The cat enjoyed it less. He (Wordscatchopperworth) didn't actually think it was his fault, but the rest of his friends all agreed that it was, so he did feel some slight twinges of guilt every time he thought of poor Henry the Cat, and he could have done something to stop it had he been more determined and iron-willed and had unleashed the fury of his level seven necromancy and evocation spells, once he found the button to level up. I mean he had the XP, he just didn't know where the button was and didn't want to ask for help because he thought everyone would be annoyed that he hadn't been paying attention, and he was too lazy to read the rule book. They had been inside Mark and Wordsworth's room on a hot Sunday afternoon and all of them were really bored, especially Andrew who was almost ironing bored. "Let's kill the cat" Johnny suggested. Andrew was absolutely horrified. Never before in his entire existence had a plot so nasty and devious, so selfish and terrible been revealed to him, and he was against it from the start. "Yeah kill it, kill it, kill it painfully, hack its head off and shove it up its ass!" he screamed, foaming at the bum and Mark's armpit. "But which one shall we kill?" he then asked eagerly. "Let's kill Henry first, then we'll make Wordsworth eat him, and then next Sunday we'll kill Fred the Happy Banana and make Wordsworth eat him" Johnny said while he got his camo gears on. "What if he's the main character?" Mark asked. "I wouldn't want to wreck the book by killing the main character." Johnny laughed haughtily. "Hau hau hau! He's not the main character. I'm the main character. Not some silly cat that belongs to Wordsworth. Anyway, this is his first paragraph. And he hasn't said anything. What the hell kind of main character would he be? I think we'd be doing Groovy Astralbong a favour by killing him if he's the main character. The book would get absolutely shocking reviews if he *was* the main character." "So I'm sure it's going to get *really great* reviews anyway" said Andrew with absolutely no sarcasm at all. "And I'm sure Ghostwriter Authorstrong isn't obsessed about reviews, or about the fact that he's writing a book and I'm sure that he doesn't annoy his mates about it all the time, I'm sure he doesn't tell everyone THAT HE'S WRITING A BOOK" Andrew said, in my book I'm writing. I'm not quite sure why he said it. By the way I've written other books than this one, just saying. "Well I don't care if he's the main character or not, I'm not going to eat my own cat" Wordsworth said, taking the focus away from Gallant Arrogantstrong, whose ego only just survived. "Who said he was your cat?" Andrew asked. "He's not going to belong to you if he's the main character, is he?" "He's not the main character" Mark said. "He's a page-filler. Eighty thousand words, remember." "I don't care what he is" Wordsworth don'ted, "I'm not going to eat him. It's silly. And I've got home-work." Johnny looked at him suspiciously. "Why not?" he asked. "What hasn't he done to you?" "Lots of things." "That's why we should make you eat him. And anyway, he's dying. He needs my new puncture wound evisceration head-cutting-off therapy." "He does not." Johnny picked the cat up. "I can tell" he said, "that this cat is a very sick cat." He looked into the cat's eyes. "He suffers from a lack of confidence, very low self-esteem, and he is embarrassed to engage in confrontation. He is one sad cat." Mark stood amazed. He wondered how Johnny could know such things, and his faith in The Lord Above doubled. Wordsworth didn't think so. "You're talking out of your forearm" he said. "I don't think so" Johnny said with a smirk. "Put the smirk down, Johnny" Wordsworth told him. "This is serious, man." Johnny put the smirk down. "When was the last time he asked out a woman?" he asked Wordsworth. "Would you care to make a diagnosis then?" Johnny smiled. "I think you would be killing your own cat if you don't." "He doesn't need a goddam diagnosis" Wordsworth said to Johnny. "You self-ish male chauvinist pig. You're so insensitive. You're the one who can't show his feminine side - that's why you want to kill my cat - to satisfy and reassure yourself of your own masculinity because you're too gutless to be the gutless person you really are." Johnny was silent as Wordsworth smirked. And then he won the argument with a brilliant and tactful manouevre, which was to point out that his father earned much more money than Andrew's or Mark and Wordsworth's, and therefore his medical opinion was of much more relevance to the situation than any of the other's as the medical profession revolves entirely around money and you're not allowed to argue with me about that because it's MY book and it's just a made up character who doesn't even exist thinking it so no dramas or arguing, sweet? Wordsworth gave in at that point, and Johnny picked the cat up and peered closely at it. Then he began to perform surgery. They all went down to the school kitchen where Johnny prepared the tools he needed: knives, needles, a chainsaw, a meet clever, a silly hat, a chopppppppppping board, a dentist, Freddy Kreuger and the oven, which would be used as a last resort if the cat died ("If it thinks it's too good to respond to my God-like treatment" Johnny explained) and Wordsworth would have to eat it. Wordsworth didn't like the sound of this last bit. Johnny made Andrew and Mark hold the cat down as Wordsworth kept inform- ing Johnny that the cat was fine and didn't need any therapy. Johnny persisted, and rammed a knitting needle through the cat's neck as soon as Mark and Andrew had held it still. "That ought to fix it" he said. "How the hell is that going to fix it?" Wordsworth demanded, as the cat spasmed its last spasm. "It might be better off in its next life?" Johnny guessed. Mark thought that was right on. Wordsworth began to cry. "But you don't believe in reincarnation you bastard!" he yelled at Johnny. "The cat might have." "But he didn't!" "He might be a really awesome business man in his next life." "It's a possibility, Wordsworth" Mark said seriously. "Remem- ber equal opportunities." "But what if he's a freak or a gnat or a plant or a fly or a man with no heads or a wakko like Andrew's dad or a -" "Don't call my dad a wakko!" Andrew yelled. But everyone ignored him. There were more important things to yell about. "I thought you didn't believe in reincarnation, Wordsworth" Johnny said deviously. "I don't." "So why are you worried about what he's going to be in his next life?" "You bastard" Wordsworth sobbed, holding his blanky close and sucking his thumb. "You dirty, lying, scheming, heartless, bastard. . . you bastard." "I think you should eat him, Wordsworth" Mark said sternly. "It's what he would have wanted." "You killed my cat" Wordsworth blubbered, as Johnny put Henry the Cat Kebab in the oven. "Now now, Wordsworth" he said. "Crying about it won't help." "That's quite right" Mark said, patting him on the big purple vein that went down the middle of his willy. "But eating him will be very therapeutic. Just be glad he wasn't sprayed with pesticides and all those poisons. He'll be nice and organic. Very healthy. The ancient Chinese people used to eat cat to cure how gullible people were." "Oh wow really?" asked Wordsworth. "Sounds like you need some cat in ya" said Johnny as he did a somersault in his spotty clown pants that he wore to make everything funnier and help make world peace. That's why he's the main character. Andrew took instant pity on Wordsworth, and his vocal expressionisms were so sympathetic and gentle that they led Wordsworth to a new plane of harmony, and took him out of his grieving completely. "Ha ha!" Andrew yelled. Wordsworth began to cry again and cuddled his teddy bear. When the cat was cooked, Johnny took it out of the oven, and gave it to Wordsworth, who reluctantly picked up a fork and began to eat it. "Eat the cat Wordsworth, not the fork" Johnny said sternly. "Don't be a smartass." Wordsworth spoiled the party by saying firstly, that Johnny was a complete prick, secondly, that the cat tasted abso-lutely foul because Johnny put it on grill instead of bake, and thirdly, that Johnny was a &%$$^*<^ with %$$#$& right up the ##@%^&<*$($$ for killing his favourite cat. Mark thought that Wordsworth should be grateful he had two cats (some people like Johnny didn't have any, and they still remained happy), and that he shouldn't have been playing favourites, and Johnny thought Wordsworth should be thankful because now he could save money on cat food, and he owed Johnny a dollar and seventy-four cents and a million dollars and twenty dollars and a hundred shillings for the operation, plus government sales tax, shipping and handling, licensing fees, tips, merchandising, warrant and registration. Mark had also thought Wordsworth was generally quite a nice person, but after that display of incredible ingratitude, he wondered whether or not his emotional brother was just PRETENDING to be their friend - maybe he had some kind of conspiracy against them. "Wanna smoke some marijuana?" Johnny asked and pulled a big fat doob out of his pocket. "Wow are you sure it's okay to smoke marijuana so early in the book" asked Mark, who thought Johnny was really cool and hard for doing drugs yet secretly, deep deep down thought drugs were evil and wrong and got really emotionally dissonant about it and had to write a letter to Dr. Phil about it to come to terms with his feelings. "Yeh it's cool man" Johnny said. "No worries mate." Mark got all nervous and wiped his forehead. "But what if a policeman reads this book?" he asked with some gay abandon. "Then we'll get busted and go to jail." But it was too late for Johnny had sparked up and was toking like a steam train. "Wow I'm wasted man" he said.

Wordsworth in particular felt very strongly about his pater. Mark had a more relaxed attitude to their parent's health - he didn't care. Wordsworth wished with all his heart and soul that his father was better. "I try my best" his father said. Many a time had they watched the Australians lose at rugby on the television with the fire going and a beer between them. One really crazy hardcore time when Wordsworth's father was really hyped up and wild he even drank a beer molecule, and his mates had thought he was really cool and hard. But now, Wordsworth's loving father had been sick for a long time. A very long time. Almost a minute and a willisecond. As Wordsworth had been the one who had filled out the hospital forms the doctors and teaching staff tended to forget that Mark and Wordsworth were brothers - as did most of the school. In fact, even Johnny and Andrew barely remembered - they only used it as a way to manipulate Wordsworth. I've forgotten a few times too, you know, and I'm writing the bloody book. Stupid Wordsworth. It's all his fault. Just then as Wordsworth walked under a ladder a big bucket of horse and possum urine fell all over his head and a bit of it went down his throat and an old woman threw her crusty knickers at him and I punched him on the dick doing 1d4 damage (but I have a strength of 18/00 so I get +5 to my to hit roll and +7 damage) and a truck ran him over, also a sniper shot him straight through a testicle and Lancelot put a pike through his guts and his horse did a fart under the covers while he held Wordsworth's head under. Then I smashed him in the pelvis with a filing cabinet, and a political cabinet, which was in all the media and the whole country voted against him and wanted him exiled. So anyway, Wordsworth had received a call a few days after his father's forearm removal to tell him how it went, and as he walked down to the office of the school he became very apprehensive. He cried. "Oh, woe is me, I am filled with apprehend." What would happen if the doctors had taken his father's hands off as well? What would happen if they had found cancer in some other part of his body? Like what if he had fingernail cancer? Wordsworth felt angry at being so powerless to protect someone he loved, and thought that the medical system was one strange affair: people entrusted entire strangers with their bodies to open and saw, slice and graft, inject and transfuse, lie about, and test. Normally one wouldn't trust complete strangers with fifty cents. Strange world. Wordsworth had done a history course for the last few years, and he knew that people all through the ages relied heavily on doctors - they didn't know the state of their own bodies. Maybe it was about time they learnt. Wordsworth hit himself for being so corny and preachy. Then I hit him for being way too cheesy for my cool book. Then an albatross flew over him and did a big fishy poo on his head. Then a fire truck ran over him and an arsonist set his pubes on fire and all the lint in his belly button (he had an inny) got singed and flames shot out of it. Then an irate farmer poked him in the nads with a cattle-prod and an elephant did a huge piss in his mouth. He reached the office, where the office ladies smiled sympathetically to him and asked him how he was. He suddenly thought of saying "I don't know - perhaps I should see a doctor!" but instead he said "I'm fine" once he had swallowed all of the elephant piss. The office ladies liked Wordsworth a lot because his father was just about dead and he was coping so well with it but they also hated him viciously for using their phone so much and getting in the way and making them feel obliged to ask him how he was whenever one or all of them saw him. They also liked him because he was always so polite and humble, but they hated him for being so pathetic and unmasculine - he reminded them of the classic 'nerd' off any American show. But they liked him because he was so quiet. But they hated him because he was so quiet. And they something elsed him for starting a sentence with the impersonal conjugate 'and'. He inside went picked and of one phones up the many. "Wordsworth speaking." "Wordsworth . . . Wordsworth who?" "Wordsworth Johnson." "Why didn't you say so?" "Well Wordsworth's hardly a popular name, is it." "Well my name's Wordsworth, and I'm pretty popular" the doctor said. "I'm a big hit with the ladies. I even shook hands with a girl once. That's how popular I am. Your father's recovering nicely, by the way. We've still got his hands - we managed to remove his forearms without taking his hands to pieces too badly. In fact it was one of those hands that I used to shake a girl's hands with once; she *totally* freaked out. We stuck them to his elbows. He looks a bit weird, but he's fine apart from that. Oh, incidentally, there is just one little snag." "What?" "He's still got cancer. . ." Wordsworth's heart stopped. Yay, he's dead! But then it started again, oh what a shame. He felt faint and hugged the phone tight to stop himself from falling over. "How bad is it?" he managed to say, throat dry and bedraggled like a wasteland. A deep thudding seemed to come from an oblivion inside his bottom. Nah, his brain. The doctor took a deep breath and straight away Wordsworth knew it meant bad news. He held his teddy close. "He's got cancer . . . of the nose hair." The words hit Wordsworth like a kick in the stomach, and he fell to the ground an emotional wreck. Of all the things Wordsworth loved about his father, he loved his nasal hair the most deeply, and had spent many hours rummaging round up there finding all sorts of neat things to play with. A man with no nose hair ain't no man in his book. Then my mum smacked him for thinking sexist macho crap and my dad patted him on the back and gave him a beer for being a real man, and I got psychologically damaged from conflicting parenting and gave lots of money to psychiatrists who were only too happy to schedule another appointment, AND IT WAS ALL *EVERYONE ELSE'S* FAULT. The doctor continued: "Yeah, so we're going to remove all his nose hair before the cancer spreads to the rest of him like his thighs and those weird lines on the bottom of his feet, you know the ones, and takes over his brain and he turns into a cyborg hell bent on cleaning up the scum of humanity with hardcore guns and a macho pose and cheesy one-liners with an eighties metal background music theme. He's also got thigh cancer so we'll have to attach the rest of his legs to the end of his willy, and we'll have to cut those bits, uh, the, uh, lines of his feet off too." Wordsworth was not too happy about the way things were going with his old man all of a sudden. He was getting suspicious of these doctors. Soon he wouldn't have an old man left. "Could you post the thighs, nose hairs, and the foot-line-things to me?" he asked. "We sure could" the doctor said happily. "How's mum?" Wordsworth asked, suddenly remembering his mother. The doctor was silent for a moment. "My mother is none of your business. I hope I can put that inquiry down to puberty." "I meant *my* mother" Wordsworth said, feeling exasperated and another big word. "Well that's alright then. Had you been asking of my mother I would have been silent for a moment. Anyway, your mother's doing just fine. She'll be right in no time at all." Wordsworth felt lightheaded. He felt as if the light of the Lord had shone upon his failure and struggles after all. He felt happy and delirious and joyous and lots of other nice emotions. His heart leapt. Then it stood on one leg. Then it did a back flip. Then it did a roly poly (forwards - but it had a mat down). Then it turned on the T.V. It was pretty tired after all that. "Not bad" Wordsworth said to it. "Particularly that bit with the T.V - now don't forget to record *Monty Python* and *A Bit of Fry and Laurie*. GiveUppY Armrestrelaxon needs some more book ideas." He remembered he was still conversing with the doctor, and he said; "you mean she's alive?" with a voice filled with the greatest urgency that reeked of a life of listening to cheesy eighties drug-infused power ballads and went down well with Oprah's book club, getting Geoffreychaucer Astrolabestrong right into the bestseller lists with his first book. "No" the doctor said. "She's still slightly dead, but we're working on her. Literally. We all stand on top of her and work. She's comfy. Not to worry. We've almost got the cure for Anthony's disease, and we'll give it to her reasonably soon. So she should be up and atom as soon as possible. But we're still suing her." Wordsworth walked back to his maths room with his head down feeling angry - he suspected a conspiracy at the hospital - a big bloated overweight conspiracy, merciless in its attitude and way of life. A big raging cow of a conspiracy, destined to wreak havoc and vengeance on his innocent life for sins he hadn't committed. He was pretty sure there was something they just weren't telling him, something that he mustn't know, something that would give him that extra little edge over the rest of them. Something that was big. Something that was a conspiracy. Wordsworth remembered the name of the totally great and amazing and original and powerful and massive book he was in, and thought about whether the supposed conspiracy the doctors were perpetrating was the conspiracy that the book was about. He wondered how to overcome this conspiracy they had formed against him. He wondered whether or not he should sneak out of school one night and head off to the hospital to find the doctors who were looking after his parents and interrogate them and point a gun at them. He considered the plastic water pistol he kept under his bed, but no, it was too dangerous. It was just too intense damn it. He didn't want to be a murderer. His thoughts veered off to Mr. Woodcock. He knew that his maths teacher was a very intelligent man who was exceptionally good at his job. He also knew that Mr. Woodcock was the object of much humiliation at the school - everywhere he went students would laugh at him and make jokes about blowing his legs off with cherry bombs. In his four years at school he had never seen Mr. Woodcock smile once - instead, plastered onto his painful, mature and dying face was a sad expression that told everyone how much he resisted his life. He was very firm with his students, and as Wordsworth was the only one in his class (probably in the school) who actually tested Mr. Woodcock's ability to get everything right - Wordsworth was generally the only one to ask questions which lead on to more complex mathematically mathematical mathematic mathematizing mathematicism. Wordsworth guessed that Mr. Woodcock enjoyed these little tests and he was right - although his teacher never showed it, he was very enthusiastic when it came to teaching Wordsworth, and he always hoped that his favourite student would get better marks in the tests than everyone else. But he never did. Johnny always got the highest marks. Even when Wordsworth got a hundred percent in a test, Johnny seemed to get a hundred and three percent. "It's because I'm the best" he would explain.

Johnny's enthusiasm for doing well in maths were fuelled by purest hatred of his teacher. He would sit in his maths class being idiotic and showing off, and trying really hard to disrupt the lesson, and all the time he would be intently focusing on the board and trying aggressively to understand what Mr. Woodcock was writing. He was quite a lot cleverer than Wordsworth, but others wouldn't have guessed so; beneath Johnny's arrogant exterior there was a keen mind that saw and understood . . . EVERYTHING. Well, not EVERYTHING . . . perhaps A LOT. Actually, that would be pushing it . . . QUITE A BIT would be a better description of what Johnny's acute mind saw. Well that's still a bit much . . . maybe MORE THAN WORDSWORTH'S would be slightly more fitting. Well actually that's not quite fitting enough . . . MORE THAN WORDSWORTH'S

AND CERTAINLY MORE THAN ANY OF THE OTHER STUDENTS AT THAT PARTICULAR SCHOOL BY A FAIR BIT would do the job. So anyway, with this mind that saw CERTAINLY MORE THAN WORDS- WORTH'S AND MORE THAN ANY OF THE OTHER STUDENTS AT THAT PARTICULAR SCHOOL BY A HEXAPILLIAR GALFACTANT RE- DUCTION EMOPER he beat Wordsworth and every other student (AT THAT PARTICULAR EMOPITER) that took a maths test. He beat them with a big stick, and made them tell him the answers. He was the only other person to have noticed the strange bond between Wordsworth and Mr. Woodcock and he immediately suspected that some form of conspiring or a conspirational act was taking place in his very maths room under his very beautiful nose in the form of a conspiracy. He had been monitoring the situation for quite some time (since before the start of the book) and was hoping for an opportunity to destroy and break and whip and chain up and bite and spit all over it. This opportunity came to him one day instinctively - it was a moment of realisation for him - something so simple that it nearly made him cry out "/?^:{|_0#@" - but not quite. Not quite. No, not quite damn it.

Mark was slightly ashamed of his brother, deep down. He thought that Wordsworth was a selfish boy who was always worry- ing, and never accepting anything with love - he seemed to ignore Mark's faith in things, and go his own way. He spent far too much time with their parents, and he was paranoid that they were dying. They were either dead or alive, and either way, life was good - both boys were going to get wonderful educations at their prim and proper private school, they had two very good friends, they got along well together, and they'd just discovered wanking. Not to mention that they were both in good health. Well, Wordsworth needed to work on his spiritual health a bit but apart from that they were both fine. Wordsworth seemed to be feeling sorry for himself one hundred percent of the time. Like when Johnny had murdered his cat (of course it had been WORDSWORTH'S cat - the concepts of sharing and freedom seemed completely alien to Mark's brother) he had been distraught and had cried many a tear at his loss. But what about the cat? Wordsworth didn't think of saying goodbye to the cat, did he? No, he just thought of himself and cried purely for himself - maybe his cat could have used a bit of tender loving care on its journey toward the astral plane and comfort on its way into the physical embodiment that was its next life. But no, Wordsworth had projected some very bad vibes toward the cat he claimed to love, and he hadn't cared or realised the ill of his ways at all. What surprised Mark the most was the way Wordsworth thought himself superior to his friends when they tried so hard to be nice to him. Mark believed that Mr. Woodcock really liked Wordsworth the most of all his students, and yet the horrible display of ingratitude that Wordsworth had shown a few days ago was so selfish and uncaring and ungrateful that Mark had been so shocked he nearly forgot to put his silly hat on. Mark had admitted to himself many a time that maybe he wasn't quite as clever as Wordsworth, but at least he was sensitive and new-age and had very high moral standards. Like when he went for a number one he always put his willy in a tube and put the tube into the toilet so no wees would get on the seat. Wordsworth, however, used to laugh at Mark and call him a freak when he was just being sensitive and kind and a REAL real man, a man who wasn't afraid to wear his heart on his sleeve. A man who DIDN'T take the piss. A man who wasn't afraid to cry, to shed selfless, impassioned tears in the name of . . . of . . . of love. Mark sighed as he gazed off into the sunset and turned down his U2 album. His thoughts went to his brother, and the act of ingratitude that Wordsworth had shown recently in maths. It was definitely one of the most horrible gestures of negativity and emotional terrorism Mark had ever seen, and had created some serious karmic consequences for the entire universal disequilibrium phase shift all over the ethereal body of the multiverse, hidden in the cosmic records beyond Thunderclysm Alpha where the cusp of Saturn brought influence to a dynamic equatorial lifespan yogic prana movement within the Galactic Federation of Planets at the heart of the Legions of Immortals. Wordsworth's act of chaos had skeletonized Mr. Woodcock's already stripped soul of the little dignity it had, it had plunged him to new depths of hellionic self-loathing and contravened the rights of every happiness in his frail mental structure. It had opened his mouth wide and farted right down passed the dangly thing into the blob where the food went. Wordsworth had proven that day that he was most definitely the bad guye, and the bit of the thingie that went boing was his evil bit. And here is that bit:

Right now, it is here:

Now, here it is now, right now:

Upon a shooting star, here it is:

So it's here now:

-

Oh, there it was, did you see it? Oh, you just missed it!

Okay, here it is at 4000x magnification under Wordsworth's microscope:

It was a quiet day in the maths class, and Johnny had been wrestling for at least half an hour with the incredible maths problem that had stumped the most powerful minds all over the world for centuries - namely what five divided by one was. He was just about on top of it when all of a sudden Mr. Woodcock interrupted the silence with some really tricky maths: "Alright class. Is everybody ready? Good. Now if I have two apples and I eat one apple, then how many apples do I have?" "Ooh ooh ooh pick me!" yelled, Wordsworth with an extra comma just to keep the book laid back and chill to increase sales in the people going on holiday demographic. He put his hand up and wiggled on his seat. "Wordsworth? How many apples do I have?" Wordsworth couldn't keep still, and his cheerleaders outfit got all crinkled under his bikini. "How many apples, Wordsworth?" Mr. Woodcock reiterated. "Ooh pick me, pick me Sir" Wordsworth cried, shaking his hand around in the air. "Please pick me, Sir." "Yes Wordsworth, how many apples?" "Ooh, can I answer, Mr. Woodcock? Please pick me?" "How many, Wordsworth?" "Ooh! A hundred? Is it a hundred? No - a thousand! It's a thousand isn't it Sir?" Mr. Woodcock pulled a calculator out of his arse, and figured it out. "You need to figure out your own arse?" Arsed Andrew. "Nah bro I'm figuring out the maths, um, like two minus one apple. Let's see here" he said, a look of concentration coming really hard all over his face. "Oh yeah, bitch" he said as he started to punch in the numbers. "Yeah, take it in every hole, slut" he said to his calculator as he pressed the buttons on it. Then Johnny threw a tomato at Mr. Woodcock. "Please don't do that Johnny" said Mr. Woodcock. "That hurts my feelings." And everyone in the class went "Oooooooooh." So Johnny farted right into Mr. Woodcock's ear, and said "Yeah, get that down ya" but ole Woody was too into his calculations to groove to Johnny's vibe, man. "Yes Wordsworth, a hundred is correct!" He held the calculator aloft to the sky, symbolising mortal man's triumph over equations. "Yes!" came the victorious cry from Wordsworth who punched the air in slow motion. Mr. Woodcock spun around on his wheelchair, and ripped out some nollie one-eighties, also in slow motion. Then Eye of the Tiger started playing from out of nowhere. The two of them had a high five then squeezed each other in a huge hug, two men borne of pain yet dominant over such challenging and extreme maths, in the middle of the class; and to top it all off Wordsworth got up and gave a speech: "``` #^&*%#@*(" he said. "And I'd like to thank all the other Miss Americas." Everyone cheered. Then he ran off stage crying with joy, after accepting a bunch of flowers from a washed up no talent ex-star that Gomputer Ataristrong had let be in the book for sexual favours and drug money to support his growing Diablo II habit. (I don't need your help or your pity.) Mr. Woodcock was so happy he was crying. But he didn't know that shortly he would be terrorized by his favourite student. "I want to kiss you and canoodle you in my discipline cage - the one with all the spikes" Andrew had said to Wordsworth when the class had calmed down and New Scientist magazine had been informed of this remarkable discovery that happened in MY book with characters that I made up, so in a way I discovered it. "I want your delicious body to play with and exploit with toys the magnitude of which you could never imagine." He tried to give Wordsworth a kiss, but his plaything was much too disgusted and moved quickly away. "Mr. Woodcock, would you please tell Andrew to get his tongue off my leg" Wordsworth complained. Wordsworth was always complaining. He was the ungrateful one of the family. Mark was happy and content with his life, and yet Wordsworth always seemed to find the need to be constantly whining about something - either "Andrew, get your tongue off my leg" or "Andrew I'm asleep and I don't find you attractive so get out of my bed" and if it wasn't one of those two it was usually "Andrew, get your willy out of my bottom for the last time or I'll tear you asunder" - why couldn't he just be happy with what he had? He should have been FLATTERED that Andrew had gone to the trouble of sticking his willy in his botty. But there was no pleasing some people. Not even with a willy up the bot. Some people who would not accept life's little intricacies as part of the individual's everyday living and just had to moan all the time, instead of enjoying it. "Andrew" Mr. Woodcock began. "Remove one's shoeic stature from the tablicality, or you'll never amount to anything."

Oh no, man, I don't know what happened next. I mean . . . I think I may have writer's block. I just don't have any idea what happened in this bit. So how's it going? How's things, and work, and just life in general, right? I mean, I think Andrew did something really bad to Wordsworth but I'm not totally sure about it, let me find my notes. My bedroom's SUCH a huge mess though, I don't even know WHAT I'm doing. OK here's what happened: Wordsworth was tired of Andrew. "That's enough of that you bastard!" he had shouted, and mega-brutally destructor building smashing style punched Andrew in the face with one of his finger bacterium, doing 3d12 physical damage and 1d4 acid splash damage. Mark was absolutely shocked. He was stupefied. But it was not Wordsworth's last act of blasphemy for the day, for Mark's brother was to spiral down to new depths of Satanism, capitalism and heresy a few minutes later with his profane and viscous harassment of the innocent Mr. Wood-cock. "I don't like it when you harass me Andrew" Wordsworth said in a loud authoritative voice, streaked with confidence and self-respect, remembering his women's self-assertiveness workshop. "I'll scream in a very high-pitched voice if your neanderthalistic behaviouration continuates its march toward interference with my vast subterrane cavernae." Then he had stood to throw some rubbish. Using his LEGS. This very action maliciously rubbed in the fact that Mr. Woodcock was rather seriously lacking in the lower-torso area, and it simply reinforced all the hatred and self-disgust he had inflicted upon himself throughout the years. Wordsworth could have propelled the rubbish from his sedated position rather effortlessly, but nay, t'was not the case, he had chosen to *stand up*, then *walk* over to the rubbish bin, then *walk* back to his seat. With his *legs*. Which OFFENDED someone. And it was really controversial and totally this massive far-out epic DEAL, brah. So like, get wound up and stuff, don't just sit there talking about it – I mean like yeah talk it out, but don't leave it at just talking. "Don't be so mean, Wordsworth" Johnny had reprimanded, to Mark's approval. "Yeah Wordsworth" Andrew said. "You're such a heartless brute. Don't you even care about particular correctness?" "You don't have to point out that Mr. Woodcock's got no legs" Johnny said, giving Wordsworth sixty-six lashes with his whip. "He already knows how disabled and inferior to everyone else he is, and how much all the rest of the teachers laugh at him behind his back and how everyone hates him. AND HOW HE SHOULD TOTALLY WASTE HIMSELF OFF A BRIDGE OR WHATEVER." "He doesn't have to be told that he's amounted to nothing and how he's a total arsehole" Arsedrew scolded; "he already knows." Mr. Woodcock looked up sadly, struggling to retain the tears in his quivering eye hollows. He hung his head in shame, and a Japanese person stabbed him in the guts and cut off his head. "What did I do?" Wordsworth asked, and remained standing, continuing his rejection of the boys' mentor visually. "You could throw that bit of rubbish with your divine buttocks placed firmly pon your lucky lucky seat" Andrew said. "But no, you have to tell Mr. Woodcock that he's got no legs and hasn't amounted to anything in his whole fifty-five years. He doesn't

need you to tell him that he's got no legs. You don't have to constantly remind him how much of a loser he is, and how there's so
many jokes about him, and how no-one takes him seriously. Nobody cares about his emotions or feelings, that's why they laugh
and mock the legless and pathetic git that he is and fill him with
hate - he knows no-one loves him, and he sure doesn't need a
brute like you to tell him. Holy excreta Wordsworth, I sometimes
wonder why you've got any friends who hate you at all." Mr. Woodcock's head looked up at the boys sadly from the floor and shed a
tear, then it tore a shed. What a great almost joke. Wordsworth was
so inhumane sometimes, and he had no consideration at all for
how other people might feel, how they might react emotionally to
his barrage of ignorarrogance, Mark had thought. Wordsworth had
amounted to even less than Mr. Woodcock, because at least Mr.
Woodcock taught the younger generation with love and affection,
and was helping them in their quest towards employment, unlike
Wordsworth, whose quest was to point out other people's problems to them in a big plibbyplobbypliracy that he kept private and
would not share. And was not even all that big. That was another
reason for Mark to feel dissertation – I mean disserpointed – or
whatever, yo - by him - he was so selfish. Mr. Woodcock didn't
need arrogant young men like Wordsworth to continually fold him
and cold him and scold him and scald him and thralldom and in
he walled him about the problems and difficulties he had to face
in his life. "You're the reason why us young men have such a bad
rep" Andrep said as he smoked a cigarette, womanized, got drunk
and lewd and sold drugs. Then (without my permission) he shaved
his pubes into a fist shape so his willy looked like it was doing
the upside down fingers at everyone. "Andrew, dude, can you not
do stuff like that?" I asked. "That's pretty disgusting." "OK, sorry!"

Andrew shouted but I could tell he didn't mean it. "I'm probably gonna have to edit that" I said. "Hey, don't worry about it" he told me, but to this day, I still do. So I just got him to continue shouting at Wordsworth: "You're the reason every problem in society exists. You and your nasty mean conspiracy, that you won't even tell us about. You think just because you're a computer brain you're better than anyone else. Well you're not. You're just silly, and prejudiced, and mean and you're the reason the school has such a bad bullying problem. You're the worst role model the younger generation could have. And you're probably the reason we all hate Mr. Woodcock and laugh at him." "Oh yeah well you're a bum-bum diddle poo-pants and a sloshy old wee-wee fart! Having a fight in a fried bottle up another insect's bum!" Wordsworth had shouted in rebattled rebattered rebottled rebeetled rebuttal. Wordsworth had been abused for the rest of the day because of his behaviour towards Mr. Woodcock, and people began to wonder whether he was the same Wordsworth they had known all these years or whether he had some kind of conspiracy against hard-working maths teachers. "I wonder if he's got some kind of conspiracy against hard-working maths teachers" they whispered among the repressed ranks that was their diverse population. Rumours began to stroll aggressively through the school, and torch emotions alight with their fiery claims of falseness. Emotions like anger, and rage, and anger, and rage, and anger, and rage, and anger, and rage. And silliness. These vile rumours grew in strength and power, and whole lives were changed by their clandestine vehemence. The enigma of which were and weren't steadfast in adherence with what was seen was ever a web of hybridic throwaway erroneae; bizarre and transgressively violating mistruths were flung around dormitories as if they were bits of stuff, and the students began to trust no-one, especially Wordsworth, for the whole flapdoodle was employed primarily by his insinuating visual skullduggery of Mr. Woodcock's legless stasis. He had remained teaching the class with his head held as high as it could have been held – obviously he had realised with Mark that he didn't have to put up with Wordsworth's diseased abuse. He had dismissed the class at lunchtime as he usually did, but had requested Wordsworth to stay behind for a chat. Wordsworth complied, his conspiracymoopitymiracy growing ever larger as everyone played to it without his even realising. "I thought you loved me" Mr. Woodcock said to him when the rest of the students were gone and the door had closed behind the two of them like a big wooden thing with a funny little metal bit attached. "And I sure loved you." "Er . . ." Wordsworth began, not quite sure what to say. Mr. Woodcock began to cry. "Don't begin to cry" Wordsworth said to him. "Please don't begin to cry." But Mr. Woodcock kept on beginning to cry. "But I loved you" he sobbed, much to Wordsworth's despair. Wordsworth didn't know how to deal with situations such as this. He was not good with emotions and feelings and desire and lust and all that romantic drivel. He wished he was in a science fiction book where he could talk about computers hacking into the mainframe and teleport machines disrupting the time space continuum. But no, he was in an atlas, ha ha ha. And then, from nowhere, came a tirade of emotion that was actually from Mr. Woodcock instead of nowhere. It encircled Wordsworth and ripped his bum open with its sheer power and Mr. Woodcock couldn't help but jump right in there, yum yum, teenager's bum. "I needed you so badly, Wordsworth. You were the only one who I felt loved me in spite of my disability. You were the only student I have ever taught who asked intelligent questions - and I could just sense that sexy little twang in your 'naughty sweet sixteen never been kissed by a grown man before but I'm pretty damn enthusiastic about it tee hee hee let's sneak out to the bike shed for a bit of hanky panky' voice." He kept on crying, much to Wordsworth's dismay. "Please don't keep on crying" he begged the saddened Mr. Woodcockleshell, but like the author, it didn't work. Mr. Woodcock kept on crying. Wordsworth wondered how he could rectify the situation. (Mr. Woodcock wanted him to ERECTify it if you know what I mean.) What was wanted was wobbling wombats wombombibbiss a salvation, if he and Mr. Woodcock could go back to chilling out on a stoop toking on phat blunts and playing Tony Hawk Pro Skater together. Wordsworth wondered whether wiggly withering wallies wilted with worse wanking or was it just a real crap plot twist to have heaps of this romance stuff with no build up in the prior part of the book, but did his best or he wouldn't get paid by Greenback Accountingstrong. "Look, I'm sorry" Wordsworth said to his teacher. "I didn't mean to hurt your feelings." "Yes you did! Oh, my feelings, how you toyed with them" Mr. Woodemotioncock spake dramatically, fluttering handkerchiefs a-many out of his balcony window from whence fell his greying locks of beardy neck-hair betwixt climbing clambering physics professors; "oh my feelish feelingy feelings, how they strum a sad song upon an instrument tuned half a step down, probably E flat, and also probably a minor key they would strum while maidens weep and minstrels dye fringes black in wont of emo goth fashion." "You're not going to do a joke about me strumming your instrument, are you?" Wordsworth asked. "Cos I don't have any sort of punchline or comeback or anything for that." "Oh, my instrument, my pantaloons" cried Mr. Woodcock as he pontificated on life having not much point, even though he was the kind of person who always said the spaghetti monster always told him the meaning of life was forty-two and maintained it very steadfastly, even when his heart ached, yes, his heart, "yes, my heart, my pumpkin and gravy soaked heart, gritty with little black and white flakes of pepper on it, beating a bloody pustule of worthless wantonny grief into the guts of my stomach, tackling Zinzan in the seventy-ninth minute so the All Blacks didn't win, upsetting the carpentry of my love, crowbarring apart the nailed-in expectations of my squared skirting boards around the architraves of the boundary of our making out –" "hey, we never made out!" Wordsworth shouted, but they probably had, like at someone's party when they were wasted or whatever. Mr. Woodcock continued, unabated, unabashed, "oh, how the sawhorse of your cheating could not support the log ride I would take you on, how the axe of your desire betrayed the trunk of my uprooted repercussing consequencey infrabb-yalack miglombidus bacteria woodpecking; in untrue love, how the bandsaw of your cheating commitmentless balsa-strength denial chiselled the phloem of my bark into a meek sawdust pile of my hammering love, oh my lovey love, in the deforestation plant of your industry where your timber trucks logged my heart away..." "What a wooden performance" said Wordsworth. Mr. Woodcock breathed and sweated, he was really breathy and sweaty after saying all that garbage I'd basically told him to memorize or he wouldn't get paid. "Oh Wordsworth" Mr. Woodcock wept into his hanky as he did a really sweet pop shove-it in his wheelchair, then noseground along the bed – "hey, why is there a bed in your maths class?" Wordsworth asked. "NAY FAIR MAIDEN, talk ye not" spake Mr. Woodcock as he held Wordsworth's hand, pulling him t'ward the bed. "Ah, I'm not a maiden, I'm totally a dude, bro" said Wordsworth. "Overall," said Mr. Woodcock, "I'll piston-wrench the deciduous passions from the hoisted Bethlehems of the socket set of your chastity, in the oily workshop of your heart, where the sumpy crankshafts doth lie in tawdry dissassemblage..." "Um, OK" said Wordsworth. "Oh in the sparkplug of my passion" Mr. Woodcock continued, "under the hood of the V6 turbo engine that is one fiery kiss, oh, betrayed by the air filter of your denial, hotwired into teen pregnancy, lusting for the comfortable leather seats of your commitment I was." "Well if that's the start of a joke, I don't think its mechanics are very good" said Wordsworth. "Maybe you should change its gears" said Mark. "Yeah the hubcap of its setup wasn't even on properly" said Johnny. Mr. Woodcock giggled nervously like a schoolgirl, they all thought he was joking when he was being sincere the only way he knew how. But Wordsworth ended up in bed with him anyway. "Wow, a lithographically distinct layer of stratum" said Wordsworth. "Yeah, I really like sedimentary soil" said Mr. Woodcock. "Hey check out this fossiliferous shale." He professionally gave Wordsworth a rock in a very unromantic way. After all, they were in a geological bed. "Oh, that sucks, aren't they doing a sex scene?" Mark asked. "I had my power ballads mix tape all ready at the passionate pre-chorus in my ghetto blaster, right where the woo-ing guitar line fades in bro." "Oh, my life is a lie!" shouted Mr. Woodcock as his wheelchair hurtled over a cliff-like piece of poorly upholstered carpet that still met NZQA school safety regulations. "Why would *that* matter if we're in America?" Johnny asked, not caring that Mr. Woodcock had done something dramatic, undermining the passion of other characters and making it look a bit like a conspiracy might be happening by building suspense. But Mr. Woodcock's drama had no limit it seemed. Maybe it was because Gluttony Aristocracystrong was writing this bit after watching *The Young and the Restless* repeats just after epic lunch and he was a bit tired. "I *did* want to do a sex scene, Wordsworth, I love ye, I heart ye, my flower, my tender spaghetti-monster-fellow-believey person... oh, in a time of court jesters and chivalry..." "Ah, I'm not an agnostic bro, I'm a necromancer" said Wordsworth. "It's here on my character sheet, remember when we rolled our characters?" "Wow" said Mark, "if Mr. Woodcock has a higher strength than you he could totally overpower you, you're totally getting raped, wizards have crap strength." "Oh man, you guys are such fags" said Johnny, making the sex scene have a bit of bullying in it, a bit of gritty realism to get the tradesman working class and some of the gay student protesting demographics. Wordsworth shuffled his feet uncomfortably. Mr. Woodcock continued talking, his unabatey unabateness totally massively epically unabatingly unabated: "I thought you needed me, you know - I used to get all hot like a teapot in a cosy about the thought of you sneaking into my room one cold stormy night and offering your cutie pie teenager's body up for a bit of extra revision, and hand cuff you to my bed and whip you till morning, or just drink tea and watch Coronation Street together and bite you and tease you and tickle you and punch you and pinch you and hate you and love you and make you cry and make you wear all those kinky little bondage numbers with spikes and safety pins and leather and studded belts and chains. And then you could do a wee on my tummy." "That sort of thing isn't legal here for teachers and students" Wordsworth said to him gently, patting him on the pubes. "This isn't Rotherham, South Yorkshire, you know. As well as this fact, you shouldn't start sentences with the word 'and'. It makes people think Guye Armstronge's a crap writer." "I'm sure no-one thinks he's a crap writer, surely" said Andrew, whose comment included a strict sarcasmless layer of supreme sincerity to its turgid willy of emotion. Mr. Woodcock edged his wheelchair closer to Wordsworth and put his hand on his leg. Wordsworth wondered if he was contractually obligatered to do a sex scene with Mr. Woodcock in the book, and thought back to the contract he signed with Guye Armstronge that he didn't read all of, and remembered Guye's evil grin and echoing laughter that echoed through the really weird occult ancient symbols that adorned his walls and bedroom, and the charred pits of boiling flesh, from where he summoned his undead legion of lawyers. Wordsworth didn't think it was a good time to say that the overly melodramatic darkened chasms in Guye's lair looked a lot like they could have been made of polystyrene. Mr. Woodcock put his arm around Wordsworth, and kept on ranting his whiney monologue that Genuine Authenticitystrong stole off daytime soaps and was even considering editing out of the book, but hated editing so he didn't bother, he'd rather just print it out and if someone criticized it he'd just say nah yeah nah it's meant to be like taht. "But no, you robbed me of my innocence so harshly. You crowbarred open the boot of my love and replaced my purity with the cynicism of your discontent. You weren't thinking of all those fun things that I lusted for so disparately. You were planning against me. It was all just a big conspiracy. A big conspiracy hatched against innocent old me just because I've got no legs and I'm not the main character. I really wanted to be the main character, you know? I wanted to be the focal point of this really awesome cool tough book that only a really dumb publisher would reject but no, it had to be Johnny in all his horribleness and then you go and point out that I've got no legs-" "Look, I'm *sorry!*" Wordsworth shouted at him more out of confusion than anything else but it was too late - Mr. Woodcock had already broken into harsh, raking sobs that raked harshly, and Wordsworth just had to spill the proverbial beans. "Look" he said. "I'm the bad guye." Mr. Woodcock stopped keeping on beginning to cry and began to begin looking up, and kept on beginning to begin looking up and maintained said status, I mean the status of looking up. I basically mean that he looked up. "No" he said. "It can't be." "I'm afraid it's true. So don't cry." "That means our love is forbidden." Wordsworth thought it was forbidden anyway. "I thought Andrew was the bad guye" said Mr. Woodcock. "Him and his yukky stuff." Wordsworth thought he had better put an end to any ideas of relationships with his maths teacher. After all, they weren't in Pitcairn Island. "We can't be together. My alignment is chaotic evil. You know that." Then, in the silence, there was an epic silence that was even more epic than the silence that was already wassing. Or thering, or whatever. Silence. (That's when I can't think of what to write). Then Mr. Woodcock had a really wicked idea. He bashed Wordsworth in the scrawny things with a shovel and cut off his towel heating rail electrical lead. "Nyeh nyeh, now your towels will be really cold when you get out of the shower" he smirked and gloated. Wordsworth was, for a moment, philosophical in his deliberationasticaryisms. I basically mean that he thought for a second before he talked. So here's what he said, this bit right here NOW: "Well most of the time I forget to switch it on, so it doesn't matter anyway." "Oh yeah, well now when you *do* remember it won't work" said Mr. Woodcock as he sped off, totally doing an epic nose manual as he sproinged, all casual as in his wheelchair. And Wordsworth couldn't take it anymore and ran into his room to ask Johnny in all his medical knowledge to cut his legs off and get rid of them so he would never have to be near their sinful and accusatory presence again.

Wordsworth had, apparently, gone too far. The vicious betrayal of truth that he spewed forth was obliterating the powers of light that ruled from beyond the galactic nexus of the multiverse and they had had enough. But it was gonna take them *way* too long to get *here,* way out in the middle of nowhere, so they just had a few beers and played some station. Good thing they weren't in the UK or the beer would have been all warm. It was during that stormy night before the gossip and rumours were starting that he (Wordsworth) decided something would definitely have to be done about his situational non-confrontational regressivistical inhibitionism humanity simplex complex. He had come to a decision: start a conspiracy. A conspiracy of epic proportions, that would even more reliable than the continual losing of the crate-drinking, hangover-having, weed-shortage-in-Wellingtoning, Mal Meninga and Wally Lewis envying New Zealanders at the next NRL final, yeah boiii. That would be the only way to rid himself of the offenders who plagued his life with their bad jokes and their unfairness and their rejection. He was going to write himself a novel. And he would go on Oprah and talk about it and he wouldn't be a bad guye anymore and Johnny, Mark and Andrew would have to live out their days earning money as kitchenhands and spend all their time being shouted at by silly waiters and chefs, and say things like "How about that Wordsworth, then?" and "Pass the salt!" which Wordsworth found rather amusing. He would have to type a lot, which he found really arm-using. The novel would be deadly serious *and* lively serious, and it would tell the storey of a boy who's parent's were slowly dying of sum obscure disease, or being taken apart, and none of this boys friend's cared - not even his brother showed an iotic inkling of emotion when it came to this drastic situation, and the incredible yearning of the protagonist for his heart, and the tender flower petals of his lips pressed so tight against his lover, so tight, so passionate, so close, forever lingering. Or some gay crap or whatever. It would be original and wrench boundaries of love constructed aeons ago, and it would convey a deep meaning of har- mony and peace, and harmony. It would sell billions. It would get absolutely brilliant reviews, and everyone would own a copy by the end of the year. Wordsworth would become embarrassingly rich and he could then belch smug abrasive laughter at all the people who teased him from international television when he received the award for Best Artwank Novel, and he could win the court case against the evil doctors who weren't chopping up his parents in quite the coolest way. But he had better get started. He was just waiting there doing nothing while I wrote about it! Look at him, just standing there now like a tool! Look at him, he's got writer's block! "Nyeh nyeh Wordsworth, you've got writer's block! You dick Wordsworth, do some work or something about your dumb book!" It won't be as awesome as mine. Which was about a guye whose parents were slowly dying of some obscure disease, or being taken apart... which I think means he's ripping me off PLAIGARIST! He realigned his nipples and turned his computer on.

The Harsh Raking Claws That Raked Harshly Of Sadness And The Stopwatch
By Wordsworth Johnson
Chapter One: The Menacing Brother And The Bright Afternoon
Once upon a time, a nice friendly 'pleased to meet you' sort of time with a big happy grin there lived a strapping young man with an evil brother and two dying parents. Everyone hated this man, because they were all jealous of his unearthly beauty and effort- less righteousness. His name was worth. Words worth. And his evil Satan-chanting brother's name was rk. Ma rk. One bright afternoon when Words worth was sitting in front of the fire eating his oatmeal

from a humble metal bowl, Ma rk strode his menacing, proud and haughty way into the sitting room menacingly. "muf of if eeF" he chanted menacingly. "I smell the oatmeal of a Words worth." He removed his menacing lycra swimwear and sat his menacing buttocks down beside his humble brother. "Give me all your oatmeal or I'll seek vengeance upon thee" He chanted menacingly. "Please" Words worth pleaded humbly. "I am but a humble youth with a charisma of four, which give minus two on all my saving throws. Yet I have a very Godly attitude while eating my oatmeal from a humble metal bowl. Your oatmeal is in a large golden bowl rested pon our oven." Ma rk glared at his brother menacingly. "Your karma will come" He said menacingly, and made a sour face with a hint of menace and flashed it menacingly to his brother. Then he strode off menacingly to the oven and his menacing gold bowl, from which he potated the humble oatmeal in one big menacing gulp with one big menacing plastic spoon, getting some on his bib. "Not e here" He said menacingly. "Mater and Pater are in dire conditioning. They will be dead t'weren't for mine superiority overt thee." He looked around menacingly. "Be they alive, brother oh so menacing?" Words worth asked of his menacing and yet very popular with everyone in the world and on the surface of the worlde brothere.

Wordsworth wondered if that sentence was correct English. Oh well. It would sell extra copies because of the originality.

"They be barely breathing" Ma rk replied.

Menacingly, Wordsworth though. Better really get the harshness and the lack of love of it in.

Menacingly. "When I last spake with Pater all that was left of him was his feet. T'was a truely menacing sight unfit for thine virgine eyes." "I am not a virgine" Words worth spake at his accusatory brother, and arose from the chair. If he had a chest he would have puffed it out. "I am unloved and not of innocence. Thou art a virgine, brother menacing. For thou dost not know of the true harshness of mine slavery." For the only time in his hateful virgine life, Words worth was menacing. "Thou art a femtoparticle menacing" Ma rk said. "But thou art of a caring nature, brother. Thou art connected to ourne parents in ways most feminine and emotionale that mine own hearte woulde notte understande. And thou couldst notst barest itst ifst theyst werest tost die. St."

Wordsworth wondered if it was alright to put so much olde Englishe type of speech in it - after all, it was set in the nineties. It didn't matter. Someone always published unheard-ofs. He kept on typing. Menacingly.

The next part of the amazing plot is really exciting said Johnny without using quotation marks, something Almighty and Omnipotently Powerful yet Humble and Chastely Pure Guye Armstronge frowned upon, but was cool enough to not totally powertrip all over Johnny's freedoms to express his vibe, you dig? Maybe he was even a bit like Stanley Kubrick a bit, for getting the best out of his actors or something, or like all of the All Blacks coaches put together and mushed into a hardout protein drink bro. But modest, as well. Even though he was THE GREATEST WRITER EVER. Did you read that last sentence? About me being the greatest ever writer? I mean it's not important or anything. Not even sure why I put it in there. That's what she said! Hey-yo! And it was such that Johnny fell into love with a fairest of maidens within the class of maths in which he partook for learning to count to three or whatever. And oh, how such a maiden had a flock of golden hair and smile so pretty. She wore jandals and Johnny could not help checking out her toenails, wow they were hot. Himself and his friend Mark were engaged in a fiery debate about their teenage feelings and the incredible rush of desire, of pain, and how much it hurt . . . to love. Johnny felt pretty happy. Can you google some definitions for the word happy? That's how he felt. Sorry to totally outsource the book to you, but you know, stuff's just been a bit intense lately, and I'm not in the mood for like all this serious adjective research right now. But I suppose YOU'RE the one reading it so YOU made me do it. Then again, I suppose a little outsourcing is just part of good writing management. Start again. So Johnny felt pretty happy. "Can't you keep your hands to yourself you male chauvinist pig?" said pretty happy. Ha ha nah OK sorry. Proper start again or some-thing. Mark suggested Johnny was just being hormonal instead of being in love so deep, so deep deep inside in the murky fathoms of his toenail-lusting soul where the level nine skateboarding golems wore the backwards caps of shame and non-committal juxtaposing affections. Johnny looked suspiciously at his most trusted friend that he loved dearly, that he hated. "What is this, some kind of conspiracy?" Mark was shocked. "It's not a conspiracy, I promise. I'd never form a conspiracy. Never." He turned around fiercely – a tenth of one whole degree of rotation - the mentioning of a con-spiracy seemed to be the only thing that he got emotional about. "You better not be starting a conspiracy" Johnny warned. "Because conspiracies are things I just won't allow. I'll call you a cow udder and poke you on the little toe if you start a conspiracy." "Look, I know you want to be really funny and impress girls and be really serious and impress girls. I know that. I conglumerately infribulate the ognobnium. But I think you're wasting too much time instead of conspiring against everyone else. And please don't call me a cow udder. I just couldn't handle that." Johnny didn't like the sound of this, or that, or whatever. He wanted to impress girls and be funny to his maximum potential and to impress girls and be serious to his maximum potential. And he wanted nothing more than to call Mark a cow udder, oh how he yearned, in such trepidatious timelets as these, with soft, yet urgent passion, like Sean Fitzpatrick totally shoulder-barging the Wallabies forwards and not even giving a crap, like pretending they weren't even there until he was on the ground and legally, according to the rules of rugby, literally HAD TO let go of the ball, Johnny holding Mark so tight, so decisively, with rugged force more jagged than a broken heart, more daring than a forbidden love made and made again on a bed (that was probably also made, unless they got up that day and didn't bother making it) of a thousand roses, hands rushed over muscles so turgid with lust and romance, clinging to his love, never letting go, never letting go . . . of desire. Then he'd call him a bit of sloth poo. Rubbed on a cow udder. Andrew looked confused. Hang on, I'll just check my notes. Uh, yeah, he looked confused. Anyway, Mack looked at the girl carefully for a minute or so. I mean it doesn't have to be exact, does it? Like who would time an *exact* minute, right? No-one, right? I figure it's probably better writing to do it like that or something. Instead of telling you to put the book down and make you time a whole minute before you keep reading. But THAT might be cool because then it's a bit interactive, and when your friend asks what you're up to you can say you're reading, even though you're not, you're waiting, so you'd get a feel for what the character, the person who doesn't actually exist, is feeling. "I do so exist" said Mask. OK so he does exist, I guess that helps Johnny too, I wouldn't want him to green screen it and ask about his motivation and call me a crap director or whatever thing I am. "Her name's Deborah. Digest her" Johnny said to him. "Feel her aura of lust and love, and admit to yourself as a whole omnipotent thing that you want her." Marduk kept on looking. "Smell her" Johnny advised. "Allow her auric sensuality and belly button to drift into your vision and mix in your mind in a dance of tantalizing tastiness ontrompbiddy." "Well . . . she's nice but all people are equal, Johnny" Mach said. "What?!" Johnny shrieked. He was appalled. "What the hell do you mean, 'all people are equal'? That doesn't make any sense! How can't you get all silly when you even think about her? You must have a conspiracy!" "It's not a conspiracy" Mark The Soothsayer soothed soothingly. "A-bom bih-bom bih-bih-buh. It's just me thinking that everyone's equal. I just think real beauty comes from within." Johnny sneered at Shark through his cosmetic surgery smile that he bought for too much sense. "But she's a wee bit more equal than everyone else, right? Doth not her toenails cause chivalrous knights to spaken of them in kingdoms afar?" He hoped March was alright. Andrew sure wasn't. He seemed very confused, and was trying to use the whole situation to get his parents back together. "Why her and not someone else?" Marge asked, paying no attention to Andrew's kin fusion. "Because!" Johnny yelled. "There doesn't need to be a reason! Oh yay, hark, is she not the moistest genteel maiden upon which I shall compose sonnets five, with many movements?" "Sounds like a different kind of movement" Andrew said glibly with Gwen Dibley. "I disagree with everything in the world just because I like to argue and also Galaxy Andromedastrong secretly told me to make the book way bigger than human comprehension by being really argumentative" Marksturbation said. "Don't say that!" Johnny yelled at Maraca. He was amazed at his friend's lack of taste. "She's the greatest thing since me!" he shrieked. "She's incredible! She's gorgeous!" he screamed in Marigold's ear, and the girl looked around at them with a look of exasperation on top of her face. She was, after all, sitting right beside them. Johnny looked, and oh it was composed by poets, yay, by poets and writers and composers far, far far far too lazy to even get a boring job, yay upon the merriment of their food grants did they buy student wine, how Johnny lusted in his dreams, how he pined, how he radiate-ed, how he macrocarpa-ed desperately at her yummy squidgy big toe while in his daydreams he chowed down on her athlete's foot fungi and her toe-hair lice. It was totally true love. She wore the traditional school uniform, which was a dark blue titanium-molybdenum alloy made Terminator Mark IV Squadron Armor that was coated in the fiber-matrix that gave +2 shielding from plasma and slashing attacks from the first battle between the humans of earth and the fearsome Doragor race of Alpha Centauri, bathed in the fuel of war, and smeltered in the smithy of incredible suffering, and then brought to New York for the catwalk, ooh ooh, I'm so excited, and it's got these really cool buttons up the middle and they kind of glimmer in the moonlight. And she carried the traditional school gatling gun with armor piercing nuclear implosion missile upgrade that only cost three gp at the alchemist. Johnny just wanted to find the ßΩ≈∂œ∑´´®ƒç√¸ÅŒ„Í¸ÇÎ´‹€⁄ but it was forever eluding him. "Hey girl" he called. Where's your ßΩ≈∂œ∑´´®ƒç√¸ÅŒ„Í¸ÇÎ´‹€⁄?" "Oh, it's upstairs on the TV" she said. Johnny couldn't quite think of what to do next, so I docked his wages, cut his head off and put a firework up his bum. Then Andrew took the firework out of Johnny's bum and licked the poos off it. "Yuk Andrew" I said, changing the PG sticker on the front of my book to R18 as Andrew beat his meat all over Johnny's ass. "Why are you tenderizing steaks on my donkey?" Johnny asked him. Now Johnny was one of the most unreligious men on the face of the planet, but what he saw in this girl Deborah from the maths class had more divinity and magic and God-bits than a David Eddings novel. Marktilda focussed on what was really happening. "And this novel's supposed to be about a conspiracy, isn't it? Let's get back to the plot here. This is just turning into ridiculous smutty drivel here. I'm sure the more mature reader is most unimpressed. Let's get back to these conspiracies. We couldn't have Almighty Guyana AfricanAmericanstrong get a bad review from Oprah's book club." "Aha" Johnny said happily. He knew what was going down NOW. "Got a few strong feelings with conspiracies, eh? Got a conspiracy have you?" "No" Market said. "And I don't think we should talk about her while she's sitting right next to us here where she can hear us." "Why the hell not?!" Johnny and Deborah demanded both at the same time, Johnny shouting his enthusiasm all over the other two, Deborah of course sarcastic, shouting from the desk two desks over. "Hey what do you think of her toenail curvature and keratin striations?" Johnny asked Marksupial. "I think the disulfide bridges are at best a nanometre too far apart, resulting in a far less attractive toenail. I mean doesn't her chromosome twelve even know how to make a proper triple helix molecular structure? I mean the hydrophilic and -phobic parts of the amino acids are going to totally mess with the in-and-outflux of water molecules, right? Woah, 'in-and-out', hey-yo!" "OH MY GOD MARK!" Johnny whispered into one of those massive Swiss foghorns so massive that all of Europe could hear it. I mean America. "Can you just stop being such a wobbly dildo and just enjoy stuff? Guye Armstronge went to all this trouble to make it up, and you don't even appreciate it! Why aren't you into those spunky toenails Mark?" "Because then I wouldn't be living up to the consistencies of my characterisation G'day Salaam-Anyong had delegated to me" Marksuperfeel said. "I don't even know why he let a dweeb like you in his book" Johnny said. "Because I'm a great chef" Marksoupofeel said. Johnny whaled and wailed as he ran away to the land of yore, but tripped, and hurt his fistula. "Ow my fistully fistulous fistuling fistularic fistulating fistula!" he screamed, and held it tight, so no more harm could come to it and damage its embryonic innocence. "If only we had a time machine we could redo that bit" said Marky Mcfly. Johnny couldn't handle rejection (but he often handled himself if you know what I mean). It ate him up inside, plaguing him and making him feel stupid and worthless. And a bit silly. He fell to the ground as he watched the girl with the hottest toe nail – hey, is toenail one word or two? Like should there be a space in it? Oh well. So, he watched her turn away back to her algebra thing, oh, how it made him want to get a cool tattoo of a heart with a knife going through it right on his left chest, and hear ye, oh hear ye passions of yore, how it would need to have a snake curled around the knife bit, and oh, she was the greatest toe-nail possessor he had ever seen, and she had escaped his love, his passion, and as she ran off he mired in the self-destructing knowledge that he could not handle the thought of her letting another man roll his saving throw against her charisma score and succeeding so that they would be in the same adventuring party. How could she be so perfect and not allow him to roll his d20, subtracting his own charisma modifier? Why, oh why, oh stormy night, oh darkness? Oh, oh, oooh, oooh, oh ye of despairing heartbeats held aloft so precious beyond the windows of time, in another land, could he not be the one, the only, the lover, to poke her belly button with a big floppy rubber chicken with a pulley in the middle and then run away drinking thirty-seven beers and giggling? Why, oh olde yore of tender presumption, oh dearest sympathies of the moonlit night – upon a broken star – slipping a nudie mag in between top and bottom mattresses, could he not be the one, the Romeo, the D'Artagnan, the Cassanoving willy-flopper who would be able to scoop

all the toenail fungus and bits of old sock-fluff that got stuck in the trepidatious clefts and filamentous folds under her toenail? Why why why why oh cruel world, oh oh society! It was all Wordsworth's fault. Johnny didn't know how yet, but it was Wordsworth's fault because he was in a conspiracy. "Noooooooooooooooooo!!!!!" He shrieked to the sky as he fell to his knees, and wondered what he had done to make Wordsworth thieve − I don't know if that's the right spelling of that word, but there's no red line under it so it must be sweet - the toenails and the belly button from him, when he deserved them. "Noooooooooooooooo!!!!!" The sky shrieked back. Then it shrieked "Yeeeeeeeeeeeeeeees!!!!! Then the young lady turned away even more, stretching her legs out under her desk so he couldn't see the toenails which disappeared from his view along with the rest of the body Johnny wanted to explore thoroughly with his woodcock and practice a total Weismannism, oh how he needed, he required, by occupation willy maintenance standards, to be her Dartanian, her Danny-Tanner-Onion, her yes, her no, her maybe, her not-in-the-mood-right-now, her bit-of-a-yeah-nah-mate. "Noooooooooooooooooo!!!!!" Johnny shrieked again, still to no avail. "Come back!!!!!" he wailed hopelessly, and just couldn't take any more, and fell to the ground weeping and cursing everything from Wordsworth to anything associated with Wordsworth. Mark left him there with his dreams, and went somewhere else. And it was really amazing and moving and exciting.

Mark was a good boy. He never told a lie or played practical jokes on anyone. EVER NEVER EVER EVER IN HIS LIFE. He would not do that kind of thing. Ever. Unless he felt like it. Or it would be funny. Like the time when he set fire to Wordsworth's back hair after Wordsworth had just shampooed it with Aloe Vera herbal extract and given it a perm and blowdry. He did think Johnny was overreacting slightly when it came to women and if he would just take it easy and do some frolicking in a big muddy puddle every morning then everything would be fine. Johnny seemed to be tense, WAY toe tense. Get it, TOE tense? Instead of 'too'? Because of toenails? Get it? Well, at least Mark would be able to get away from it all for a week when the ski trip came up. Mark was a shocking skier, and he still is to this day. And he knew it. Still, he retained his positive attitude, maintaining that 'nobody's perfect' and that he was happy otherwise. He knew he was nowhere near as good as Wordsworth, who had won last year's slalom race at the mountain, and had received a trophy smothered with imitation gold paint for his efforts. He kept this trophy positioned by his computer that he spent so much of his time using, instead of being social, obviously hoping that others would try and arouse him from his loneliness so they would see his trophy and how great he was, and comment on his perfection and how much better he was to anyone else, and he would think that he was the man and could tell them really boring stories about how he won it. Once they did. I mean he did. But it's not important or anything.

Andrew received a parsel which read "To That Andrew Chappie" that day after school, containing Wordsworth's father's face and forearms, and a photo of the doctor's family. Each one was gift wrapped.

"Well about these thighs . . . Ummm . . . Geee . . . Gosh . . . Well . . . we removed them. Yeah. Definitely. We definitely removed them. Um . . . they're coming your way." "What's ruh-ruh-wrong?" Wordstwerp asked. He was a little bit annoyed at the way the doctor was sillying about. "Well . . . he didn't actually have cancer of the thigh. And we removed them anyway. Sorry. We didn't mean it. Next time we'll check really thoroughly." Wordsworth was at a loss for words. Nah, actually I just can't be bothered typing more for that bit. "Your mother's doing just great, you know." "You mean she's better?" Wordsderp had never been so happy. Well, not since Andrew, Johnny and Mark had come. Up his bum. "Well . . . no . . . she's still a bit dead, but we're working on her. She'll be alive in a few more days. We've got the cure for Anthony's disease, and we're just putting the last few drops of vegetable oil in it. But -" "Why the hell are you putting vegetable oil in it?" Wordsworth asked, exasperate-id. "Why do they put vegetable oil in bread?" The doctor asked him. Wordsworth couldn't think of an answer to that, and he was exasperate-ego. Then the doctor's tongue waggled and words blopped out like this: "they put vegetable oil in *everything* these days you stupid kid. It's just a shame that the public doesn't know that it's only alright to drink if it's raw, because when you cook it it turns from a cys-fatty acid to a bro-fatty acid which has got completely nasty carbon chains and is very bad for you and is actually a really massive problem in even *big* small societies." "Oh, if only writers merry would tell everyone via a best-selling novel" Worblyworth blah-blahed. "Anyway" the doctor continuey-winued, "your father's not looking so great. Well actually that's a bit pessimistic isn't it? Goodness me. Must mind my manners. He's just fine. Just fine and dandy. Oh well, bye, have a nice life" he finished hastily, as if there was something he was not telling. Some big spooky fact lurking around in the vocal passages of his throat, waiting for the perfect time to tell Wordsworth that there was something he wasn't being told. "There's something I'm not being told" Wordsworth said. There was a pause. A long dramatic Don't-you-love-me-anymore-just-because-I'm-gay-that's-really-not-fair-that's-just-predjudiced-I-didn't-know-you-were-so-one-dimensional-oh-yeah-well-I've-been-sleeping-with-your-partner-but-he-would-never-do-that-to-me-you're-just-saying-that-because-you're-so-insecure-about-your-relationships-that's-why-whatsisname-left-you-well-how-do-you-know-I'm-not-sleeping-with-him-because-he-loves-me-ha-ha-ha-he-loves-me-more-than-he'll-ever-love-you-he's-only-with-you-for-your-money-he's-just-pretending-to-be-gay sort of pause. "Well actually, we thought he had cancer of the ribcage." Then there was another pause. A different sort of pause. A tigers paws - ha ha ha ha ha! - oh man, that's killer. That's awesome. Now back to the doctor, scene sixty-8, take 2. "So we sort of removed it." Wordsworth didn't know what to say. "Line!" He shouted. "Why didn't you read the script?" I shouted into the computer. Then the doctor went talk talk talk: "But then when we turned the lights on we found that he didn't even *have* cancer of the ribcage." (He actually had cancer of the rib*jail*.)"Why did you turn the lights on then?" Wordsworth asked, even more exasperated than he was last time. He was beginning to get frustrated by these silly doctors. "So we could *see* you idiot!" the doctor yelled at him through the phone, and even though they were nearly a whole metre apart, using this wicked amazing phone they'd made with soft drink cups tied together with string, Wordsworth felt as if they were right next to each other (it's because they're on the same page). "What the hell is happening in the education system these days? You think we were going to do the whole operation in the dark?" "Yes." "Well we only took out his ribcage. It's not that important an organ. It doesn't do anything.

In fact, a study by this guy in Aberdeen showed that really clever people don't have ribcages and that ribcages just restrict circulation." "You put it back in though, right?" Wordsworth asked. He couldn't believe what he was hearing. "Well we were just about to, but we actually had some drinkies last night - only a few drops of the old port, and we sort of forgot that we should stick it back in. And anyway, the drinkies were damn strong - I reckon somebody must have spiked it with milk in first or something - and anyway, we sort of mailed just about all the cancerous organs from just about all the cancer patients to that Andrew chappie. Sorry." "So he didn't have cancer of the ribcage then?" Wordsworth asked. "Well he might have. But he did have cancer of . . . the . . . ummm . . . liver. Yeah. Yeah that's feasible. Cancer of the liver. Definitely cancer of the liver. Right. Cancer of the liver. Damn I'm good on my feet. Yeah, cancer of the liver. It's all black and filthy and dirty and crusty. Disgusting. That man's on death's door if his liver stays inside him. So anyway, we removed the ribcage to prevent it spreading to the organs like the heart and stuff. Because the liver's just next to the ribcage, which is just next to some of that other gloopy stuff, which is full of those blue things that are full of that red stuff that's always spraying everywhere -" "You mean blood?" Wordsworth asked, scared. "I don't know what they tell you to call it these days at high school, you little snob, and I don't care. Stop interrupting me. I'm doing a damn good job saving your father's life, here, and so don't you go around telling me what to do and what to call gloopy stuff that's always spraying around into all the other patients. They can't keep it to themselves. I spent a whole day at med school, and I deserve a bit of respect. Any way . . . where was I? Oh yeah, the ribcage - we figured that if we removed the ribcage we could prevent it from getting to the pumpy thing and the stuff that sticks to hair and the grey thing that smells bad. But you probably don't get it, you being just a stupid dumb little kiddy. Get lost." Wordsworth ignored the insults. "So did you remove the liver?" he asked, feeling rather put out by the whole schenanigan. "Well as I said" the doctor began " . . . Get lost." And he hung up.

"That Words worth character is so harsh and brutal and menacing and karma - creating" Mark said after reading Wordsworth's novel. He was moved by the levels of expression and the courage with which his brother spoke of his struggles. He felt red-faced and a bit silly that he might have to lie down because Wordsworth's book was so totally heavy, man. "Scaring his brother like that by being so menacing and spooky." "Did you like it?" Wordsworth asked. He valued his brother's opinion in spite of the fact that they hated each other bitterly, and their detestation for each other was intense to say the least, yet he loved Mark and hoped wildly that one dark stormy night when the hail was pelting down and the rain was fiery and rugged and aggressive they could explore each other's young man's bodies in a big orgy of passion. Again. "Well I thought that despite the rudimentary odoaceriumuscusness and the scandiumotry, not to mention the stakhanovitic inyalaicalitiousness -" "But did you *like* it?" Wordsworth interrupted. "Well, as I said, the aurignacian recrudescence capofrigulates into the transpontine-" "Yes yes yes, but did you *like* it?" Wordsworth interrupted again. "Well I'm not-" "Stop urinating me around, Mark, and tell me whether or not you liked the damn thing!" "-" "You bastard!" Wordsworth screamed at his brother. "*I knew you wouldn't like it!* You're a male chauvanist pig and I'm leaving you!" Then he ran out of the room sobbing, his dress trailing behind him. "-" Mark said again. "_{--#-\;+|>!!!" He then shouted at his already hurt brother, raking the wound unforgivingly open and letting it hurt and sting and be really painful and squeezing a bit of lemon juice and cider apple vinegar in it and putting a plaster on it and tearing it off really slowly a few days later so all the hairs came out at the follicles and the skin went all pink and sensitive and then slapping it while he wore jeans so the denim scraped on the tender skin and he went ouch. Wordsworth was in horrific agony, all thanks to Mark's bitter crusade of criticism against his Magnus Opum. He sobbed bitter tears and went yah boo, sucks to you. "Don't say 'sucks to you' to the reader Wordsworth you dicky-bum!" I shouty-blahed at him, but it was too late.

Johnny was enthusiastic about the coming ski trip. He was also happy and joyous and smiley and giggly and funny and cheerful and talkative and some other adjectives that he was. He had put his name down on the list, after making sure that none of the friends whom he hated had followed him to do the same. He went skiing with his school every year, and it was always a very jolly time - schools from all over the country entwined in the ecstasy that was each other's alpine company, principals and teachers met and shook hands, students won and lost trophies, medals, competitions. They hurled snowballs at each other amidst their stays at the mountain, they created teams who would strike out at others with spheres of arctic matter, they had inter-school snowball wars that went on for years, they raced against everyone else's best times and their own, they fought each other for spaces in chair lift queues, they vied with each other for the attention of the oppositationedalnessly gender, and they made snowmen. And they wore silly hats. Johnny was not a good skier, although his arrogance and his height in the unwritten fashion empire took care of the opinions of others for him. What Johnny didn't want was for Andrew, Mark and Wordsworth to come on the ski trip. He hated them, he decided. He hated them bitterly and aggressively, with a passion that was nearly fanatical, he found. They were impeding and worsening his chances to find pretty girls and have really long gossip sessions with them and write down the names of all the cute guys in the class.

Mr Pizazz was a badass biker and he needed something cool to do to make him look tough while he threatened Mr. Woodcock. "I know what" he thought. Then there was a knock at the door. The door of the office that they were in I mean. "Who's knock-knocking on my do-door?" asked Mr. Pizazz and Mrs. Pizazz together. "I am" said the person who knocked. "Who are you?" they asked. "I'm me, ya morons" said the voice. "Who is me?" they asked again. "I'm the voice that belongs to the person who knocked." "Which is whose voice?" said Mrs. Pizazz while Mr. Pizazz dreamt up a conspiracy that involved finding out who was knocking on his door, or, more precisely, whose knocks were generated by firmly applied pressure in a direct physical medium upon the door, not up *on* the door but side long, or penetrating the door from a frontal angle perpendicular to the widest opposite-to-them plane of the door. "The voice is mine" said the person. "Well who are you?" asked Mr. Pizazz. "I'm the one whose knocks are penetrating your door from a frontal angle and causing a sonic wave to be generated that's going plop into your ear." "Well you should come in then." "I will come in. Just as soon as you invite me in." "I already did invite you in so come in." The door opened, or rather, to be more precise about it, technically, from a quantum mechanics standpoint, electrons or whatever in the door manipulated anti matter, or were manipulated by the opener of the door to open. So now the door is open. The way is open. It was made by those who are alive. Mr. Woodcock had been the one knocking, or creating the knocks via the spatial medium of the time space continuum that we call reality but which is just a fragment of multidimensional space and coolness that Mr. Woodcock inhabited. He sat in the doorway in his wheelchair and said hello to the Pizazzes. "Listen Woodcock" Mr. Pizazz said. "I know what you're up to. You've got a conspiracy. You know what we do to people who have conspiracies. "I don't have a conspiracy" Mr. Woodcock lied. Mr. Pizazz knew he was lying because he didn't trust him. The only person Mr. Pizazz did trust was himself. And his pet frog, David the Bald Eagle. "I want to keep you here, Woodcock, but I don't know if you're worth it. I think it would be better for everyone if you had an accident." Mr. Woodcock said "bro I already totally skinned my elbow pulling an ollie fakie in my wheelchair to show off to this fly as chick, G." "No I mean it would be better if you had an 'accident' kind of accident." "Do you mean like pooing my pants or wetting the bed like a little kid?" "No I mean it would be better if you got all chopped up and mushed in a meatworks and twenty-two adult elephants with obesity epidemics jumped up and down on you." "It wouldn't be better for me" Mr. Woodcock said. "So what" Mr. Pizazz said. "Who cares about you?" "Well I care about me" said Mr. Woodcock. "And Guye Armstronge needs me in the book for a bit yet I think." Mr. Pizazz looked sheepishly at the floor at the thought of betraying his royal highness of wonder and perfection, and shivered with fear cos Guye was business-like and brutally ass kicking, and was NEVER all talk and no action, even when he was having epic sleep-ins. Mr. Pizazz could relate to Mr. Woodcock on a level of emotion that both of them could understand - neither had any form of love, but Mr. Pizazz at least had a job he could think about all the time, while Mr. Woodcock had a job he would rather not have at all. "Nobody cares about you, you fat old git" Mr. Pizazz said to him in uncharacteristic emotion, that changed the tone of the book subtly and made it even way more better which most people thought was impossible, but Guye was just totally about pushing the envelope. Mr. Woodcock began to cry. "Don't begin to cry" Mr. Pizazz commanded, but he knew it was pointless. He would no doubt sob until it was time to go home, and Mr. Pizazz didn't want him hanging around his office while he delegated menial tasks and smoked cigars, and called his boss to talk about spying on Mr. Woodcock's private life, and flash new conspiracies with names like 'The Flash New Conspiracy' and 'The Conspiracy I Thought Of While I Was On The Toilet'. He would impede upon Mr. Pizazz's contribution to world conspiracies. However, to tell him that he had one minute to suppress his emotions and shut his fat mouth up before he was shown the way out, and that Mr. Pizazz had Johnny Henderson waiting outside to commend him on his performance in the mathematical field would help 'sober' Mr. Woodcock up when he was politely asked what Johnny would think when he saw Mr. Woodcock sobbing his legs that he didn't have off. "I'm calling Johnny Henderson down to my office to commend him on his performance in the mathematical field." He reached for his special phone, and proudly and skillfully and and and and and delegated a menial task: "I would like to speak with one Johnny Henderson, please." He placed the phone down on the plastic thing with all the buttons in symmetrical formation that looked very pretty. "Think about what he would say if he saw you crying." It was an act of mercy and wonderful intelligence on behalf of Mr. Pizazz, and he congratulated himself on it. "Congratulations." Mr. Woodcock looked up from his wheelchair with a look of total hatred towards his commanding officer, and wheeled his geriatric old self out of Mr. Pizazz's office.

"Your attempts to ever amount to a credible life form is most unfetchingly rare" Mr. Woodcock said to the six of them. "Well at least I know what nineteen divided by two is" Johnny said. "NYEaaaaaarr" said Mr. Woodcock, rattling his fist at them. (Then he fisted them with his rattle.) Johnny tried to get the grandmas to unhook themselves from his wonderous bod. "Please" he said. "Unhook yourselves from my wonderous bod." They burst out laughing, and said things like "Ee hee hee hee hee" and "Ee hee hee hee hee" while Johnny just stood there and lapped it up outside Mr. Pizazz's office door. "I'll be back . . ." the grandmas gasped at his cuteness, and he found himself wanting to grab some armpit hair.

" . . . In a minute" He continued. The grandmas went wild and fell against each other giggling. One of them fainted. "Come in Mr. Henderson" He heard Mr. Pizazz say, before he even touched the door. Mr. Pizazz filled Johnny with a sense of awe and he was bursting with pride as he stepped into Mr. Pizazz's office. Mr. Pizazz was the kind of man who had more conspiracies than the guy off the X-Files, and he reigned supreme over all else because he knew who the hell Gwen Dibley was - not the person Mr. Woodcock had been before he had become Mr. Woodcock, but the OTHER Gwen Dibley, who lay hiding around every corner, forever emerged in a conspiracy of some sort. Johnny knew that Mr. Pizazz would be facing the window with the blind pulled down as he always did, letting a very little amount of light into the room, sitting in his La-Z-Boy, while puffing on one of his cigars. He would be wearing a black suit and a deceiving look that said "I know more than you" and one could be as sure as anything that Mr. Pizazz knew exactly what was going on, even though no-one had ever seen him leave or enter his office. Even when he was going into the staff room to delegate menial tasks to the teachers, no-one ever saw him leave his office or go back in (he had a secret tunnel – that's what she said). He was too brilliant for them. That was why he was the principal. That was why he could smoke cigars and not get questioned about it when it was against the school policy for students to smoke. Johnny remembered back to the first time he had been called in to see Mr. Pizazz: it had been during a very interesting English class four years ago, and he had been complaining about the usage of clothing required on behalf of the female students, and was doing fairly well, until a messenger was sent up to him telling him that Mr. Pizazz wished to see him. As the girls began putting their shirts back on, Johnny told Mark that it was because of Johnny's brilliance and perfection that Mr. Pizazz wished to see him. Johnny didn't know why he had been asked a group of silly questions, and what surprised Johnny was the way Mr. Pizazz had handled the conversation without spinning around in his La-Z-Boy - he had spent the entire ten minutes facing the window. He was good at his job. But the questions must have been for some reason, as Mr. Pizazz was the sort of man who was absolutely unsilly. So into Mr. Pizazz's room Johnny marched, and as always, Mr. Pizazz was facing his window. He turned his La-Z-Boy around slowly. He puffed on his cigar. He looked Johnny in the eye. He didn't sip any tea. What a master. "I see you have absolute control over the fairer gender" He observed. "You bet your vast reservoirs of knowledge that you use to delegate menial tasks and control sad pathetic people like Mr. Woodcock" Johnny said, feeling tip-top about the way the day was going, especially how Mr. Pizazz had noticed his absolute control over the old ladies without even using any elements of role play and bondage gear, even though later on he was going to get them to call him their mistress. "Use it wisely" Mr. Pizazz cautioned. Johnny nodded, nod nod went his head. "You may go, Mr. Henderson" Mr. Pizazz said.

Johnny left, and rehooked the grandmas onto his wonderous bod and grabbed their earwax, wishing like crazy that they were as perfect as the girl from heaven's. But of course they weren't, no, they had hard flaky earwax, and Johnny wasn't that much of a hard flaky earwax man anymore. He was a waxy hi-lipid concentration gooey earwax man. He liked earwax that was all mushy and slopped around his fingers when he got it on with his grandmas from Mars.

"Your mother's up to her usual tricks again" said the doctor to Wordsworth. "She doesn't even have one water atom of Anthony's Disease. She doesn't have a disease anything like Anthony's disease. So we're suing her. For two million this time. At least. It'll teach her to mess with us. But we'll still cure her. Even though we don't really want to any more. She deserves to die, you know. She's made a joke out of the whole medical profession, as I might have said before. Or maybe that was some other guy's mother. Probably was actually. Well it doesn't matter. Anyway, we're still suing her. So there." Wordsworth decided to ignore these idle threats and find out what she had. "What does she have?" "Well, we pulled out the books, and we reckon she's dying of this thing called Wordsworth's disease. It's a really horrible one that. She'll die nice and slow. Serves her right. Serves her damn right. That'll teach her to mess us around. Ha ha ha." Wordsworth felt guilty instantly. Surely he could not have brought his mother's death on? No. Never. For he loved his mother so much, and had held her close, so close, *too* close, on too many winter evenings. "Is there a cure?" he asked, with EXACTLY the same urgency of Colin Meads' favourite Slazenger boots – the size sixteens with ten mil sprig – pelting into the wet earth narrowly dodging the Wallabies under the nightlights and roaring crowd at Mt. Smart Stadium, even though they were some-where in America. "Well yes, there is, as a matter of fact. There definitely is. But we'll just let her die for a while before we give it to her. Show her what it's like to be messed around. We'll leave her lying on death's door, then we'll pump her full of cure, and she'll apologize, and everyone'll be happy. Now your father's in a very different state indeed. We sort of sucked out his liver and sent it to that Andrew chappie, but we were a wee bit too late. It had spread to his arms and his hands, so we cut them off. And the spleen. But apart from that he's great." Wordsworth was relieved to hear that his father was so healthy, and hoped that some day they would be back on the couch drinking beer and calling each other mate and watching the kangaroo-eating, David Campese-1991-classic-try-against-the-All-Blacks-in-Ireland-showing off, VB-swilling Austra-lians lose the rugby.

I drank a potion of magic protection. Deborah was another person who existed. She was of a good alignment, and her char-acter class was paladin. She was the one who Johnny had a total crush on for like ten minutes or something. And it was true, yay was it true... that Deborah *did* kind of like him. BUT DEEP! OH SO DEEP! – In the unrequieted fathoms of the spelunking depths of the vast feloobriance trah-trovvedying Kalashnikov war massacres of her heart, she was so timid and fragile, so gasping, how broken she was... by how much... it hurt... to kind of like. She was a Carbon-Hydrogen based being, and she too was about to be torn apart emotionally by society's ills, oh society, oh The World, oh oh the muchness of blind rules and schooldom and unemployment levels and ridiculing social graces that are probably way more of a hassle than they're worth, oh Deborah, oh the three dimensional-ity of your character class, oh oooooh society, society oh oh oooh, how I doth bequeath ye... with desire so powered by willies of all the other guys in her maths class, and possibly a really rubbish cliché-intense sequel... if she survives... The Conspiracy. Deborah was fifteen years old. So she wasn't legal, which kind of sucks. She was intelligent, persuasive, gentle and warm, she had much compassion and a good heart. Wordsworth leaned out of my com-puter, cleared his throat right in my ear, and said "Do you mean in a biochemical and/or physiological sense of muscular structure and histoarchitecture of the atria, or does it mean in a metaphor-ical sense, as in conforming behaviourally within a spectrum of socially moral norms of her own free expression, for the greater good?" I pushed him away and said "I already SAID she was a good person you dickhead Wordsworth can you shut up and stop inter-rupting my amazing adjective third person thing?" Anyway. One day, Deborah sat in maths class – "Is this the same Deborah in *our* maths class?" Wordsworth interrupted. "Yes it is" I said. "It's still the same Deborah, there's only one of them, Wordsworth." "Oh, I thought part of someone's conspiracy might have been a cloner." It was the same Deborah, and there was no cloner. Well, one day – "She's actually a very able student" Mr. Woodcock interrupted, and I got annoyed. "Bro I'm trying to keep it STRICTLY third person instead of breaking the fourth wall ALL THE TIME" I shouted at him, my God I was so sick of telling these twerps to just stay in character so I didn't have to break the third person out of the narrating dimension to tell you, the person reading this THAT I ACTUALLY EXIST NOT JUST IN THIS BOOK I ACTUALLY EXIST IN A REAL LIFE LIKE YOURS EXCEPT I'M NOT YOU. I think. (Proofreading this bit was really confusing and heavy, man.) Deborah was kind and thoughtful, dignified, and raised well by her parents. Also her tits were MASSIVE. Word bro, like, no sag. Deborah was in the same maths class as Johnny, Wordsworth, Mark and Andrew, and Mr. Woodcock. "Hey I don't mean to be really annoying but you already said that" said Wordsworth and there was a sneaky look on his face that suggested to me that he DID want to be annoying, like really annoying but not telling me about it. I got my d20 ready for a two-handed sword attack if I needed to. So. In their maths class – "Wow the whole thing takes place in a maths class" said Andrew, who I hadn't seen until then. "We're really taking the world by storm here, aren't we?" he said with no detectable sarcasm at all, and I really appreciate that he said it without any sarcasm. There was also a sixteen-year-old in their maths class called Fred, he was mighty and powerful. He was a barbarian with a strength of nineteen, almost as strong as a Frost Giant. "Ah, hang on, Frost Giant strength is twenty-nine" interrupted Wordsworth. "That's *way* more than nineteen." OK so according to Wordsworth, Fred's strength was actually closer to a Fire Giant, sorry about that. Anyway, along with the story and – "Hang on again, hang on, sorry" interrupted Wordsworth AGAIN, "but Fire Giant strength is thirty-one, it's not accurate to say that his strength was like a Fire Giant!" Wordsworth yelled at me, sticking his stupid head way out of the computer right at me when for once I was actually concentrating on doing writing stuff, for once without using ANY writing enhancing substances. So Fred had a strength of nineteen, which was as strong as an Ogre Mage. "Hey actually" Wordsworth shouted at me again, his nasal voice being really annoying, "you can just say the same strength as an Ogre. It doesn't have to be an Ogre *Mage* – that would imply that Fred had magic, and he doesn't have magic." Fred, who was as strong as an Ogre and who did not have magic because he didn't need it, only sneaky weenies are magic users, was incidentally stronger than a necromancer. "Ah, I'm not sneaky, only thieves have sneak skills" Wordsworth told me while I was trying to write about someone other than him, someone who was incidentally way more interesting and layered and Deborah-attracting than him. "If Fred doesn't have any magic he wouldn't do well against undead, heaps of undead need magic weapons to destroy them" Wordsworth rudely interrupted. "I think you mean heaps of undead CAN ONLY BE DESTROYED by magic weapons Wordsworth" I corrected. Anyway, on with – "Ah, actually yes, that is what I mean" Wordsworth interrupted again, because he was a dick and Deborah definitely did not have a crush on him. "If she saw my undead army then she probably would get a crush on me, like I've got five liches that I've summoned. That's more liches than Bill Clinton has! She'd be impressed by that, women are totally impressed by power." "You don't have five liches Wordsworth" I told him. "You don't even have one lich." Wordsworth, who did not even have one lich, and had such a low strength it did not even bear mention, went away from me somewhere else so I could concentrate on writing the bit about Deborah being interested in a character called Fred. Deborah was interested in a character called Fred. There. "I don't mean to be annoying, but why is she interested in him?" Wordsworth, who I'm pretty sure actually WAS meaning to be annoying, interrupted, even though I had psychically commanded him to go away. "I mean a necromancer can have a really big strength if I cast the Strength spell." Wordsworth cast the Strength spell in front of Deborah, who wasn't really looking anyway, and even after casting it his strength was still a lot less than Fred's strength, also, Deborah didn't ONLY care about strength. "Well you should say how much it is!" Wordsworth shouted, and it was really weird that I could hear him when I was pretty certain he had gone away. "Yeah I've gone away but I'll just cast that spell heaps so I've got more strength than Fred." In their maths class, a sudden – "Hey actually –" Wordsworth interrupted AGAIN, "actually I have a really high charisma score so Deborah *would* be attracted to me, and if Fred's a level twenty Barbarian then his charisma would be really low because he's probably been in heaps of fights and got cuts all over him and wouldn't he be weakened? Like wouldn't it be more realistic role-playing if he was a bit tired of fighting, and ready to give up and... you know he doesn't sound like a very good character." Fred was, actually, a pretty cool character. "You should probably delete him" said Wordsworth, who had somehow stepped out of my computer and was pouring me a beer. "Just move him to the recycling bin, and then click empty the recycle bin, that'll be fine." I had a bit of the beer, and you know, it wasn't bad. "Thanks Wordsworth, I guess maybe you're not the bad guye after all." "Wow, PLOT TWIST!" shouted Wordsworth as he asked if he could have one of my beers but I saw I only had eleven left after this one so I told him I only got enough for myself. Yeah nah uce wait until WINZ puts my bene in. "Well, ah... shall we delete Fred now?" he asked, and I secretly thought he should probably go down the shops and get me some more beers, and also stay the night so he could go to some job interviews for me in the morning, so I could have a sleep-in, like I'm not lazy or anything but I totally need a recharge, like I've written like two pages today. And, and – AND I looked at some old stuff I wrote ages ago. Some of it needs editing but I'll do it tomorrow. Wordsworth moved a bit closer to me on the couch, and I saw him looking at the last bite of my pie that I didn't want to give him, even though I was full. He moved his head closer over the keyboard and his stupid hair-cut got in the way of the screen, and I had a bit of dissonance because even though he was a dick, he did actually go all the way to the fridge and get me a beer. "So can you just give me a turn..." he said as he wriggled his fingers under my hand with the mouse, and stupidly... I let him. After all, there was some beer left, so I drank about three swigs. He started scrolling through the document, and he grabbed the keyboard off me as well. "Let me just help you out with the characters, Guye..." he searched for all the parts in the document with Fred in them, and I knew he was up to his old non-beer bad guye tricks again. He wanted to conflict me, in the flaming bong of my pericardium, where the epic quest of my inner gauze bit got all clogged up with the weed residue of his hatred, and the paranoia of... desire. My desire to call Wordsworth a dick and make him go away again. After he went and got me some beers and a tinny. "Hey Wordsworth can you go away again off the couch and go get me some more beers then get back in the computer immediately without arguing." "Hang on" he said, "I'm... juuust..." and he had double-clicked on EVERY mention of Fred in the book, he'd selected every instance of Fred's name and I said "bro stop taking over the book it's mine and you're already writing the really gay claws of being sad or whatever so piss off." But then his eyes blazed a fury, his bikini charged with a molten depravity-blast of evil magic AND HE CAST LARLOCH'S MINOR DRAIN AT ME! I stood, immediately – well OK not IMMEDIATELY, but I did sort of get up a bit, the missile rebounding off me and knocking over my beer and then into my rubbish bin, that I could see the corner of under all my rejection letters. "You'll never have me alive Wordsworth!" I shouted. "How do you deny my necromantic magical necromance!" he challenged, in the face of my defiance in the face of his defiance. "WORDSWORTH YOU HAVE COURTED OBLIVION!" I shouted, standing to like mostly my full height, but one of my knees was still on my couch cos there was heaps of junk on the floor and only space for one of my feet. I pulled out my druid staff, which did +6 to hit and damage to Wordsworth and threatened him with it. "I drank a potion of magic protection Wordsworth, I knew you were going to try something like this!" I shouted. He stood, glaring, awash in the abject lust of his misery, feeling the trepidating fury of my control-freaky autonomy, in the rejection letter of my magic protection, in the mess of my bedroom. Even the really gross carpet fungus in the corner that I had my bookshelf over that I think my dad hadn't seen. The evil sorcerer was humbled. "I'm not a sorcerer I'm a necromancer" he said. "OK well you're gonna have to go and do romance in a different book mate" I said, and THEN he was humbled. I sat back down on the couch, I was tired from doing a standing up bit. "Hey Wordsworth after you go down to New World and buy me some more beers with YOUR MONEY can you get back in the computer so we can finish the bit where Fred beats you up and everyone including Deborah sees AND THEN FRED AND DEBORAH START MAKING OUT?" Wordsworth fumed, hanging his head in shame. "You don't have to put they're making out in capital letters" he grumbled. "Just shut up and get back in the computer" I saided. "OK I'll get back in the computer but can you..." he looked around to see that no-one else was in my room or anything, then he said "can you download a bit of porn for when you turn the computer off? And then copy and paste me into the porn folder?" And he grinned at me really sneaky and I just firmly said "Wordsworth I absolutely refuse to do that and I don't want to do that and I never ever use porn to get book ideas. Now get back in the computer!"

The students got every third weekend off to go home if they lived near enough, and many of them used this time to see loved ones and relatives. Deborah had been enthusiastic about going home and seeing her loved ones, but she had entangled herself within a rather nasty argument with her father. She had commented on the very teenage idea that educations weren't all that necessary. He hadn't liked it. "Sweetie honey-pie lemon tart cuddle joy darling bitch" he had said as he whipped her sumptuous eary ears with his mouthy mouth, him wearing her high heels and she wearing his, "you can't expect to be happy and have fun, especially in a septic tank like this place. Now the only way to get a hot education is to be incredibly good at maths. Maths is a REAL man's way of life." He unruffleded his paper and crossed his legs and put his lipstick on. "But I'm not a man" Deborah said. "What do you mean you're not a man? You haven't had an... operation have you?" "No. I've always not been a man." "What the hell do you mean you've always not been a man? You're starting to sound like someone out of a Guye Armstronge novel." Deborah's father was most definitely not a Guye Armstronge fan. He thought Guye's ideas were silly and absurd, and that the man was a most notoriously unhygenic and inappropriate defecatory splatter on the toilet bowl of bad writing, needing to be flushed down along with all the other bad writers. Deborah's father didn't have time for Guye Armstronge novels. Blimey, Guye didn't even start his books with capital letters. And he was so inconsistent - only telling his stories from the third person part of the time, imposing his own silly points of view over those of his "characters" who were so pencil thin and dirty-minded it just showed what sort of things "Mr." Armstronge was fixated with and with what sort of things went in on of at his bedroom - the man had no sense of control over the things that happened in his books. Still . . . . Deborah sometimes wondered if it all *was* just a Guye Armstronge novel. "I've always not been a man, that's what I mean." Her father sighed, and started paying some real attention to his daughter, the first time in a long time... oh, the might of her daddy issues... oooooh, the unsatisfaction of the cataclysms... in her heart... oh, the turbulent rage struggling to be free from her love, oh the myriad pounding of the 1987 Irish World Cup rugby forwards scoring the tries of desire in the pouty lips of the touch judges of her passion. "I wish you could've told us" he said. "We are your parents you know." "I thought you already knew that I was a girl." "I knew no such thing. You've brought shame to this family, and to the Shaolin Temple. What do you think all our relatives will say when they find out you're a girl?" "They should've already known!" she yelled in disbelief, hoping that some prat would leap out at her and say that she was on the Best of Candid Camera, and she had just won something really useless. At least she might be able to USE something really useless. Her father sighed again, and opened the mail. Deborah noticed one of the letters was from her school, and she became scared as her father read over its scratchingly uncomfortable statement, and widened his eyes in a look of shock. "Do you know what this note says?" He asked her. "No" She replied. "It says that on this very day, you, Deborah Cable used blasphemous ungodly Satanic Christian-killing Bible-defying gospel-threatening cross-inverting language in your maths lesson today. What have you got to say for yourself?" Deborah's parents had always been reasonably strict when it came to religion, and almost as strict when it came to school. Adorning the walls of their humble home were arcane symbols, things about stuff, rules, bibles, commandments, lessons, quotes, jokes, knicknacks, spikes, collars, hand cuffs, and other religious stuff. It was totally nematocystically lophobranchiatingly streptomycining and a real xerophthalmiac on the really sensitive purple bit of my stramonium. Deborah became scared, as any sixteen-year-old girl would. "I thought she was fifteen" said Andrew, who didn't seem to take any enjoyment in interrupting my blah blahing at all, no, I'm sure he hated pointing out any inconsistencies in my writey-waffle. "Yeah, hang on, so is she legal now?" Mr. Woodcock asked. Mr. Woodcock could manipulate Deborah's life in his evil ways that would get her in trouble with her parents, and with Mr. Pizazz. He could, if he wanted, get her expelled from school. "You've brought disgrace to this humble home, Deborah, and to the Shaolin Temple" Her father said. "Why Deborah? First you say you've always not been a man like some ridiculous inconsistent idiot then you start to use blasphemous ungodly Satanic Christian-killing Bible-defying gospel-threatening language in your maths lesson, thus indicating your lack of hunger to be absolutely perfect. Tomorrow evening we'll go and see Mr. Woodcock. I want to clear this bad language problem up. What would your mother think?" "You forgot cross-inverting!" Deborah shouty-shouted. Her mother would no doubt think her daughter had lost her childish innocence (which she had really lost four years ago to Johnny who had enjoyed their little game of monopoly immensely). Deborah wasn't very scared because she really *is* just a made up character and doesn't have emotions. She's just made up okay? She's not real. All you people at conventions can just chill out man.

Johnny went home to his mother, who wanted to know whether or not he was still dating that nasty girl Andrew, and how well he was doing at school. "You're still not dating that nasty girl Andrew, are you?" his mother asked him. "Andrew's a boy, mother dear" Johnny informed her. Andrew went home to his father, who wanted to know whether or not he was still dating that nasty girl Johnny, and how his novel was going. To say that Andrew was a stupid boy would be *awfully* politically incorrect, and horribly predjudiced, and simply not on, and not to be tolerated in a politically correct and sensitive composition such as this. Andrew was a stupid boy. And he still is. He lives just down the road from me at No. 47 and his IQ test just came in the mail and it turns out that his IQ is minus one million and a twenty-sixth. He was easily the stupidest person in this book. He was happy to be one of Johnny's friends. He too was writing a novel on Wordsworth's computer. Soon his friends who hated him would find out. Andrew wasn't all stupidity. Oh Yes. Andrew's becoming of friendship with Johnny was just the start of his master conspiracy - he knew Johnny wouldn't mind if he used and abused Wordsworth's computer, and he often slinked stealthily into Mark and Wordsworth's room during the daytime when the lights were off and no-one could see him and write his novel deftly. Yes, soon Andrew's *The Cleverest Book In The World* would hit the bookstores. He would be rich before the end of the year. Very rich. He already had some ideas:

The Cleverest Book In The World
By Gwen Dibley

It was going well.

Wordsworth was deep in thought. Mark, Johnny and Andrew shouldn't come on the ski trip because it would be bad. Because if they did, Wordsworth would be in hell. Especially if Johnny came. Wordsworth could put up with Mark's small talk, but Johnny and Andrew had always been very annoying to be with. If Johnny was to come along the two of them would no doubt gang up on Wordsworth and make him cry, like the time when Johnny had poured ketchup on his vita brits. "They're *MY* vita brits Words-worth" Johnny had said, but it didn't stop the pain, dammit. Once again Wordsworth desired solitude. So I threw a party for him. It would be so beneficial for him to get some "time off" - he wasn't handling the stress at home very well (I think he just doesn't like being in my rad book). "I don't like being in your stupid book" he said. Wordsworth had formed a conspiracy preventing the evils of Andrew and Johnny, but it relied heavily on luck. In fact it was totally luck. Bummer for him that I hate him, bwah ha ha. What he wanted was for Mark, Johnny and Andrew to not hear about the ski trip at all, or think it was for weeny nerds like Wordsworth, which wouldn't matter because Wordsworth was an exceptionally brilliant skier, and everyone would go home singing his praises, and he might even get a nice lady friend to do strange things with his bits and pieces. "You're so horny Wordsworth" I said to him. "Always thinking about shagging and doing it. You're totally gonna ruin my posh upper class romance Jane Austen style novel." "Well if you'd just give me a sex scene, then I could relax, man!" he shouted at me, but I want him to learn some self-control. "OK, OK, just give me a shower scene then" he begged, taking a far too casual attitude in his mannerisms toward Almighty Guye Arm-stronge, Slaughterer of Evil, summoned by the peoples of the Cult of Dorageur aeons before, in an age of might and battles, when men were men and hard-working women were getting at *least* seventy-five cents for every dollar a man made by slush funds and offshore tax havens. A lightbulb appeared above Wordsworth's head, and I mean the other head. He sighed, and sidled up way too close to me. "Guye, *bro,* can you just give me a shower scene with that Deborah chick? Just... you know, come on man. I wanna totally squish her earlobes around, it'll be awesome dude, I prom-ise. You won't even need to write any dialogue for it, just put it in before the ski trip bit. If you gave me a shower scene I could totally rock the book out. And make a ghetto blaster and we'll play some eighties music with real wicked lead guitar while we're shower-ing" Wordsworth continued as he flexed his forty-seven-kilogram stature to make the bottom of his ribcage poke out, not noticing my right pinky getting ever closer to the unfathomable nemesis of the delete button in the upper right corner of my mum's eighties Macintosh LSII, which is way better than IBM Bill Gates Windows bollocks so don't even go *there* girlfriend. "Yeah, a shower scene's the way to go, Guye, just check out my Mel Gibson-esque bum-bum." "You might need to scrub the "ANDREW WAS HERE" graffiti off it before I cast you in a shower scene, Wordsworth" I said, his farty aroma pungently tantalising my nostrils and doing more damage than a thousand cigarettes all at the same time. My pinky was hovering over the delete button while I desperately tried to not obliterate him from the greatest book ever that only stupid publishers with no taste at all would reject. "Yeah, me and Deborah in a shower scene would put you into the highest publishing per-centile and the 'wealthy over-forties single women reading about relationships' demographic, dude" Wordsworth told me, unaware that I could beat him up in a fight so easy, like I can just about do seven push-ups and once I even went for a run to the dairy and almost back. Inputting the security code into his Anal Alarm System, Wordsworth closed his poos from the world. "What - " he began, as he saw my pinky fingernail tickling the delete button, and the faint smile on my face...

AND NOW . . .
THE NEXT BIT . . .

And oh, in Mr. Woodcock's dream, in a dream not real life so it couldn't be called illegal, yay it was written, in starlit brimming hopey tears of empassioned brastrap-twanging softcore, where freedom was free, where maidens did frolic, that Mr. Woodcock held Deborah so tight, so even and close, so warmly that her pleasure was a red-hot brimstone of primitive passion and looked deep into her light-blue ears. "Why's all this weird blue stuff in your ears?" he willow-the-whispered. The firmness and passion of his wisp took her heart soaring ever closer to meaning, to purpose of life and love. He cleared his throat and finally picked out the really annoying bit of spinach that had been stuck in his teeth all day since the omelette he had for lunch. In such a roaring tidal wave of love, passion and lusty weirdness, in the forest of her soft hair, he pressed his tender lips to her ear, and whispered words he hoped would propel her pulmonary trunk to new levels of idiopathic enlargement, diagnosed by x-ray, yay into the waxy caverns of her earlet so tenderly, in romance, in soaring pashes of passionate love did he whisper: "Mal Meninga was one of the greatest players in NRL history." She fought against him, pushing him away, and in the dream he almost lost her. "I actually prefer Cliff Lyons" she said. "I mean, as someone who ran the ball a bit more down the wing, instead of just smashing through the forwards." Mr. Woodcock's heart slammed to a stop: "No, no, oh noeyest no! Say it is not soey so!" "Oh my maths teacher it is so and yay, I doth say it." He put his arm over his eyes. "Ye are..." he began... alas, he could not say it! Her mighty bosom heaved, and any teenage male reading this bit totally thought I was about to describe her boobs really graphically, but I wasn't. Her voice wavered with lost love, with a puzzled, pulsing heart so broken, so torn, so divorced, and in a really frustrating passive-aggressive way with heaps of communication breakdowns and arguing over who was gonna get what, and the divorce lawyers were changing secretaries and there was all this hiring and firing and layoffs, and so many notations got lost that it totally stressed out both parties... I guess that's the corporate world... sorry, lost my train of thought... something... from love... that she felt her bonnet was ensmashed with his wacky old man's boner 'accidentally' rubbing against her in the nightclub while he asked her what she was up to and pulled his new cellphone out where everyone could see so they knew he was cool. When she spoke he felt nothing but emotion, he measured it on a galvanic skin response meter: "It is true...!" she cried. His eyes poured a slush of tears upon his gentle mathsy mathsish skinletty wrinkle-bottoms on the muscle most buccinatey. "We cannot be together!" she shouted. "No" he cried... when he spake his torn words it was with such a quiver of sorrow that seas divided and mountains fell: "Ye are a Manly supporter!" "I am, it is so!" she shouted. "But Meninga was one of the most difficult players to tackle in the history of rugby league" he said, fitting a new 240V donkeypower engine onto his wheelchair so he could totally do one-eighty tailslides. "Oh, in the Campese-goose-steps of your betrayal" Mr. Woodcock dream-whispered to dream-Deborah as he balanced one of his dozen Foster's cans on her boob to show how big it was, sitting in the dream-carpark, his proud blond dream-hair and flowing dress billowing out behind him as he ran (he had legs in the dream). There was a knot at his maths room door which brought him out of his dream and back into reality. Which was a bit weird because he's totally a fictional character. "Oh reality, oh polynomials, oh hyperbolic graphs, oh reduced reductionism, oh Darwinian mechanics of biological processes" he gasped, tongue and wheelchair aflutter. The knot upon his door was a structural weakening of timber cleavability, and had no real impact upon maidens fair, or the epic romance of anyone's heart. And upon this knot that was not even worth mentioning; I mean I have no idea why you're reading this sentence all about it, but anyway G upon it came a knock, a fist rapping with the urgency of a dude who was maybe a bit bored, like not really too worried what was going on, like pretty chilled out bro. And I didn't really approve of laziness in my awesome book, but he was just an extra, so whatever, like we'll just get this scene done real quick then no worries eh. They walked into Mr. Woodcock's discipline room at the sort of speed one would have expected from such a religion-obsessed family - a biblical pace set by Deborah's father Mr. Cable, and the rest of the family followed. They seated their heavenly holed holes upon the chairs Mr. Woodcock had placed around the room strategically - his wheels were in the centre, the other three positioned strategically so as to allow for the best acoustics - one was in the window, two were under his desk, and three was in a different room. Mr. Woodcock shook hands, shoulders, knees and toes with Mr. and Mrs. Cable and then knocked back fifteen shots of vodka. "Skull, skull skull" Mr. and Mrs. Cable chanted, following the viking roots of their vodka-in-the-nostril worshipping philosophy. Mr. Woodcock jumped out of the window, ate a huge steak to sober up, and rode his wheelchair back, doing a really gnarly handplant but not showing off or whatever. "Well your daughter's always been subjected to a most impolite profanity problem, Mr. Cable" he said sternly as he bounced his wheelchair down and up on a pogo stick in a gumboot, and for the briefest of seconds, in the cavern of denial, in the quarterpipe of aching bereavement, over the railgrind of abnegating loss, did his skateboarding mates believe that he didn't think skateboarding was cool anymore. Deborah could not believe what she was hearing. She had simply said "Oh my God" in that usual high school girlish fashion, and was being punished for it. She worked hard in maths, except for the few times that there had been good goss that just had to be told, and she was in the top twenty percent of her class. She always did her homework. Mr. Cable nodded sternly, and ran his finger over the image on his Bon Jovi T shirt that was probably a knock off that he bought in some third world country for two bucks, that I hoped I didn't get sued over and didn't actually approve of him wearing but like whatever let's just get on with it. Deborah thought sometimes it was as if her father was still immature - normally she could have quite interesting and involving discussions with him, but whenever he had his mates around to watch the New Zealanders and Australians and Canadians lose at every sport, because they wanted America to win, because they were in America, he would take up the customary tough guy attitude, and lose his sense of maturity. He would slouch in his chair, drink beer, put his bondage outfit on, crack his whip, and say rude things to Deborah and her mother - he was still a teenager really - worse, even, as there were quiet, humble teenagers becoming young men, who were sensible and knew where they stood – at least in the unspoken hierarchy of school fashions. Deborah wondered if they were denying their own personal power, instead of taking charge of their own lives, and standing up for themselves more. There was no way they would try to impress the loud, arrogant, mocking, ignorant, horny, racist pigs that made up some of the other less desirable parts of the population. It was a bit unfair that they were treated so badly - always by themselves, reading books about science fiction and fantasy and computer programming and how the world had been visited by aliens from Uranus. They deserved better. Much better. Pre-judging definitely ruled when popularity was concerned. Not that *she* was going to go out with some uncool loser who wasn't in the first fifteen. I mean grid iron. Deborah vomited inwardly as she realised how cheesy her bits of the book were getting when she hadn't even been in it very long, and I punched her in the vag for letting my cool book get all corny and rehashing all the eight-ies teen angst movies, without even getting her boobs out once. "Deborah continually releases the most awful and expletive word patterns" Mr. Woodcock continued. "Every sentence she gives to the world and to the classroom is littered with the most repugnant and dodecasyllabic monophrases of a plop. Her evil mind seems to filter the perfection of nice words like 'cat' and 'flower' right out of her voice container. It is simply dipterous to mendeleviate a mesembrianthemum of saying bad stuff. Her mouth seems to be one huge constantly-orgasmic linguatic phallus, copulating its souring toxins into the shrine of my maths class, impregnating the other students with their foul cornucopia of yukky-poo and defil-ing the very basis of numberdom. Deborah tries to emulate "cool-ness" and be "trendy" - may I suggest to you that you tell her off? I think I may. Tell her off. She normally works quite hard in class, except there are some times when she finds it necessary to gossip about a young barbarian called Fred, I believe. I think she's just trying to fit in with her friends by this sort of behaviour. Maybe it would be better for her education and the ozone layer if she didn't sit with them for a start." "Yes" her father agreed. "Yes yes yes you gorgeous hunk of an old man. She's always wanted to be accepted by her friends. Rather immature behaviour really." Brenda or whatever her name was could not believe what rubbish she was hearing. And this time her father was trying to impress Mr. Woodcock with his display of "maturity" when his study machine of a daughter was trying her hardest, and not caring really whether or not she fitted in. Her father was a hypocrite. Of the lowest calibre. *He* was the heretic. "How would that be Deborah?" her mother asked. "Do you think if you didn't sit with your friends you'd do better work, and none of this blasphemous lingual ingsgwerkulous?" She was already doing very good work, and Fred had nothing to do with it. Even though he was level twenty, and his constitution was so high he rolled 2d8 for his hit points every time he levelled up. "I think so" Mr. Woodcock interrupted. "Deborah's mouth is as resemblent to a substandard recycling plant that did not deal with all subtypes of plastics. The rest of the class seems to exist to her as no more than a napkin or kerchief forced to ensoak a cacophonic verbal phlegm. The number of students that have caught the diseases of expurgatory disrespect is phenomenally dreadful - vast numbers of persona have defiled our sacred and innocent school by their horrific extrudement of tainted English." "I'm doing just fine" Kendra or whoever her name was said firmly. Fred just didn't care. He was a bragging show off, whose personality nobody really would have liked if he didn't always use a two-handed sword in every attack phase and get critical hits all the time. "As you can see, I'm disabled"

Mr. Woodcock said accusingly, as if he was going to blame Deborah for his loss of legs. If he was, she would no longer know what to think. The world was going mad, and Deborah was the poor sane one left to sort her life out. There could be no way Mr. Woodcock could blame her for his disability, and she prayed to God in all his loving glory to not let Mr. Woodcock tell such whopping lies. "And it's all your fault" he continued. "Nah, just kidding. But there are a lot of amusing and humorous students who seem to think it amusing and humorous to find amusing and humorous things which have quite a lot to do with this most unfortunate disability, which they consider to be amusing and humorous. Which is one thing I definitely do not find . . . neither amusing . . . nor humorous. Not even when I totally bring the mad fakeys, brah." Her parents nodded fiercely and agressively, their jaws set like cement and their eyes semi-closed in a look of hatred at anything resembling even a vague touch of amusement or humour. They would have made great English teachers. "I have to say that I don't find this sort of behaviour appropriate in the classroom" Mr. Woodcock continued. "I find it entirely inappropriate! Now Deborah here was once a nice girl, but now I am beginning to think that maybe she would rather be one of the students who are wasting their lives away by failing all their subjects stubbornly and arrogantly and trying to write a best-selling novel about problems in society. I hope for the sake of everyone involved here that Deborah has not taken this course of action." Deborah had not taken this road - the thought of writing a best-selling novel about a problem in society had not occurred to her, but now her maths teacher had shown her something she could do in her spare time, apart from gossiping about Fred and his +1 diddle. "You're not writing a best-selling novel about a problem in society, are you?" her mother asked her, sounding very scared.

"No" Deborah said. "I think the first problem we have to address is this blasphemous ungodly Satanic Christian-killing Bible-defying gospel-threatening cross-inverting language. We're religious, and so of course we take this sort of heretical attitude very seriously" Deborah's father said. Mr. Woodcock's eyes lit up at the thought of getting Deborah into even more trouble than she was already in. He put his eyes out before Mr. Cable could notice anything strange and resembling to The Dark Lord in them. "Well of course it is to be taken very seriously" he said, but he didn't care. He said swear words all the time. He was a hard case. Once he even said . . . . poos. "I think first that some form of punishment should be given to Deborah so she knows what you think of this sort of behaviour. You should let her know just where she stands." "I'm actually sitting down" said Deborah. But Mr. Woodcock ignored her. "I can imagine a lot of your relatives and friends not wanting to know that Deborah is made of the dark side." "Yes I agree with you there completely" Mr. Cable said. "Deborah, you're not going on the ski trip." This was followed by evil laughter. "Evil laughter." Deborah had been looking forward to going on the ski trip all year, and having it taken from her was the one way directly to crush and squeeze and rub salt against a paper cut in the web of skin between her toes and make her eat soaked Linseed for breakfast, instead of one weet-a-bik with fifty spoons of sugar on it. She loved to ski, and had since her first time on the mountain that had captivated her with its turbulent tumultuous passion, its soft lips and its... its... its love. She wanted to always be near it, to live on it, to ski on it full time, and write her novels about problems in society from atop her peak, ignoring the fact that she wouldn't actually be *in* society if she was bollocking around and having a really chill placid life *away* from society not even worrying about all its problems on top of mountain peaks. "When are we gonna see *her* peaks, hey-yo!" Wordsworth shouted from Character Jail. Deborah thought oh oh oh again, again again, oh so much fervent turgid againing, about the mountain she was not at. The feeling of gliding down upon such marvelous snow that the mountain had, the feeling that she could relax completely and still go jolly fast enlightened her in a very unique way, and she found the skiing experience magical. But thanks to Mr. Woodcock's evil conspiracy, her favourite past-time had been taken from her like mushed up spinach from an old lady, and she would have no chance to ski for yet another long year. As her parents were devout traditionalists who they went skiing very often - never before, in fact. She had been up to the mountains many a time, with her uncle and aunt - nice, good people with personalities who enjoyed constructive activities like skiing and arguing, and eating the yellow snow. Unfortunately, the year before she enrolled in her high school, these people had been shipped off to Mexico, and had given her no notice whatsoever, except a silly little postcard that said something about Mexico, and being shipped off. That was how she knew - she was a bright one. The good thing was, the school she now went to had a ski trip that when selected, went up to a selected ski field that was selected at the start of the ski selection season every year around the time Winter became whatever Winter becomes, and she had not missed a trip once because of her selecty selectingness. Skiing was the passion that enthused her, it was what she wanted to spend the rest of her life doing, and any chance to ski that she missed would not be a happy memory. She so desperately wanted to ski. She had never done it before. Naturally, being told that she was not to go and advance further in her favourite activity was not something she wanted - she would rather have anything of her physical possessions taken from her, so when her father exclaimed that she was not going, her reply was understandable, even for someone like you. "Daddy" she whined in her prettiest voice, giving him the sweetest smile she could conjure up on such short notice, "I work really hard, and I never swear. It just happened this once - it sort of slipped out." Her father looked down at his feet in a gesture of shame and dishonesty and guilt and horror, but like, pretty B grade acting. I probably shouldn't have told you about it. Anyway, she figured she still had a chance . . . . . .

She would *not* spoil his fun. He had come this far, and he would go further. None of her "Daddy's little angel" crap would be force-fed down Mr. Cable's throat. Mr. Woodcock was going to win this one. He felt slightly guilty about sentencing her to such a tremendous punishment - it was a typically miserish thing to do, and it just confirmed his suspicions about whether or not he really was a nasty old git. No wonder everyone hated him. Even his best friend hated him. Even his wife hated him, and he wasn't even married. Even *he* hated him, and that was not funny in the slightest. It was about as funny as someone who had just realised that they had not yet amounted to anything in all their fifty-five years, and had not seen the funny side of it. In fact, it was exactly as funny as someone who had just realised that they had not yet amounted to anything in all their fifty-five years, and had not seen the funny side of it, as that was what had happinned – OK I mean happpind – OK *happenned* to Mr. Woodcock. It was nearly as funny as telling the old "a man walks into a bar and says ouch" joke, and it was a bit funnier than getting your foot run over. At least he still had his brains. He must have still had his brains to come up with a realization as cunning and as subtle as the one that he had just come up with. I mean with which he had come up. He knew that the guilt would never go away, and so he wished that the reality he lived in would change forever, and he wished that this OTHER Gwen Dibley would come out of the woodwork and explain what the hell all this crap about conspiracies was. He wished that the sad, confused, un-deserving, beautiful girl that stood in front of him would smile one of her smiles that made his day worthwhile. Still, for the sake of cheap misery and selfishness, he had given a young girl, a young, beautiful, girl who deserved far more than what her parents could or would ever give , a sentence that she did not want to have, and a sob nearly escaped him when he thought of the fun she would miss out on, and as he gazed into the sunset, holding his teddy bear so tight, his passions so confused by my totally God-awful writing and his own hormones, he knew, oh so deep inside, oh so how his heart was in aching pains in the endocardium even when he took heaps of disprins, and smashed back a mean-as bucky, oh that his life was over, that he would never love another, that he was destined for a life alone, and dark tears fell down his cheeks, and his teddy cried with loss at jealousy of his weird potentially illegal obsession with Deborah, and sobbed such epic viaductish wails, oh how it did wail in scraping agony-romance for it knew not how to tell him that it was HIV positive. Probably from rooting this truck driver in a public toilet somewhere, but whatever, right? Mr. Wood-cock knew from the gossippish, sweet, enthusiastic conversations that Deborah held with her friends who were continually trying to set her up with some creep called Fred, that skiing was what she wanted to do with her life, and he, Mr. Cockwood, was taking this pleasure from her. Still, her parents would be happy, but it did little to consolidate him and he wondered why he had let himself ruin the only student he liked, and the only student who he hoped had once liked him. He wished he had said something that made her laugh, instead of telling her that she was a heretic. She was no heretic. She was perfect. She was the one in four billion that loved everything unconditionally - not for some reason no-one would understand, but because that's what she was. In a way, no-one could understand her - the notion of loving *everything* seemed very silly and mythical to people these days. Deborah was the survivor of a lost race - a race of lovers, and Mr. Woodcock had helped pull her down into the junk food and double digit ppb arsenic level centralized city drinking water that was most people's thoughts. Oh, how those digits stood in double side-by-side wackity obliqueness. Uncorrupted and innocent, Mr. Woodcock had given her the hate that had been dwelling inside his body for so long, which was one thing she did not deserve. The Deborahs of the world were not heretics. It was people like him, Mr. Pizazz, and Johnny who were heretics - everything had to be negative for them. He could have considered her a friend before, but now, that was one thing he could never do. He would never have said that she was his friend, but he would have known - or at least hoped in blind love that she liked him, and didn't just smile when she saw him because of some joke she had heard. There would be no more of that, though. The guilt struck at him like a really big thing that would strike at someone, and it hurt like nothing else he had ever experienced as he said "Does not the holy Bibble of Blibblington say . . . don't let things just slip out?"

Deborah knew that Mr. Woodcock was no Bible-reading religious philosopher. She knew that he was a maths teacher whom she felt sorry for, and that there was very little resembling happiness in his life. She wondered again what she had done to deserve the treatment he was giving her, and looking at him in a confused look of love and confusion. She did not hate her teacher and her parents yet, she simply had no idea why they were being so hard to her. "No" she declared at Mr. Woodcock's ridiculous assumptions of the Bibble. "Yes, I've read that part" her father said, ignoring her completely. "I know that one well." "Well in that case, maybe you could refresh us on that particular . . . bit" Mr. Woodcock said. "My memory isn't what it used to be. I think instead of using the normal method where we at the school think up a punishment for Deborah here, it should be up to you parents to decide a fitting thing for Deborah to do." What a greaser. "Yes" Mr. Cable said, rubbing his chin. "I think it goes like this: ". . . Don't let things just slip out." "Well that is useful" Mr. Woodcock said. "Any experienced Bibblical personification would of course forbid any involvement in the ski trip, but you're the parents so it's really up to you." Deborah knew that there was no Woodcock bit in the Bibble, and she also knew that her parents had not read the Bibble for years. They were even more heretic than her. She was suddenly consumed by anger, and decided to never forgive her parents for being so gullible - and if they were just putting on this crazy act to be part of Mr. Woodcock's evil conspiracy he had with Gwen Dibley, then Deborah would have to fight back with a conspiracy of her own.

Mark was feeling his adolesence, he wanted so desperately, no, he NEEDED so incredibly to fall, to fall, to fall so far, so deep, like a rugby ball dropping from the hands of someone tackled by Graham Mourie on a wet, overcast day at Carisbrook, into mild, homeostatic relationshippy weirdness with a human. A woman or a man. But he wasn't too fussy, anyone or anything would do really. He wanted to pony up and settle down. He wanted a palace for his phallus, a tepee for his peepee. He wanted to live in a small community away from Johnny, Wordsworth and Andrew. Mark got excited about the ski trip again and again as he imagined the type of vegetable, animal or mineral he would fall in love with. The girl he would marry would stand by him through thick and thin, short and fat, rugby and cricket, and their love would never die. Until the end of the book where Mark and Wordsworth die by getting killed but it's a secret so don't tell just forget it. Mark was one of those goody-good types who thought it was wrong to do anything wrong. He did fairly well in school (he tried so hard), and wanted to join a noble and patriotic profession, such as writing best-selling novels about modern-day crises and problems with society. Of course, he simply accepted all the lies he was told by his teachers and his peers, and bothered not to research the truth in anything unless it was for a school project, and even then ignored it - he was just too stupid, not too nice. I PROMISE I'll kill him off, maybe get him squished in a mincer after he's hacked up with a chainsaw and then cut his fingers off and poke really cold ice cream up his nose. "I feel that western society has always placed an unnecessarily strong emphasis on monetary value and material gain. This is one of the main reasons the world is in such a harsh ecological state" Wordsworth said. "You are absolutely correct, my recycling friend" Mark told him. "We need to care more for this planet than we do - there are far too many pollutants in this world for us to survive much longer. How many years do we have until complete ecological breakdown?" "It is a relevant point you have raised to our discussion" Johnny said; "and I feel that society as a whole need to know the truth of what they are doing when they buy a something." "That's absolutely right" Andrew said from atop his wooden chair, that had once been a tree, and it yearned, oh how it yearned so deeply, to be in the arms of the earth, to be and to feel and be alive and play in a meadow with true love, dancing and spinning, its woody heart paralysed ... by love... instead of having Andrew's non-wiped bum on it. "I don't think people realise but every time they make a purchase, they cast a vote. I do not wish to point fingers and the such, but I think that people should know that every time they buy meat of any form, they are voting that it's OK to cut down trees to make farmland, therefore decreasing the amount of Oxygen in the air" he said as he ate some free trade tofu with organic lemon marinade sauce as he bragged about how healthy and ecological it was, when really he was hanging out for some BK, and was going to meet some dudes there later for a Whopper with like five extra beef patties dipped in liquefied bacon. "I mean, it's only about eighteen percent Oxygen at the moment, and with all the deforestation going on it's just getting worse. The deforesty industry is completely lying to the public when it comes to factory-farmed meat being healthy. Yes, it does have a vague smattering of Iron, but apart from that, it has toxins which destroy enzymes, which are the basis of life and the most important nutrient. They want to make more money so they lie to the public, and people just swallow it whole." "I'm really glad you differentiated between factory meat and natural meat" Mark said to whoever was talking before. "And always remember that the lack of one nutrient can cause up to ten diseases." He looked deep into Wordsworth's eyes, and held him so close, tenderly, but with such passion. "Always always remember that." "And the minerals, Andrew" Wordsworth said, shaking his head sadly. "I think that the public has a right to know that they can't get anywhere near enough minerals from vegetables and fruit because of all the pesticides that destroy the nutrients. The only good fruit and vegetables used to be organically grown, but now even organic food is often not so good." "Don't forget that the growers only put three minerals in the soil when they plant the stuff - Potassium, Phosphorus and Nitrogen. So you miss out on the other minerals. The growers only put in what they need to make a big plant. They get paid by the quantity, not the quality. And they pick the fruits long before they ripen so that they last longer, yet by the time they reach the supermarkets there is just about no nutritional value left, and even organic fruit and vegetables are often deficient in this way - what we've been told is the best is quite inferior." Just then the door to Mark and Wordsworth's room opened, and in strode a beautiful young man, who wore not leather. Some cancer patients went into total recovery and regeneration as he entered the room. He rode bareback atop an animal that emitted not gasoline nor harmful fumes, that had not been tamed from the wild, instead the animal had consented via a signed document with the equal, not superior, human that rode it in the form of a contract that was fair and just and had no fine print and had been drawn up by both parties whom each held original signed copies of said contract, were independent and responsible for their decision-making that required not lawyers; unless as a last resort when one of said parties, fully exercising free will and under the tenets of responsibility, that is, the willingness to be both cause and effect, the ability to respond to outer stimuli in a manner befitting the pathway of greatest compassion and freedom, decided to "break" said contract by defying its language, the word meanings of which inherent within many different dictionaries, available from libraries because purchasing said dictionaries would remove more wood from the rainforests thus creating an imbalance in the abode of the animal, this word "animal" being used purely in a meaning that enhanced the equality of it (the word 'it' not intended in any derogatory manner toward any defined or non-defined point in an entire spectrum of gender possibilities, the privacy of which were completely recognised) and all within the genetic pedigree that consisted of its specie, and absolutely definitely vehemently not in a manner that accosted or betrayed or stole away from recognition of the multifaceted aspects of the three and a half billion years of evolutionary mechanisms and DNA hierarchies, while certainly not offending young earth creationists. "Hey it's Greenie Arbore-aldong" Johnny said, but Greenhouse Atmospherestrong wasn't in the mood for any hey. Or for being serious. "What the hell is going on here?" he demanded. "You're not supposed to be talking about modern produce not meeting basic nutritional requirements demonstrated by symptoms of malnutrition, and you're not supposed to be talking about how it's impossible to be maximally healthy through a balanced diet because the nutrients are no longer in our food chains. You're supposed to be silly. Have you done the dinosaur joke yet?" The boys looked at each other guiltily. Johnny, who thought it was all a red herring, spoke up gilltilly: "Yeah, we ahhh... hang on, didn't we do the dinosaur joke millions of years ago?" Wordsworth the Naughty called from character gaol gaoltily: "We think it's more relevant to society this way" he said. "Well I don't care" Gaseous Azeotrope-Combustionstrong said, waving his manuscript about at them. "This is the bit where you tie Wordsworth to a bulldozer and drive him into a farmyard and his face mushes into a horsepat." "But we want to say a few serious things about the health of the planet." "But nobody cares about the health of the planet" Groundwater Aquastrong said. "That's pretty obvious, I would have thought. From the amount of people who do all the bad stuff. And the sewage. And the ozone layer. And all the whaling and all that. So shut up and be silly. People don't care about living healthily. They just care about satisfying their own personal reactive patterns by making more and more money and eating lots of crappy food. You see they only care about their immediate satisfaction - the average person is about ninety-nine percent reactive, you know, and controlled totally by unconscious and uncontrollable desires, and has little desire to break out of this invisible prison. Anyway, you guys are supposed to be doing silly stuff. Do something silly." "We don't want to do silly stuff anymore" Johnny said. "We think it would be good if you had bits in your novel about society and all that. And anyway, you haven't taken the extremely important evidence produced by Weston Price, and give a very unbalanced view of the vegetarian/vegan diet that you don't even explain, you are becoming just another addition to the misinformation out there, and you make judgements upon the size and shape of people which is a huge generalization and offensive to those types that you mention, and I find it interesting that you don't mention that you embody some of these "weaknesses" that you so focus upon and preach, yet how are you helping by putting this in your totally rockin' and kickass novel?" "Well it's my novel" Guye Armstronge said to them, feeling very angered at the thought of having his hefty manuscript being so openly disobeyed. "If you guys want to be sensible, you should write your own novels. I think you shouldn't so openly disrespect my manuscript by being so disobedient." "We will when this novel's over" Johnny promised. "I'll write a book called *How People Can Live Well Past a Hundred and Still be Strong and Healthy*." "And I'll write a book called *How There's a Cure for Cancer*" Mark said proudly. Andrew strode forth on his mighty warhorse. "I'll write a book called *How Chromium and Vanadium Have Been Proven to Replace Insulin And Cure Diabetes*

*And Hypoglycemia; I Know it's True But I Can't Remember the Study
I read it in.*" "And I'm writing a

book called *How Doing Anything Is Really Bad and Open to
Criticism from Anyone So You Might as Well Just Go To The Pub*"
Wordsworth said. "Well I personally don't care about all that rubbish" Guye Armstronge said. "Now do something silly." The boys
thumbed through the hefty manuscript looking for some form
of entertaining silly act in which to engage. Then they fingered
through it. Then they toed through it. "That's much better" funGi
Ascomycotastrong complemented. "I guess you're right about everything Guye, and absolutely perfect and above any criticism"
Johnny said, shaving Guye Armstronge's legs with his Ladyshave.
"We'll just keep doing silly stuff from now on."

"Well yes . . . about that Wordsworth's disease cure. We left it
a bit late. Sorry." It hit Wordsworth like a really big heavy thing.
Could Wordsworth's mother be dead? Could the woman who had
nurtured him from baby to wanker be up in heaven? Could the
woman he would have died for be gone? Could he have killed the
mother he loved so much? "What happened?" he asked. "Well, we
waited for a while - till we thought she was just about dead, then
stuck her full of cure. And . . . nothing happened. Obviously she
was tricking us again. She didn't have Wordsworth's disease at all.
So now she's dead. Dead as a dead thing. Dead as a rock. Dead
as that Andrew chappie's dead thing collection. Dead as a writer's
social life. Dead as a writer's sex life. Dead as a writer's bank balance. Dead as one of those recurring jokes that just won't go away.
Stone dead. Dead as another dead thing. Dead as a joke that's been
done to death. So dead. So, so dead. So anyway, it's all her fault.
You know, if her and all those other women had been honest with

us, none of this would have happened. We could have made them better, sent them on their way, and taken their money, but no, they have to be all up themselves and trick us into giving them false cures, don't they? Bloody conspiracy isn't it. Like that woman who came in for the common cold. Well, it turned out her head had been cut off. What a tricky tricker! Anyway . . . sorry. Promise it won't happen again."

Two weeks later, neither Mark, Andrew, Johnny, and especially Wordsworth had not said anything to each other about the ski trip. Deborah and her parents had not spoken nicely to each other, Deborah's father had still not yet shown her the bit in the Bibble, and Deborah's novel was forming chapter after heading after sub-heading in its electronic womb, and Deborah was commanding her thoughts and her powers of emotion into it, and fertilising her composition with her epic blah blah blah of passion. She was moved to tears at the thought of missing what she had been look-ing forward to for almost a year, and a lot of her faith in 'manifest-ing your desire' websites and information from ranty loud people in pubs on Friday night had gone. Would she ever ski again? Would her parents let her ski again? Oh, it was so so moving and dramatic. Before Mr. Woodcock's evil trickery, she had been sweet and innocent, uncapable of hate, but afterwards, especially after writing so much of her novel, which was focussed on problems in society, she now found it relatively simple to think negatively towards the ones who said they loved her. She had started stay-ing up late, and found the idea of getting up in the mornings boring and tiresome - normally she was enthusiastic about almost everything, but since her encounter with Mr. Woodcock she had started to drink coffee, and was taking Panadol and other drugs she originally would have been against. I don't mean against like leaning against them physically; sitting on them in a position that might scrunch up the shirt-cloth on her shoulder or whatever, I mean morally against them, not totally though, understanding their potentiational appropriatenessisms's. She no longer cared about her health, which was good, because she now fitted into society. She drank lots of milk, and didn't even give a crap that the dairy industry hadn't even bought PS4s for their most milky cows. And she drank hardout vaccinated water. Her novel had started off well, and it was continuing at breakneck speed - she had been working on it every day after school for the past two weeks, and it would be finished very soon. It was a brilliant novel, and she took no enjoyment from writing it - quite often she would break down in front of her computer in a fit of despair, wishing that she could have back the innocence and wondrous enthusiasm she once had, but these bouts only came after a deeply emotional paragraph. Unfortunately, every paragraph in her novel so far was deeply emotional, and showed up problems in society like no other novel, not even the really hardout preachy ones. Deborah found she had a natural aptitude for writing deeply emotional novels and para-graphs about problems in society. Her novel was not in the slight-est bit happy, and she was dead certain that the novel would sell millions of copies, giving her the opportunity to devote her life to skiing, and living with nature, as long as she ignored the fact that skis had plastic in them. By herself. With no other people around, forever. It felt great to write her preachy blah blah and she went full ego about it. But she didn't want to get too cocky. She read over it a last time, and felt a burst of smug happiness - something she had never felt before, and found herself very satisfied with the way it was going. Every paragraph, every word, every sentence, every little bit was interlaced with another stunning bit that would revolutionize the way people saw themselves and their society. It was a brilliant novel, and it was called *The Most Problems In Society's Book In The World*. She read through it slowly again, taking her time, making sure that everything was perfect, and that the common person would be riveted, and would find it incredible.

Wordsworth was talking on the phone with his mother's doctor. "I've got the school ski trip" Wordsworth said. "Well that is a shame" the doctor told him. "You'll have to come and visit her afterwards then." "Is she better?" Wordsworth asked hastily. "Oh yes" the doctor said. "She's completely alive and well. Just before she was having a sing along and moonwalking all over the ward." Wordsworth felt wave upon wave of pleasure cascade over his wacky necromancer's undead body. His testicles jiggled in their bag, and danced around and took the day off. Their first day off in ages. And man did they need it? Yes.

NEW TOPIC

Finally the woman he loved (his mum) was alright. "I cured her completely" the doctor continued. "That ten minutes at med school paid off." "Can I speak to her?" Wordsworth asked. "No, she's asleep." "But I'm just about to leave on my ski trip." "Well you go and have a good time skiing while your only mother's in bed then, you selfish little brat. Up yours." And before Wordsworth could say "Tell her I love her and cast Cure Medium Wounds on her " the conversation had ended.

"You're not coming on the ski trip are you?" Mark asked Andrew. "You're not coming on the ski trip are you?" Johnny asked Mark. "You're not coming on the ski trip are you?" Andrew asked

Wordsworth. "Is my hair ok?" Wordsworth asked Johnny and took his make-up mirror out of his handbag. They were relatively stupid questions to ask - each had a large pack, skis, and various other items used for alpine sport. And Wordsworth of course, had hair that was definitely not OK. "Wordsworth, why are you having a bad hair day?" I asked. "This bit's, like, really important, bro." "Wordsworth man, you're totally ruining the book!" Johnny shouted. "Shut up, it's not my fault I'm having a bad hair day" Wordsworth did his lipstick and pouted. "I don't think appearances are important in a book anyway" my rules he flouted. "You don't even get what my book's about" I abouted. "BY THE WAY MARK'S A FAG, EVERYONE!" Andrew outed. Mark didn't have a girlfriend, or anyone to kiss. He would just have to kiss himself. "Oooh yeah, ooooh can I, can I?" he questioned Guye Armstronge with a question mark. "Don't be revolting Mark!" Non-Revolting Guye Armstronge exclaimed with an exclamation mark. "No one wants to read about that." But Mark disagreed. "Maybe I could do a really romantic scene looking into the mirror, then kiss myself and we'll maximize sales in the lonely gay dude demographic." Almighty Sales-Maximizing Guye Armstronge thought for a second. "Because there isn't enough gay stuff going on here already" Andrew said without any sarcasm at all. The sun was just coming up over the school library and so the library melted. Wordsworth ran over and jumped in it and got stuck in the library goo and got his botty burned by the sun. It was a big trip from wherever they were to wherever they were going, so they all had books and magazines to read, crosswords, cards and travel scrabble. After all, it was a big ole bus trip to the mountain - a whole two minutes' drive. At about eight-thirty the teachers undertook their usual behaviour: shouting and moaning at the students about their pay until whatever it was they

wanted to be done was done. This time they ordered the next generation to squeeze onto the bus. I mean *inside* the bus. And then
it happened: they were talking about the lesbian, gay, bisexual,
transgender, endosex, vibrosex, hand-holding, pornstache, and
biker-bummers community. What was absolutely miraculous was
that they were holding such a conversation WITHOUT OFFENDING
ANYONE. Not even all of the people on the internet! So NO-ONE
complained to Gropey Mammary-Wrong about it or bugged him
about using the wrong word for gay fags, or lezzies, or gave him a
crappy review. "You guys are *obsessed* with gay stuff" said Johnny.
"I'm offended by that." One of their classmates was offended by
some of Johnny's offence. "That offence is very offensive" he said.
"But just because I'm not gay it doesn't mean I should be prejudiced like you. That's the problem in society." Mark whirled his
ornately carved and furnished antique pubis around in his seat at
the mention of problems in society. What would that other boy
know about problems in society? he philosophized angrily. Mark
knew about problems in society. Mark was into society. It was one
of his interests. Discussing society was fun for him. That other guy
was completely wrong. Other people always were. And Mark was
right. I mean I'm not saying he was LITERALLY right, I mean whatever I don't care, that's just how he felt. I guess I'm showing up his
narrow-mindedness, which is a big problem in society. But Mark
thought the problem in society was that people like the one who
was offended by Johnny's offence kept on pointing out problems in
society. As long as they kept on moaning about problems in society
like the crappy violence, the annoying people, the other people,
the bad problems, the bad health, the bad breath, the arrogance,
the selfishness, the conspiracies, the prejudices, the half-truths
about food, the eighty-five percent negative thought, the mineral-

deprived food, etc, etc, and wrote really bad novels that just weren't funny about them, the problem would stay. People should focus on the wonders of modern life. As long as people weren't focusing on the problems in society, there wouldn't *be* any. THAT was the problem in society. "What, so we should all just be ignorant and not address anything?" Mark asked me. "Just shut up and get on with it" I said. "Just read your lines or whatever. It's Johnny's turn." "Well I better get paid" Mark said. "I mean you better sell some copies of this thing, OK?" "Just hurry up and DO IT!" I shouted at him. "It's Johnny's line." "OK but do you think Johnny will be good?" So I shouted "go Johnny go!" "I'm not prejudiced" Johnny said. "Yes you are. You're bigoted, you hate everyone." "That's a load of crap! I don't hate everyone!" Johnny shouted hatefully at everyone and was warned by the teachers that if he spoke that loud again, Andrew and Wordsworth would be thrown off the bus and would be ordered to walk the rest of the way to the mountain. "That's not fair" Andrew said. "You didn't expect it to be fair, did you?!" Johnny shouted at him. "I sure as hell did!" Andrew shouted at him back. "Excuse me" the other boy tried to interrupt. "Well it's not very fair the way men like me and you are always trying to take advantage of everything?" Johnny yelled, always trying to take advantage of everything. "It's not very fair the way I'm going to hit Wordsworth in the eye, is it? It's not very fair that some baby in Romania has been born with AIDS and won't get a shot at life is it?" "Is that a really poor taste insensitive dead baby joke about sharing needles?" asked Wordsworth. Everybody stopped what they were doing and stared at him. "No Wordsworth" said Johnny. "Yeah Wordsworth, how could you be so insensitive?" Mark asked. "Well I am the bad guye" said Wordsworth, shuffling his feet and looking at the floor. "But you knew you had gone too far" Mark began, "you knew, oh how you knew, in your heart of hearts, in the veins of the atria where the gluggy blood-bits goes glug glug glug into that steamy chamber of passionate empowerment where all the top NRL players have they're names written. And on a wild night, cuddled by the fireplace, two lovers, two souls-" "Ah, hang on, hang on" said Wordsworth. "I think you mean *their* names written. Not *they're*. That means *they are*." Mark readjusted his Shakespearean hat with which he hoped one day to wear around maidens fair. "Don't you mean *Advance Australia Fair?*" Asked Wordsworth. "You mean America" said Andrew, but Mark was too in touch with his feelings to worry about geographical locations, he was too 'in the moment'. He cleared his throat with Clearasil daily throaty-jizz-remover. He put his arm out, holding a skull in his hand outstretched for amateur dramatic effect. "In a time of yore" he began, "in a time of maidens and chivalry, in a time where a kiss was a promise and holding hands was as big a deal as third base, two lovers held each other, fighting the problems of society, fighting every last hope and breath, for written – nay tattooed, nay *scoured* over their in they're racing past the ten metre mark up the wing of there hearts was Cliff Lyons' magnificent bootprint; even in-" "Hang on Mark" said Andrew. "Yeah hang on Mark" said Wordsworth. "Don't copy me" said Andrew to Wordsworth. "Or people won't feel that each one of us is fleshed out and realistic enough. And then everyone will complain that they didn't identify with any of the characters." "OK *fine* then... OK *hold* on Mark" said Wordsworth. But Mark couldn't hold on... to love. He mounted his podium and once more began to spake his emotional effluent: "surely, even in Manly's 1997 loss to Newcastle, Lyons stood out over their in Aussie yet again as one of the greatest NRL players..." "Mark!" Johnny and Wordsworth and Andrew and Grousemate

Australiastrong and Mr. Woodcock and Mr. Pizazz shouted. Oh, and
Deborah. She hasn't been in it for a while, so... give her a shouty
bit. "Can you get your words edited so you don't get confused
with they're and their and there?" Johnny asked. But Mark ignored
him, and finished his tender, eighth-beer-of-the-evening-without-
even-having-a-pie drenched soliloquoy: "... one of the greatest NRL
players ...in your heart, right they're." But before anyone could say
anything, Goodonyamate Allblackstrong appeared. "OK no more
from you Mark, for at least, like, three pages or something."

"Hey is it OK if I talk now?" Mark asked when it was actually one
of Wordsworth's lines. "Dude can you just shut up?" Johnny said.
"It hasn't even been one page and you're being a dick again." "OK
it's my line now are you ready?" Wordsworth said. His lip wobbled
and it looked like he was about to cry. "Look, I got the highest roll
on the d20 when we rolled initiative so it's my turn." "Hey I've just
been reading this really amazing book about self-empowerment"
said Mark, who was obviously an infiltrator from some other
author trying to plug his or her book in *my* book. "OK everyone
listen to me it's my line" said Wordsworth. "Mark are you ready?
Are you ready for my line?" "Wow" said Mark. "You're such a dork,
Wordsworth." So Wordsworth got all in Mark's face and he was like
"What's up bitch?" and Mark was like "What you gettin' in my face
for bitch?" and then Wordsworth's like "Oh yeah bitch" and Mark's
like "Yeah bitch" and I'm like "you guys are both bitches" and
the crowd was all like "Jer-ry! Jer-ry! Jer-ry!" and Mark's like "Gee
you're so anal and intellectual Wordsworth" and so Wordsworth
goes, he goes, he goes, "what you lookin' at me wrong for, bitch?"
and so Mark's all like "You're so wussy and you're just like Steve
Urkel off Family Matters" and Wordsworth's all like "Oh yeah?" and

Mark's all like "Yeah what you gonna do about it bitch?" Johnny got up and hit Mark in the face, knocking him out inside the bus. "That's how wars start." The teachers informed Andrew and Wordsworth that they were walking on very thin ice indeed, and that their parents would be told they weren't amounting to very much. "It's not my fault you haven't amounted to very much" said Andrew, who had become a bit cheeky. And that's why they threw him and Wordsworth from the bus, leaving them to mutter about conspiracies. And how disgusting soaked linseed is for breakfast. And how it's even more disgusting if you mix it all up with bee pollen.

"Nice one, Wordsworth" Andrew said. "Getting us kicked off the bus like that. Real smart move. Now we have to walk to the mountain. This is your fault, you know." "We weren't *on* the bus, we were *in* it, so we couldn't have been kicked *off* it we had to have been kicked *out*. You should keep to a stricter parameter of logic, and learn your lines. Like read the script or something." "OK well can we start again then?" asked Andrew, and fidgeted uncomfortably as was his nervousness and oblivious fecund-smasher. Andrew and Wordsworth's bags were heavy and uncomfortable, and they weren't there yet. "Are we there yet?" Andrew asked. Wordsworth looked around. "No." They walked another few metres. "Are we there yet?" Andrew asked. Wordsworth looked around. "I don't know, are we?" He asked. "No Wordsworth, we're not there yet." "Stop asking me these silly questions or I'll tickle your tootsies. I've got a real tootsie fetish I have I have." They walked a few more metres. "Are we there yet?" Andrew asked. "No." "Are we there yet?" Andrew asked. "No." "Are we there yet?" Andrew asked. "No." "Would you stop talking to yourself?" Wordsworth said. "It's really getting on my tootsies." "Sorry" Andrew said. "Can I just say it one more time?" "No you may not" Wordsworth answered, wrapping his bikini tighter around his skin. It was snowing, after all. They were getting close to the mountain. "Are you going to win like last year?" Andrew asked him. "I don't really mind if I win or not" Wordsworth said. "I've always been happy with second best. I just ski for the love of skiing." "There you go again" Andrew said. "You and your filthy bragging. Bragging about how you're going to win, and beat all the losers. You know I'm not a good skier." Andrew glared morosely at his friend that he hated. Wordsworth seemed to create a sort of sullen cloud that showered doom and negativity down upon Andrew, soaking him all over with it's ice-cold pessimism I mean ITS pessimism, without an apostrophe, if you're totally a grammar fascist or like editing or whatever. Andrew sulked and cried slightly as his friend undermined his confidence even more, and definitely more than necessary, Andrew's poor thimble of a self-esteem measurement that was already not at all large. Wordsworth knew he only went skiing out of fear of not fitting into the other students' fashion - skiing being a trendy and more sweeter tasting dip of sport into which the richer and upper class parents dipped their crackers of children during every winterous phasure, so they could embark upon pleasures countless while their offspring were absent. Like aggravated spanking and riding around on each others's's backs like horseys and the time when she slid down the bannister onto his willy. Andrew prayed to whatever controlled his life for mercy, and he hoped and hoped that there would never be the day that he would return to them and for some bizarre reason they would wipe him from the face of their clique with the conceited dermatology that was their abuse, and leave him alone to face a world that hated him and would bash the knees of his independence from behind without the assistance of any friends who hated him to help him walk the walk of trepidation over the brimstone of glee, beyond the chasm... of his epicardium. He stood out like some strange form of maculic displacement on the pure white skin of the ski field, marring the fashion that Mark tried so hard to emulate and the fashion Johnny didn't need to emulate thanks to his fashion emulator, that he made Wordsworth make for him, in Wordsworth's nefarious lair. With magic. He lacked Mark's faith that everything would be alright as soon as he just accepted it with positivity when regarding uncoordinated and failed attempts to ski well. He lacked Johnny's arrogance and his sense of humour, and he had missed out somewhere along the line of life on the respect he commanded, and was given. Johnny was not a good skier, yet he bragged and bragged and could get away with it. But most of all he lacked Wordsworth's grace, that seemed to flow naturally and instinctively from his friend whom he hated. He tried to second Wordsworth's skill that embellished his skiing style - long and short, slow and quick turns that were always perfectly circular; and that seemed to always spray up great soft wafts of perfect powder snow that hung in the air as if in suspended animation, Wordsworth's speed that would have killed any lesser man, and a silly hat. Wordsworth embellished his skiing mode with these faculties that were the macrocosm of Andrew's jealousy - a huge, throbbing, pulsating, writhing, uncomfortable, massive, degenerative, piercing, blackening, filthy, mutating, frustrating, annoying, molesting, harassing, belly-flopping, dive-bombing, back-slapping, haranguing, disgusting, datgusting, gusting, stinging, singing, inging, sting of vexatious jealousy that filled his emotional veins with its vast ugliness and brought him to his knees and made him feel so bad about himself that he got a job at MacDonalds working for a really bossy guy whose initials just might be CS or PF and would always make him work late so by the time he got home he had missed all the good TV. Andrew was not a good skier. He rode his skis jerkily and lived life on the ski slopes in cowardly and part time and full time and zero hour shift (because of too much corporate influence on labour laws) fear of being knocked over and having his brittle bones snapped, crackled and popped liked a beer can on a shooting range that was getting molested by all the other beer cans. And it would slip and fall over and all the other beer cans would apologise really hard when they heard its bones break but hark! T'was too late, too late... for desire. The six or so hours he spent each day for seven days a year were hell for him - he was ever watching behind him, making sure nobody was sneaking up on him and about to crash into him if he stopped too suddenly, then picking himself up as he had just crashed into something because he wasn't looking where he was headed. Also he didn't have any neck muscles and his head was attached mechanically via a swivel-thing and the ball bearings were really lubed up so his head just spun around 360 degrees all the time, especially when he put an industrial wind sock over his face. And Andrew sure as hell didn't need his friend who he hated reminding him of the ability he had never had, *did* never have, and *would* never have, and causing all the pain to surface by forcing his enormous egoic state around at innocent little Andrew, and down poor Andrew's throat, where he rubbed its bulbous mass with his vocal condescension until it sprayed its evil tadpoles of self-conciousness that swam away to marr the egg of Andrew's perfection with their horror and fertilize him with the gut-wrenching incompetence of rejection and wash away his self-esteem with its caustic emotional acids, like a goat stuffed full of napalm and rotting eggs exploding on a politician's tummy. Wordsworth saw what kind of look Andrew was wearing and said "I just said I skied purely for the love of skiing, not to prove I have an ability. It's one of the few things I enjoy. That's all I said." He even showed him in the script where t'was wrote. BUT OH NO! ANDREW DIDN'T BELIEVE HIM! "See, there you go again. It's so obvious you're the bad guy without an E. You're too horribly horrible for words." Andrew turned away from him and began to cry, his tear ducts working hard at forcing the salty water from him in mighty gushes of depression, down into the chasm of neglect, down and a bit to the left past the waterfall of hope, into the bumholes of despair, inhaling the farts of despair. "You're awful!" Andrew shrieked at him. "You don't even deserve to be in this book!" That had been a second trespassing of Andrew's rights, all so Wordsworth could get ever closer to desecrating the pure flowerbed of Andrew's innocence with the urination and defecatory essence of his criticism. "You use so many cuss words" Andrew said to him. "The bits of the book with you in them should be censored." It had only been the year before, when Wordsworth had sidled up to Andrew on his skis and said "Hey Andrew, how's it hangin' ya bodacious swingin' party animal mate bro?" like some git off a crappy TV show. His insult had barged into Andrew as if it were a battering ram, and had knocked the drawbridge of his confidence off the hinges of his belief and into the moat of his doubt where lay the piranhas of his evil and some got splashed onto the damsel of his innocence and went up her dress and on her left minge-flap and it was all icy cold and made her go eek. "I bet they heard your ego in Switzerland." Wordsworth didn't have anything to say about that. If Andrew wanted to be like Johnny and talk about how Aberdeen didn't exist, that was fine. "In fact" Andrew continued, "I bet they heard your ego in America." "We are in America, silly" Wordsworth said. "I thought we were in New Zealand" Andrew said, feeling perplexed. "No, no, we're definitely in America." They granny stepped closer and closer to the mountain. Andrew wanted to know if they were there yet. "Were they there yet?" he asked. "No" Wordsworth told him. "Were they there yet?" Andrew asked again. "No" Wordsworth told him again. "Were they there yet?" Andrew asked again again. "No" Wordsworth told him again again. "Were they there yet?" Andrew asked him again again again. "No, they were here." "That's a pretty bad joke, Wordsworth." "It's a pretty bad book, Andrew." They walked on, taking shelter under Wordsworth's bad joke. It was getting dark, and they were nearly at the mountain when their fragile lives became broken and the whole infra-structure of their egg-like realities cracked open, and the clean white of their consciousness mixed with the evil 'just-after-the-use-by-date' asparagus juice of Satan's 666 yolks. Wordsworth saw the bogey bungy-jumping from Andrew's crevatic and spookily dominating nostril and let it have a few jumps before he decided his mind couldn't take any more of such filth and slander on one of *his* pages and he told Andrew of its horrific presence subtly before its first jump. "Would you like a tissue?" he inquired, his quest to rid the world of Andrew's bogeys finally underway - the dream of dreams, the adventure of adventures - his final goal in life - The Bogey-Cleanse. "No thanks" Andrew said. The bogey filtered its evil and morbid laughter through to Wordsworth through its oratorial aperture, its head see-sawing back and t'ward as it diabolically rendered Wordsworth's conspiracy redundant and a bit silly. The bogal fluidic embodiment swung to and fro from Andrew's noscular cavity, singing Ring-A-Ring-A-Rosies to its cheeky self. As it was partaking in vocal utterances such, an abundance of bogeys slid down the bungee cord to join yonder with their elusive singing bogal compatriot. "I said:" Wordsworth said: "Would you like a tissue?" "I said:" Andrew said: "No thanks." The bogeys poked their tongues out at Wordsworth and laughed at him and maddened his senses for he was not silly enough. "You're not silly enough, you're not silly enough" they chanted meanly. Wordsworth began to cry, and the bogeys began to keep teasing him. "Why were you offering me a tissue, Wordsworth?" Andrew asked. "Have I defiled mine nasal perfection with the obtique and plagiostome boge?" "Thou hast, beloved one." "Well why didn't you bloody well say so?" Andrew looked at his friend who he hated irritably. "You selfish uncaring bastard." he said. Wordsworth felt guilty, then he felt himself. "After you wash your hands after you finish feeling yourself can you give me one of those tissues?" Andrew grabbed a tissue from Wordsworth's tissue fridge and held it at its most dangerous angle. Then, in one deftly quick and skilled flowing stroke, he smote yon bogey from the land, and banished the vile enmitious one t'where't belonged - Cthol Murgos. And they all lived happily ever after, even though it wasn't the end. "Wow I'm really glad Gridiron Americastrong edited that last bit of the book out, that bit sucked" said Andrew, as he giggled gleefully galloping galoshes on Wordsworth's dad's bum, totally riding him like a pony. But a naughty pony, that needed breaking in and disciplining. "Yeah Gridiron Americastrong's so amazing" said Wordsworth, not even noticing that his dad was totally being ridden and broken in, he was so in awe of the amazing editing that Guye had done. "He's totally taken out all the bits that sucked and there's only just plain awesome left." "I dunno, you're still here" said Andrew, who had become a bit cheeky, and I don't mean Wordsworth's dad's

bum's cheek. "Yes you do!" shouted Andrew, and Wordsworth pretended to not hear, because he was totally in denial. "No I'm not"
he said.

The emotion was so emotively massive and hardout bro as
Wordsworth screamed through the agony of a million sobs, the
aching torment within the rostrum of his heart, in the front yard
having a barbecue of his heart but without ANY of his mates, in
the desire of his wanton lust and irreparable silly heart, unleash-
ing the Bart Simpson of his fury upon his tears that were so many
he spoke as wept he did with such emotive emotion: "wow there's
so many tears it's biochemically impossible for the human body to
lose so much essential salts with hydrogen and oxygen, I'm going
to have to rehydrate, in order to facilitate adenosine triphosphate
production via the Krebs cycle." I paused the book for a minute.
PAUSE. "Hey Wordsworth, I don't think that line's really getting
the intensity of the emotion that I want to convey to the reader.
I mean you know the situation, right? You've lost everything and
you're really sad. Don't forget we need to get the single-women-
over-forties demographic, dude. Can you do another take but with
more passion?" Wordsworth nodded, he knew what he had to do.
UNPAUSE. "My broken love is so intense" he began. "Oh my heart
is grieving, bereft of all hope, awash with saddy Mcsadness. The
intensity of its grief, measured in cubic tearage, would take an
entire physics department a minimum of three and one half minutes to calculate, if all minds were communicating via a stream-
lined network wherein all minds could speak to all other minds
and listen to all other minds simultaneously. Allow x to represent
the number of minds in a human network. Artificial intelligences
are represented by a variable, depicting an average, or fluctuating

level of AIs and their practicality, operability, and nuances for individual variation, resulting in an impossibility in assigning my grief a rigidly defined numerical value, however, if said value *was* capable of existence, it would be a high number, close to a hundred if expressed as a percentage of the entire representation of a neurobiochemical network of brain tissue with fully functioning sodium/potassium exchange through lipid membranes in cellular matrices." "No, that's not quite what I meant Wordsworth" I said, really tired of having to interrupt my own book just to make it reach peaking levels of good, or even get a simple point across, like Wordsworth being sad. Wordsworth was sad. "Don't just write it like that!" Wordsworth shouted at me. "You're supposed to *show*, not *tell*, remember? Let me show the reader with my characterness." I sat down the wrong way on a chair to look cool, and told Wordsworth, "I want you to talk about your feelings and how much you're hurting inside so I get the teenage girl demographic. Maybe it would be easier for you to deliver an emotional performance if I got Johnny to drive a really heavy old plow made by an extremely practical grumpy Amish man over your nutsack, and then ride you and push you around." "Ummm..." Wordsworth thought about it, and I wasn't checking him out or anything but I noticed his bulge get a bit bigger, like he was getting a stiffy or something. He scratched his head, and I could sort of see he liked the idea of Johnny treating him badly. "Yeah I think that might help" he said, he's such a weenie he needs to be dominated and equates control with love haha. "Hey do you also want some old Reader's Digest magazines?" I asked him. "I've got heaps of ISSUES." "Sure" he said, not even getting it. "Here have some ISSUES" I said as I gave him some off the pile. "Do you have enough ISSUES?" "Oh wow no I don't" he said, still not even getting it. "Maybe I should take my top off if you want the teenage girl demographic" Johnny suggested. "Nah it's cool I already took mine off ages ago" I said, and flexed a bit. "Maybe I should just take mine off anyway, just to maximize the sales" Johnny saidgested. "Nah it's OK it's OK" I told him, "my muscles are enough." "Are you sure?" Johnny asked me. "I mean I've been working out heaps and getting a tan and stuff." "Yeah me too" said Andrew. "Oh well you didn't need to cos I've already done all that" I told him. "Oh really I thought you've just been sitting there drinking too much coffee and procrastinating and mucking around and going to the pub instead of writing" said Andrew. Johnny grabbed the bottom of his shirt and began pulling it up, exposing not really any abs or anything- "yeah I've got heaps of abs" he said, and I pushed his shirt back down and said look mate I've got it covered. "You forgot the quotey marks on that bit, are you a bit threatened there or something, scared I'll show you up? Are you a bit nervous?" And I just went "no I just wasn't in the mood, and don't worry about it. We're gonna do the mountain scene soon and it'll be really cold so keep your shirt on. I'll take care of the teenage girl demographic myself." Then Wordsworth said a thing but just ignore it, it doesn't matter. "OK I'll start rehearsing these amazing emotion-lines or whatever" he said, but I had already started the next bit: "oh hang on, just one more thing" said Wordsworth. "WHAT?" Johnny asked. Wordsworth put a really sincere expression on the grouping of sensory organs about the maxillary bones of his skull. "I just want everyone to know that I'm going to combine marketing and brain biochemistry in calculating the precise amount of emotion my heart will generate so we get the maximum sales in the horny women demographics." "OK well whatever" said Johnny.

They were at the mountain. "It's about time I was at the mountain" said Mr. Woodcock. "I'm gonna put my wheelchair on a snowboard and go for a spin on the halfpipe and totally smash out some seven-twenty cannonballs, and land them revert." "Ah…, you're not actually in this bit" said Guye Armstronge, casually putting a comma after a suspension point like it was no big deal. He even yawned a bit as he did it. "Well which bit am I in, then?" Mr. Woodcock asked. "You've been in so much lately it's not even fair" said Mark. "Can you stop using your disability as an excuse to be in more of the book?" said Andrew. "Everyone thinks you're like puritanical correctness gone mad." "I'm not doing that, shut up." "Look, Mr. Woodcock, you're not in this bit" said Johnny. "Me and Guye Armstronge edited you out on Friday night." "Wow sounds like you writers have really amazing Friday nights, wish I'd been invited" said Mr. Woodcock without even one nanomole of sarcasm times ten to the power of minus twenty-eight. "Yeah well we edited you out of this bit, you're supposed to be having a really passionate sad bit right now" Guye Armstronge said as he put another couple of hundred rejection letters in one of his many rejection letter shredders. "So how come I'm here then?" Mr. Woodcock asked. "And maybe I am really passionate and sad" he said; "maybe I am a tirading torrent of terrestrial tapestrised tear-ducting torn-apart, unrequieted, fifty-something maths teacher, who yearns, nay, who famishes, for divulgent incombompriums of a lover gone, a lover with the commitment of a Grant Fox conversion in stormy weather -" "yes, a lover with the tenacity of a thousand David Campese goose-steps hurled into the presence of a semi-depressed John Kirwan, homesick for Remuera in the Italian countryside, so remorseful he was ignoring a brisket of tender maidens forward-passing his gallant balls and all off-side"

interrupted Mark. "So we've been sidetracked a bit from the mountain that's right in front of us and that we're at, in America, not the
Marist Old Boys Rugby Club" said Johnny, cupping his hand over
the mouth of Mark, whose lust for sonnets and maidens of yore,
whose desire was weaving in and out like the footsteps of Smokin'
Joe after a scrum against the 'Boks, and oh, how, how how how,
and Johnny was disappointed in him for losing paragraph tactil-
ity, how it betrenched his despairing heartlet beating so soft, so
soft, how it infrompillated his dismemtia into ultimatizing, ultima-
tish, trepidarius, ultimate gloonge. "Wow, look at that mountain"
Johnny said, grabbing everyone's heads and pointing at the mountain. Yes, how desperately his heart beat a hummingbird's flutter
at the thought, nay, the LUST for more focussed, more organized
paragraphing, how tenaciously he needed to slam his cock and
balls all over a better paragraph with minimal sidetracking, no,
with no sidetracking or unnecessary bits that slopped around the
reader's eye, at all, at all, forever, for ever and ever, till end of book
did he part, or at least end of chapter or end of this bit. "Can I
part at end of that last sentence?" he asked. But he wasn't allowed
to. He looked again at the mountain. "It's the mountain that we're
at." They were at the mountain. "Yeah I just said that" Johnny just
said. "Shut up Johnny" I said, "it's my book and I'll narrate it however I want just let me do it however I want to do it OK?" Johnny
didn't say anything after that. "Yes I did" Johnny said. They were
at - "It is a mountain MOUNTAIN MOUNTAIN" said Mark, unaware
that he was interrupting me, the narrator THE MOST IMPORTANT
PERSON, easily the coolest one, the one who was telling you the
tightly decisive and focussed story, such an awesome narrator I
was that I was telling you about him interrupting me just so you,
the person whose eyes were looking RIGHT HERE RIGHT NOW,

would know every tiny detail. The feathers in Mark's hatlet were jolly and gay, as was the pounding his arse had taken the night before a la Johnny's curious side. He talked, but you can skip it, it's not important. "It is a mountain of sorrow in my heart, it is a mountain of snow and ice and a symbol of games being cancelled at Eden Park because of the weather, oh how my belly squeezes a plop of soupy-poo into my intestinal plant, how wacky it is the feath of my underhat, in the bosom of my scalpy bregma." "Do you mean you crapped on your head?" Johnny asked. Andrew, who hadn't talked in ages, told Mark to focus. "Let's you and me get together and be precise in defining a spot where we are, so the person reading knows that we're at a mountain" he said. "I've got two pens for us to use." He gave one to Mark. Then he gave him a pen hahaha. "What's that supposed to mean?" Mark asked. "Nothing, slut" I said. The two chaps made a big circle and an X where they were, which was at the mountain. "Look what I drew" Andrew drew. "Look where I'll put the mark" Mark marked. "Hark" Mark harked. They kissed. Andrew said "yaaark, Mark's plaque." Then a fisherman walked by with a shark. "Hey I gotta pull over and park the ark" said Mark, moving the ark in an arc. "I'm gonna parallel park" said Parallel Mark. "Should we set up a bulwark before we disembark so we don't cark?" one of the boys asked of Mark, I know because he narked. Finally, with the engine sparking, and no-one carking, the Markling did his parking. Then a physicist walked by who was quarking. "Is it just a lark it's not dark?" larked a notdark carparked Mark. "The whiteness is absolute." They looked. All around them it was white. "Do you mean the snowy mountain?" Johnny asked, happy they had heard his harking of mountain focus. "Nah he means this MS Word document" said Wordsworth. "Maybe you should stop breaking the fourth wall" said Andrew. "It stopped being worthwhile ages ago." "Nah shut up it's still worthwhile" said Guye Armstronge, as he wriggled on his makeshift sofa made of boxes full of rejection letters. Andrew said he'd like to buy a vowel to describe the mountain, but realised he needed a whole word. "Hey Wordsworth if you're a writer can I buy a whole word off you?" "I don't know what a word's worth" said Wordsworth. Everybody groaned. "That was so terrible Wordsworth" Mark said. "Can you stop being such a massive dickhead?" "Bro I'm just reading my lines" said Wordsworth. "I'm just reading them how they're written." "Well I say it doesn't sound very good" said Mark and Andrew and Johnny. "I say it too" said Mr. Woodcock. "No, you're not in this bit" said Johnny. "Maybe we should change some of the lines" said Mr. Woodcock. "Maybe I should be in this bit and I'll totally deliver some really gnarly ad libs with some characters I've been working on." "There's nothing wrong with the lines, it's in the delivery" said Guye Armstronge, who was not insecure about his writing in any way, and who was not worried in any way about how this bit of his book was going, and he didn't think anyone was ruining it, and he wasn't in any way worried about his future career or mental health. "Aardvark!" Wordsworth shouted. He stood there, grinning. They turned and looked at him. "Why did you say that, Wordsworth?" Johnny asked. "Because of Mark" Wordsworth said. "Mark's aardvark, am I right Mark?" "Not really" said Mark. "I don't have an aardvark." "Mark's aardvark from the park?" Wordsworth tried to lark, but instead he just said it. "No-one cares about that anymore Wordsworth" said Mark. Wordsworth giggled while the rest of them had a coffee and ciggy break. "You're marked, you've been aardvarked Mark" said Wordsworth to Mark, who just wished Wordsworth would reembark the ark, drive away and cark. Though Wordsworth had made attempts at larking, up the wrong tree he and his aardvark were barking. "Aardvarks can't bark" said Mark from the park, who knew the subject of bark. "Well geez, fark" said Wordsworth, disappointed, and tired of Mark, who of course had tired of his brother's remarking, not to mention his wasteful aardvarking. "Wow, look at the mountain, so foreboding and majestic" said Johnny, who was focussed on the mountain that they were at. "Yeah, look at this mountain, it's so amazing and splendid and verdant" said Andrew. "Yeah wow, the mountain is so tender and sensitive and showcases nature's might in a really masculine way not a gay way" said Mark, and it sounded a bit like he was complaining about it not being gay enough. "Yeah it's so incredulous and herculean and all-encompassing" said Johnny. Wordsworth stepped up; it was his turn to describe the mountain: "using geophysical extrapolations I calculate the density and largess of the mountain topography to be exactly this: AWESOME AND RADICAL, DUDE!" He turned around to high five the other guys as he put sunglasses and a backwards cap on, but they looked away as though they didn't know him. "The mountain is cosmic and infinite in its shape" said Mark. "Dude, don't use up all the adjectives or Guye Armstronge won't be able to describe it" Johnny said to Mark, squeezing his nippy-nips with peggy-pegs really tightly and twisting them around so Mark's chest-skin got all wacked but Mark was a freak and barely noticed any pain, instead he just winked at Johnny. "Yeah don't use up all the adjectives describing the amazing powerful wonderful glacial icy-cold, cold, cool, magnanimous mighty mountain" said Andrew. "But it's such a brilliant, well-formed, spiky, edgy, tall, wide, long, cliffy, chasmy, spasmy, craggy, raggy, waggy, baggy, ag(riculturalresearch)gy mountain" said Mark. "I mean you couldn't blame me really if I used up all the adjectives up saying how high and air-compressive and sublimely beautiful

and regal and holy and perfect and perfidious and fluid and rocky
and limestoney and granitty it is." "You know what Mark?" Wordsworth asked. "What Wordsworth?" Mark reply-asked. "I calculate
that I couldn't blame you even if you did use up all the adjectives
saying how sayey and telling how telly it is" he blah blahed. They
were at the mountain. "Oh wow is it the bit about the mountain?"
asked Deborah, who actually wasn't there. "Shut up I think he's
describing the mountain now" said Johnny. "Oh wow I wonder
what adjectives he's going to use" said Wordsworth. ...They... were
at... the mountain. "OK everybody ssshhh, he's describing it NOW"
ssshhhed Wordsworth, getting a bit of dribble in Johnny's popcorn
and Mark's drink, that he probably stirred with a gay dude's cock
or something. It was a mountain, and it was so mountainously
descriptively mountainous that its description became the reck-
oning of the chosen revelations of the mountainational describey
describers in descriptive description of its mountaineity. "Sounds
like the cock I stirred my drink with, HEY-YO!" Mark shouted,
winking at everyone. "I thought I wasn't in this bit, why is Mark
winking at me?" asked Mr. Woodcock. "I'm only winking at everyone *in this bit*" Mark said. "Well it says just there you're winking
at everyone, so I just thought..." Mr. Woodpedanticcock shrugged.
"Wow, *pedantic* cock, get me some of that" said Mark, "give it to
me like a jackhammer big boy" Mark said, rubbing his hands together in glee and winking at ONLY THE PEOPLE IN THIS BIT AND
DEFINITELY NOT ANYONE ELSE. "So am I in this bit or what?"
Mr. Stupidannoyingtimewastingcock asked. "I mean just ask if you
want me to not be in this bit and I'll go be in a different bit." They
were at the mountain without Mr. Woodcock who was DEFINITELY
not in this bit, not even to interrupt. The mountain, and nothing Mark had anything to do with, was wonderful and amazing

and spellbinding and incredible and nobody interrupted or broke the fourth wall or did anything to annoy Guye Armstronge ever again. "So does that mean that Guye Armstronge lived happily ever after?" Andrew asked. "Far out that's a bit cliché, I hope that's not the ending. It's pretty cheesy." "No it's not" said Gruyere Accasci-atostrong. Andrew kept on complaining: "I don't think you should mention yourself so much! Stop being such a proser!" "SSSHHH" Wordsworth and Mark and Johnny SSSHHHed. Johnny put Andrew in his place. "He's about to describe – I mean the mountain is there and if there was a person narrating, and I'm not saying there is one because only us are here, but if someone was narrating he or she or it may just be describing this mountain for it certainly is worthy of description-flopping awesome-ny awesomeness" Johnny said, brushing really hard with a massive pile of hammers pushed by a bulldozer up against the fourth wall and giving it a cheeky pat on the bum but not actually breaking it. The mountain stood splen-did and mighty and totally far out. Wordsworth yawned. "Bro what are you yawning for?" Johnny asked him. "It's the mountain bit, it's really exciting." "Oh nothing, yeah, nah I'm really excited to be at the mountain, just need a coffee or something or like a wake-up spliff. I mean the mountain's really exciting and all." "I didn't even WANT to be in the mountain bit" Mr. Woodcock said. "Yeah well you're not" said everyone in the world and everyone on the internet, especially all the really skeptical science websites about evolution and stuff. "Well I'm just saying that's good, it suits me, I think mountains are actually pretty lame. They're not cool and radical like when I draw parabolic graphs and pretend I'm doing sal flips and late flips all down them when I've got my wheelchair on a skateboard. So I don't know why you needed to say I wasn't in this bit in big capital letters." "BECAUSE YOU'RE A MASSIVE DICK" said Johnny and Andrew and Wordsworth and Mark. "No I'm not, don't say stuff that's not true, where's it written that I'm a massive dick in capital letters?" They said he was a massive dick because HE WAS A MASSIVE DICK. "Right there" said Mark. "Trust you to know where massive dick is Mark" said Wordsworth, catapulting a very politically incorrect insulting innuendo in Innuit in insalubrious insane inwardness in Mark's ear. "Yeah stick it in really hard" said Mark, who was a bitch. "Bark" Mark barked. "OK that's enough you guys don't appreciate the mountain" said Johnny. "So get away from the mountain." They were not at the mountain anymore.

They were at an as yet undisclosed place, they were not at the place they had been earlier, absolutely nobody was at that place, especially not Mr. Woodcock absolutely definitely categorically not not not times a hundred. "Oh, maths, yeah, times tables! I *must* be in *this* bit" shouted Mr. Woodcock, revving his wheelchair and taking the cap off his big failing red pen. "Just because we're not at the mountain doesn't necessarily mean that you're with us Mr. Woodcock" said Andrew. "We don't hang out with our teachers, it's a bit creepy." "I thought I might be like the token older, cool friend" said Mr. Woodcock. "And I could like bring you alcohol and tobacco and stuff like that, like yeah, I could steal it, I could go steal some guns and motorbikes, I'd be like a real badass, like not the alpha male but one of the cool people." "You better not hit on me again" said Wordsworth. They all put on their preachy faces, and at the thought of what was forthcoming, Andrew's willy drooped. "I thought you were the token disabled person" said Androop. "And don't you know about the harm alcohol and tobacco cause?" asked Masked Mark. "Don't you know that tobacco companies practice ethics of highly dubious morality?" "Yeah, don't you know about alcohol-related problems and stuff like that?" asked Wordsworth and Andrew, poking Mr. Woodcock's tickly tummy. Guye Armstronge gently moved some of his beers away from the computer screen so none of the lads would see them and tell readers about them and probably exaggerate how many there were. Johnny cleared his throat, hoping to kick some ass where they were at. "WOW IT'S REALLY INTERESTING WHERE WE ARE AT RIGHT NOW, RIGHT GUYS AND NOT MR. WOODCOCK?" Johnny asked this in a big loud voice, and it was as if, it felt to all of them, not Mr. Woodcock who was definitely somewhere else, that Johnny was perhaps suggesting that if someone was narrating their lives, or about to narrate their lives, that that person should use Johnny's thing he said as a lead-in to a narration, IF in fact a narrator of their lives did exist, but the way Johnny said his bit sort of suggested that perhaps a narrator was a little tired of narrating their stupid dumb gay dumb lives that were getting a bit annoying to a narrator, who may or may not have existed, if one was to believe the emotional insinuations of Johnny's Johnnying. There was a really long pause, and if the four or whatever number of them were in the middle of a conversation it stopped mattering, so, like, don't worry about where it was going or if there was a point to it or whatever. If a narrator had existed, he would have taken a deep, long breath. And then another. And finally, when he was ready, he would have continued. They were not at - "Oooh Guye Armstronge hey Guye Armstronge please please if it's not at a mountain can I be in this bit?" Mr. Woodcock asked and asked, tugging at Guye Armstronge's elbow. "No you can't be in this bit" Guye said. They were not at the scenic viewing area of the mountain, they were ON the mountain, on the SIDE of the mountain INSIDE a cramped little hut on the side of the ski field, WITHOUT MR. WOODCOCK who had died or was about to die in a really horrible yukky graphic mutilating way without ANY cool people or saucy sex bits so no-one would really care or bother remembering it. Johnny, Andrew, Mark and Wordsworth were on the side of the mountain. It was a nice place to stay because it was close to the main part of the ski field - one just needed to put one's skis on and groove one's way down to the chair lift and groove one's way up to the top and then groove back down. One of the few good things about the hut was that it had a huge common room, where the eager students could brag about their skiing ability and hope that the weather was bad so they wouldn't have to show anyone how untalented they really were. "I'm off to ski Satan's Bowel Movement and Hell's Really Cold Metal Tampon" they would say to their peers, and ski off by themselves so they could spend the day at Happy Valley falling over. Having packed their belongings in their rooms, they began to frightfully commonize in the frightfully common room frighfully. There they found that the teachers had something special planned. They had been seated for almost an hour, and commanded not to speak, for some reason the teachers would not say why. "Why the hell can't I talk?" a boy had asked before, and had been told to shut his big ole mouth up. "But *why?*" he asked again, and was told to shut his big ole mouth up. "Because" one of the more patient teachers said. His voice got really low and hushed, as if telling a scary story, and what he said next put a massive chill up their funny bones... "Because of our conspiracy." "Wow, about time someone talked about a conspiracy, I was getting a bit worried there" said Wordsworth. For some reason he was tapping his watch and pointing at the page number, I'm not totally sure why though. "I thought Guye Armstronge said no more breaking the fourth wall" said one of the other characters. "Gloat gloat" Wordsworth bwah-hah-hahed. "I'm the evil necromancer bad guye and I do whatever I want in the whole world and I don't follow the rules, unless they're rules of physics and chemical properties of solids, liquids and gases, and I do agree with the arrangement of the elements of the periodic table, at least as far as electronegativity is concerned, but I don't agree with any other rules, not even Darwinian mechanisms because mineral depletion in bones of the dead, via soil bacteria, makes weaker skeletons with d4 hit dice instead of d8. This is compounded by soil erosion and tectonic shifts, so I don't believe in the laws of geology either." Guye Armstronge wiped his brow and leaned back on his extremely comfortable couch as he exposed one of his creations, his bad guye, his chief villain, half of the good and evil dichotomy, again to the world. "Oh wow, good and evil, that's really original" said Andrew. "I wish I could think up original stuff like that" he said without sounding condescending or sarcastic at all in any way or like a snobby wanker wanker critic wanker who couldn't even do anything himself and just talked bollocks about everyone else. "Yeah well, it's like, I'm reworking the good versus evil concept in an original way" said Ghostwriter Articulationstrong, who didn't sound frustrated by the whole process at all. "It sounds like it's something that's really worth doing and definitely not a complete waste of time, Guye" said Andrew, without even a tiny speck of sarcasm or arrogance, no, Andrew was definitely absolutely not a pompous up-himself so-far-up-his-own-arse-he-couldn't-even-see literary critic, who was definitely not jealous in any way of anyone else's achievement or ability to create simply for the joy of creating. Andrew then said "and it's definitely not onanistic in any way, and I can say that with a totally straight face." Guye was really happy he had got someone like Andrew to tell him that stuff, because Andrew was a very sincere person and not rude or sarcastic.

"Wow thanks Andrew, your feedback means a lot to me" said Guye, also without any sarcasm or wanky I'm-a-suffering-artiste-so-treat-me-special-and-different pompousness or snarky arrogance in his attitude. Wordsworth giggled, got all excited, wriggled and audibly reignited, "hey Mark, a bit of snark! Shall we take it down to the park?" Said Mark to his brother "Wordsworth get back in our mother! Can you stop trying to be funny? Your brain's gone all runny and it's hurting my tummy!" Wordsworth looked shamed at the floor, his demeanour unsunny, he said "I guess I just needed more hugs from my mummy." "Well if you want to continue, go and shout at the dunny." Johnny said, out of his head, "can you buy some new words, do you need any money?" Wordsworth's lips turned south, unlike a bunny, he was emotionally unyummy, "I guess in my mouth, it's gone far too runny, probably because I'm secretly glummy." "Well can you piss off, you sound like a dummy." Said Andrew from school "Wordsworth can you stop trying to be cool?" "OK but when I see Mark I just start to bark, I guess I'll try keep set to park the automatic gearbox of my lark." Johnny told him "dude it would rule if you'll stop being a tool. Sometimes I think, and it's not just when I drink, your tongue's wrapped in a spool and your words are all drool."

Grabmeballs 'Arrasmentstrong looked at his drooly book. "I want to go to a fair!" Johnny shouted. He jumped up and down, then he folded his arms in front of his chest and looked a weeny bit grumpy. "I think the fair should come to us!" Mark shouted also as well as Johnny. "Yeah, advance New Zealand fair!" cried Words-boobypoosworth. "I hope Australia doesn't get hurt when New Zealand advances" said Andrew. "God defend Australia" he sang. Git Garble-drone-all-day-long ignored the lads, and their cacophony, they were, after all, and before all, and even during all, a bunch of cackling phonies. He told Wordsworth to put some sensible clothes on, which of course didn't happen. He told Andrew to stop being cheeky which also didn't happen, and he told Johnny to be even more arrogant and self-centred, which did happen. He told Mark to go away and die somewhere crappy. "Do you want to erode his lifespark?" asked Wordsworth of Mark.

It wasn't going well.

NEXT SCENE: TAKE FIFTY

"Hey Mark, are we going to totally party tonight?" Johnny asked Mark while they were both wearing extremely fashionable clothing in the swankiest part of New York. "Yeah it'll be really cool because we're millennials and we'll take selfies and text each other asking what we're up to." "You guys are probably gonna end up sucking some tranny's cock" said Wordsworth in a sudden fit of smut. "Wow yeah I wasn't expecting anyone to get smutty" Andrew said without any sarcasm. All were aghast at Wordsworth's crudeness. Mark held his +2 sword aloft, threatening his brother. Wordsworth prepared his eight-sided dice for casting the Chill Touch spell, but in a way that didn't break any Copyright with TSR or get Guye Armstronge in any kind of legal difficulty. "OK I'm attacking you now Wordsworth!" Mark shouted in the ski hut (in the swankiest part of Chicago). It was really incredible and dramatic. Andrew yawned, trying a little to hide it. "Andrew, dude, don't yawn!" Mark shouted, but Andrew didn't appear to care. Mark was about to make his attack roll, when he was stopped by a level fifteen teacher with twenty constitution, wielding a +7 red pen. "Plus seven? So unfair!" he protested, knowing his d20 roll would be worthless, as Wordsworth the evil necromancer escaped another blast of holy vengeance that could have destroyed him. "Is holiness really into revenge?" Andrew asked, his voice taking on a sudden philosophical hue. "You know it seems a bit extreme, maybe there is the possibility of forgiveness and reconciliation, instead of just annihilation." I forgot what I was about to type in this bit, Andrew had thrown off my bollocky-focus. "I guess I'm just criticizing the quickness with which the 'forces of light' resort to violence – if they really are about doing good works. I mean wouldn't they try and talk to him first, instead of just destroying him, like get to the root cause of his pain?" I leaned back on this kind of weird, semi-comfortable armchair made of paper mashayed together rejection letters and sighed. I was getting tired of all this second guessing my awesome plotty plot and narrateyness. I guess there was some-thing to be thankful for; Andrew in his criticism was not the least bit smug or self-satisfied with the fact that he had pointed out a potential hypocrisy, oh, in the flappy rindy bits of the vagina of his heart. "I think the forces of light should run Wordsworth over with a ski plough" Johnny said. Wordsworth cackled with glee, the lightning and evil oroborous of the interdimensional void opened to the gates of chaos above him. "NYEEAARH HAR HAR!" his wicked laughter boomed out in necromancey enfathomish blastisizing trumpets of brutalizing evil, as he straddled the crappy pool table in the hut common room, once Mark had made sure said table complied fully with all legal and recommended safety regulations and had the proper amount of dick and balls drawn underneath it. "Can you young men just BE QUIET!" the teachers shouted at them. It made no sense to Mark, and it never would, but the teachers insisted that they be quiet, or they would be told to be quiet again. It was going to be a long night. Mark waited. And waited. And waited. And weighted. "Hey!+!!" one of the teachers yelled at him in a +2 shout. "No weighting!"

Two days into the trip, Johnny was absolutely exhausted absolutely. "Oh, how even my personified absolution has abs" he ab-libbed. He had skied the whole mountain, even the slopes that were forbidden to him (Medusa's Eyes, Michael Jackson's Face (BEWARE OF AVALANCHES) and even Unhappy Valley). He had even skied THE MIGHTY FISTULA, a slope that was for experts only, and a slope that Wordsworth had beaten every other student on. Thus it had caused Johnny great anguish and literally tore apart his mind when someone spoke of it. The next day it was a bit boring – "oh wow, what a surprise" said Andrew without being sarcastic at all. "Shut up Andrew" I said. I mean it was a bit boring UNTIL Johnny had a really cool idea: "let's do an exorcism" he said to Wordsworth. Wordsworth wanted to know why. He wanted to know why with a big burning passion no other soul could possibly comprehend in the entirety and history of the whole embrocating consuetudinary ortolanian. His desire, montbretia and dreyfusard haptateuched with dotterely moquette mashie and opprobrious auscultation. It was most definitely a complete imfrantonkitusswoompyboomp, possibly even an iffwobbamamimmyaplobbaaeeueueuewaoeuioaa. And yet Wordsworth still wanted to know why. "Why?" he asked. That was what gave him away. (Then it gave him a bit closer.) "Be-cause I'm bored" Johnny explained. "And there's nothing else to do." "Is this one of your attempts at getting famous?" Wordsworth asked him, slightly amused. Which annoyed Johnny, because he was grumpy at the lack of activity that surrounded him. "I just want something to do, OK?" "Well what are we going to exorcise?" "Let's exorcise Mark." Mark began to front away. "Don't exorcise me" he said. "I'm just a little foreign girl. I'm only doing it because I need the money. One day I'm going to give it up and become famous and battle heroin and overcome manic depression and wanting to kill myself and make a movie about my life." "But your life sucks, and you don't even exist" I said. "So why are you talking to me then?" Mark asked me. Anyway, on with the story, and Johnny said: "We need to exorcise you to prepare you for the gates of heaven. It won't hurt." So they lay Mark down outside in the yellow snow. It was a lovely day, and the lovely boys had returned to their lovely hut after a lovely day of lovely skiing on the lovely mountain. It was lovely. The sun was still beaming its rays at them from across the nothingness, and there was not a cloud in the sky. "We're not in the sky" the clouds said. "We're in the ground." Anyway, it was a lovely day, blah blah blah, and Mark was lying on the snow outside the hut. "Which bit of me is the demon in?" he asked. "The bit that . . . that I'm going to cut off" Johnny said. He pulled a knife from his Calvin Klien Superbritches. Just then something strange happened. No, not then... just *then*! No, *THEN*! Oh, you missed it. Something that the four of them thought was the strangest thing they had seen. Something that shook the rattle of the real world violently and unforgivingly. It tore a large, ominous hole in their fragile realities and beliefs, and from that hole came an endless horror. Mark began to growl. "He's beginning to growl" Wordsworth said. "I know that silly" Johnny sneered. "I can read." Mark started to writhe around on the yellow snow and his voice became deeper and his tummy thrust out like a basketball. "Let's record this on that skinny guy's video camera with all the kinky buttons" Wordsworth suggested. They told the skinny guy banjo jokes until he gave them his video camera, which Johnny proudly operated proudly. "You're looking rather proud there Johnny" Andrew said. But Johnny did not listen to Andrew's parenchymatically enhanced oratorium of mucronatiousisticallyotious seignioragely poos and wees. He began recording as the other students gathered around him. Whispers began to circulate through the group like blood through veins. Mark began to speak in obscure guttural noises. "Grrrrrrrrrr" he said. "Grrrrrrrrrrr. rrrrrrrrrrrG" Then he lay still. Then he said "Boo." Then he said "Pop." Then aliens invaded. "Pizza Delivery" was written on the side of the spaceship. "Anywhere, Anyhow, Anywhen, Anywhat, Anywhy" was also written. Not on the spaceship, just there on this page. As it landed, Johnny, Wordsworth, Andrew and Mark looked at it feeling puzzled. Wordsworth had an intelligence of eighteen so he was very exited about all this. He wet his bikini over it. Andrew thought it was time for another fart. It had been too long, and he was getting bored. He huffed and he puffed, and squirted a billowing cloud of highly concentrated eight hundred thousand ppm gaseous botty-resin from out of his bum, and all were amazed. "That fart's almost eighty percent purity!" cried Wordsworth as his lungs turned black and he coughed like a smoker. A door opened on the side of the craft, and a horde of little pink men with broccoli-shaped heads came out wearing T-shirts. "You guys like T-shirts, eh?" Wordsworth asked them, feeling a pretty swish dude. "Get your hands off me you pervert" the swish dude said to him, slapping him. Had Wordsworth been any less enthused he would have cried at such unfairness, for the pretty swish dude was very pretty, but he ignored it and stared in rapture at the T-shirts. He would go out and buy himself a T-shirt as soon as the opportunity was presented to him from the great fun barrel of life. "Yeah" they said. The two groups stood standing still and looked at each other for a few hours. Looking looking

looking. "This is pretty exciting, standing here looking at each other" Andrew said after a few hours were up. "It's how Govinda Maharma-Bharata-Sarong makes his book so exciting" Johnny told him. "nothing is more exciting than standing around looking at stuff like some arty ponce going glingyglongywakwagyulouswoop." Johnny trounced about fifty bananas all over his narcissism, he hated everyone else and only loved himself else. He wanted everyone else to be living in a less desirable way because if they were he would feel better than everyone. Winning at life, by pure human ego and selfishness, seemed to be the only way he could compile more bananaey goo all over his own tenacre, and basically have more happiness, this of course, being only true, reprehensibly so, if one were measuring human happiness in bananas. Maybe make some banana wine? Mmm, that would be yum. Johnny drank a glass of water, pretending it was banana wine, while they relaxed and talked one evening in the totally epic and incredible ski trip they were having. It was so thrilling and dramatic, and anyone hearing about it was on the edge of their seat. Mark was reading a book about problems in society, specifically about children who were living rough, in squalor and poverty. Johnny was just about to remind his friends how important he was, how only he mattered, out of everyone in the world, how he was even more important than material things, even Stu Wilson's All Blacks jersey from the 1983 Bledisloe Cup, when Mark said "imagine what life would be like for these children. They're living in the heart of a problem in society, and they can still put on a brave face. It's so romantic. And the hardest thing about it is that it could be happening right now." "What about me!?" Johnny the attention-seeker yelled, getting everyone's attention. He even got the attention of people who weren't reading this book! "Nobody writes novels about me! I've got problems too, and nobody's ever going to write a novel about me!" "There there" Andrew said, patting Johnny on the willy-vein that looked like a little bit like a nematode. "One day someone will write a novel about you." "No they won't" Johnny said, burying his face in his hands. "Nobody will ever write a novel about me complaining from my point of view" he complained in my novel written about him from his point of view. Wordsworth also wanted some attention. "A-skiggidy bak-ta-boo, moop-moop me-moo" he said, snapping his fingers. He had little round Lennon glasses and a beret on. "Skibbidy-skabbidy-skoo!" "What the hell are you doing Wordsworth?" we all asked him. "I'm acting like this to get the beat-nik demographic, can you dig daddy-o? Don't freak out, man, don't say I'm too far out!" "Yeah…" I said, leaning back and scratching my chin, wondering the best way to tell him to forget it. "You know the beatnik demographic isn't really a big deal anymore, it's not one of the mainstream demographics, I don't think it has an influential market share." "Don't frippity-frown, no need to shut me down" he said, snapping his fingers a bit more and being a bit of a weird awkward dick. "Yeah look Wordsworth, you're ruining this bit, we don't need any beatnik crap, it's a waste of time" I said. "Is this one of your evil bad guye conspiracies?" Johnny asked him, rising from the table with his banana wine, which was actually a potion of Storm Giant strength and undead protection, in case Wordsworth summoned any undead minions. Wordsworth the beatnik necro-mancer put his +5 lab coat on. The table. "That's just a put-on" said Mark. "You're not a beatnik!" "Yeah, beat it!" Johnny shouted. "You've been nicked!" Wordsworth took off his lab coat. The table. "You mean I 'took it off the table'" Wordsworth said. "Yeah Ok well whatever Wordsworth" I said, "just because you've got an intelli-gence of eighteen doesn't matter to me or whatever." Wordsworth stood up nice and tall, asserting himself, and said "I actually drank some intelligence potions so now I have intelligence of twenty-five." And he sounded like a ponce, all hoity-toity like he was the queen or something. ("I'm the only queen around here" said Mark.) "You mean you have *an* intelligence of twenty-five" Andrew said in response to Wordsworth. "Damn it Andrew!" he shouted, all frustrated and we laughed at him. But it wasn't the only time in the history of the universe that Andrew annoyed Wordsworth by massive cruelty and sadism and being a tosser. "Look what I've got" he said an hour later, holding forth what looked to Wordsworth like a piece of pom-pom. They were standing in the main hallway of the hut, just outside the common room, two hallways down from the uncommon room, which was next to the rare room. It was NO-WHERE NEAR the limited edition room. In fact, I mean in *point* of fact, pointing *at a fact,* I mean, totally making my point: the limited edition room was not – and still *is not* – actually relevant. I don't know why I'm even bothering telling you anything about it. You probably made me, or tricked me into it, didn't you? Like most of the problems in my life, it's probably YOUR FAULT. Wordsworth and Andrew had been kicked out because Johnny had raised his voice yet again. "Got your pom-pom there mate?" Wordsworth asked him. Andrew shut the door and locked it with the key he had stolen. "This kept me really really warm" he said. "Ha ha. Warmer than any pom-pom. Ha ha. Woof woof. Cluck. Meow." Wordsworth looked at it closer. "What's that red stuff?" he asked. "Blood!" Andrew shouted happily, and unraveled what he was holding. It was Wordsworth's other cat, Fred The Happy Banana. The bastard. The psychotic bastard. "You *fuck*ing bastard. . . . " Wordsworth managed to say, all conscious knowledge of his nervousness and the 'No Swearing Rule, Promise, Pledge, Sly Wink and Secret Handshake' of this book gone. His mouth sobbed massive heartachey sobby sobs, spraying tears everywhere while his eyes let rip with rivers of hot salty teeth. A hysterical, grieving noise escaped his quivering lips. Wordsworth felt utterly lost, betrayed and faithless. In the flavourless pith of the boobs of his heart, Wordsworth felt as though he had just been staunched out by Wally Lewis, at the pub in front of all his boys. Andrew had no right to live, killing such innocent and sweet little animals brutally like that. "What's a bastard?" Andrew asked, just before Wordsworth's puny, weak, feeble, and generally not even the weeniest particle aggressive hands closed around his fat, flabby neck with the saddening and disastrous emotionally unsettling cry of "Fred The Happy Banana to whom I showed an obvious degree of favouritism!" and shook him as violently as they could till he calmly said "Lower down, Wordsworth. Definitely lower down. I didn't know you cared, you kinky little dolly." Wordsworth could take no more, and as Johnny and Mark came rushing through the door to see what all the obscene language that had seemingly come out of nowhere with no warning at all, dirtying Guye Armstronge's virgin and most usu-ally pure paragraph was about, Wordsworth leapt at Johnny, and grabbed his hair, pulling it as hard as he could, which did abso-lutely nothing, except make him even more pissed off that he was such a wimp. "Lower down, Wordsworth. Definitely lower down" Johnny said calmly, and Wordsworth could take no more and fell to the floor weeping and cursing absolutely everything. "Nice one, Wordsworth" Johnny scolded. "Now it's not a kid's book anymore." "Yeah, nice one Wordsworth" Andrew said. "Take the first swear word for yourself. We were going to have a big group profanity page at the end of the novel and all take turns, but you had to say it first, didn't you? You're so selfish. You even broke rule one of the No Swearing Rule." "What's rule one?" a big plate asked. "No swearing." Wordsworth looked up at Mark with big sad eyes that told a big sad story, but big sad Mark was not all that sympathetic. He looked rather menacing. "I'm ashamed of you, Wordsworth" he said, and mashed his midriff with a massive iron spike in a way that was really insensitive to Wordsworth's needs as a woman. Then he mashed Wordsworth's midriff with it. "It was very selfish of you to take the first swear word without asking anyone else." "I'm supposed to be the main character of this book" Wordsworth complained THAT WORD I CAN NEVER REMEMBER THAT'S GOT A 'U' IN IT AND ENDS IN -LY. Johnny slapped him with a big slapstick comedy rubber chicken. "No you're not" he said. "You're the bad guye. It says here in Guye Amstronge's notebook. So there." He put Guye Armstronge's notebook that was made from recycled paper back into Guye Armstronge's pocket made from environmentally friendly fabric that was placed gently on his virgin buttocks that knew nothing of sin, and copped a feel of Guye's tight buns, that were sculpted from being sat on all day watching Neighbours and Shortland Street and Flying Doctors reruns, even though he was based in America, looking for Illuminati symbolism and writing to politicians about it instead of getting a job. Johnny bonked Words- worth on the nose with a bit of two by four. (Tickle tickle tickle.) "Ha ha. You think you're the main character of this book, do you?" Johnny asked. "Well like I said you're the bad guye. That's why all the bad stuff happens to you. You're the evil wizard. And you're going to fall out of your castle and land in your moat and be eaten by Andrew's pet fish at the end of the book. Your spell backfires when you try to infuse your soul with Satan in your selfish quest for immortality because you're secretly scared of dying." "Wow, Sa- tan, really original Wordsworth!" shouted Andrew WITH sarcasm.

"And I'm going to push you out of the spire of your black castle and into the moat and you'll be eaten by my pet fish. That'll teach you to take the first swear word." "Didn't you say exactly that on the first page, mate?" said Wordyboobsworth. "No it's totally different said Androowoowoop. "I thought I was the good guy because I care about stuff" Wordsworth said. He didn't want to be encased within the ever-constricting and cacodemonic thralldom of being the bad guy. "I thought I was the good guy because my parents are dying and I've got no friends and I'm a dweeb and I'm the victim and we'll get the working class demographic by catering to people who care about the underdog." "No" Johnny said; "I'm the good guy! You're the bad guye because you smell funny! You've been wearing that bikini since the first page. You didn't even change it after walking to the mountain in the cold and being attacked by Andrew's evil bogeys and after we exorcised Mark." And the other students filled Wordsworth's shrinking ego with their laughter and squashed it even flatter that that skinny guy, for bikinis had gone out of fashion in the eighties. And Wordsworth was too sad to remember the dress that had trailed behind him on the day that Mark had said he hated his novel with a big bitter hatey hatred. "And you're the bad guy because you killed your mother" Johnny said. "*Wordsworth's disease*, remember? Don't you try and get out of the blame, because it's all your fault she's dead." "But she's alive!" Wordsworth yelled. "She's totally alive - the doctor told me!" "Well that's because I cured her!" Johnny screamed - he was having the time of his life, hardly even realising that he was lying yet again. "Why didn't you tell me that our mother was alive?" Mark asked. "I guess . . . I forgot in the heat of the moment?" Wordsworth guessed, remembering in the heat of the moment. He felt terrible. "Too selfish to share some good news, eh?" Johnny said. "So why didn't you go and visit her when I spent all that time curing her?" "Well I had this trip . . . and she would have wanted me to go." But it didn't sound very genuine. "You could have come up a day late." "I wanted to visit her" Mark said. "If I had known, I would have spent the whole week with her. I wouldn't have been so selfish. Like you." "Hey, watch the ole truthometer, Mark, you're talking ploppy poos and wees" Wordsworth said maniacally, tearing asunder the pre-bruised innocence of Guye Armstronge's pages, rendering them coarse and blackened with his oratically vulgar filth. "That's enough!" Johnny yelled at him, because that WAS enough.

Johnny looked around. He looked out of the computer at me and said "hey Guye, I meant enough rude words from Wordsworth, not enough of that whole paragraph bit." Johnny was lenient with what went on (after all he *was* the main character, and had been given by that great fella, that bona-fide humanitarian, that wonderboy, that superman, that God-believing, the one, the only, here he is ladies and germs, Guuuuuuuye AAAAAAAAAAAArm-strooooooonge a certain control of the sub-plots, although he was definitely sure that he wasn't going to have *ANY* more of the politeness-battering peurility in the book of which he was the protagonist). He screamed "get out of the book!" But Wordsworth could not leave the book for he was central to the ever complex plot, but Mark thought it was good of Johnny to tell him off for all his despicable coarse language. His behaviour was just awful, and he deserved having his cat killed, Mark deduced. The cat, however, was not the one who should have been experimented on by Andrew's bizarre treatment, and it was a real shame the way its life had to be ended to show that Wordsworth was silly, and was going against the laws and ways of society by being such an idiot, and putting a food processor on his head and trying to kill Andrew by falling out of a building upside down head first gravitying onto Andrew's head, even though the food processor would become un-plugged, he hoped that the momentum would be enough to chop Andrew up on his face, maybe chop his hair a bit or something. Or at least make him go what the hell was that. The ski trip was going just fine until Wordsworth decided that he wanted to throttle one of his closest friends, and Andrew was handling the situation very well. "I'm handling the situation very well" he said. That was what gave him away. "I don't know why he cried and all that. It's just a silly cat." Andrew would need a lecture on right and wrong and up and down and left and right and good and bad and in and out and washed and dirty and door and window and baaa and cluck and key and lock and go on Jerry Springer and Rikki Lake to sort out his massive epic of biblical proportions of depraved previous lifetimes of evil and not reincarnating as the right animal and not complying with whatever the meaning of life is bro. But not until Wordsworth had been dealt with. The evil bikini-clad necro-mancer was sitting in the far corner of the common room looking extremely annoyed with the way things were going, and staring bleakly at the wall. He hadn't even asked if the wall wanted to be looked at. "Would you please stop looking at me?" The wall asked of him. "I'm having a bad paint day." He was so selfish. Mark was with Johnny, and two of the teachers, and they were doing their best to console Andrew. "There, there" Johnny said to him. "Where where?" him said back. Nah OK sorry. "Here here" Andrew said, removing the cat from his pocket, splaying it forth on the table. It was not a pretty sight. Poor Fred the Happy Banana, Mark thought, and felt sorry that there were people like Andrew in the world who were incredibly stupid, and didn't know about right and wrong. It was a good thing Mark wasn't as dumb as Andrew. Mark knew all about right and wrong. He wore a cow around his neck, and he had "LIVE TO RIDE" etched into his handcuffs. "Put the cat away, Andrew" Johnny said. "I was thinking you could do some acupuncture on it to make it come back to life and stick his head back on and close his bottom up and put the intestines back in" Andrew said to him. How considerate. Andrew had realised his wrong, and was trying to make up and pay his debt to society. Because it was the nineties and society was important back then. Wordsworth hadn't said that he wanted Johnny to do acupuncture on himself and Andrew, because they might be hurt. What a meany. "Well I suppose I could" Johnny said. "I don't know about this" one of the teachers said. "I really don't know. I don't know. I just don't know. I just don't know. I don't know. I don't know. I just don't quite know. I simply just simply just simply just don't just just know don't know just. I don't know. I don't know. I don't know. I just don't know." But then again teachers just don't do they? He grimaced. "Trust him" Andrew said. "It's Johnny, remember. And he's the good guy. He's the big superhero we can outsource all of our responsibility to." The teacher frowned. "Johnny might not have rich enough parents to have a worthwhile medical opinion." "Trust me" Johnny said. "My parents have heaps of cash. Why do you think I'm so popular?" And that was that taken care of.

Wordsworth thought of his parents. "Don't think about my parents!" said Johnny. "He means I thought of *my* parents!" Wordsworth shouted. Wordsworth thought of his own parents. He definitely wasn't thinking about Johnny's parents, especially not about Johnny's mum, especially not about totally plowing Johnny's mum in heaps of wicked positions, no, he was definitely not thinking about squishing Johnny's mum's boob in his hand so all of her scoopy boob-fat slopped out between his fingers while they shagged, he definitely would never think stuff like that.

"Someone fetch me a sharp thing" Johnny said. "Acupuncture needs sharp things." One of the inferior junior students fetched Johnny a sharp thing, and he began to hack the cat to pieces, then he threw it in a blender and did a burnout on it in a snow-plough and flung it against a wall heaps of times, and just totally wasted it. "It's not responding very well to my brilliant and sur-gically precise treatment" he said, after shoving the sharp thing through its head and out its ears and waiting for a minute. "Trust one of Wordsworth's cats to not respond. They're just as bad as him - so selfish. They've got his superiority complex - they think that they're above responding to your perfect god-like treatment" Andrew said. Mark peered in awe at the generosity of what his friend was doing. Johnny was helping Wordsworth's cat back alive, even though Wordsworth had tried to kill him, and had dirtied Guye Armstronge's virgin paragraph with his obscene, unsavoury language. "It's no good" Johnny said. "Someone's going to have to eat him. Someone like Wordsworth. It's our only hope."

Wordsworth ate the cat without too, much, fuss, this time, and it made, Mark suspicious. Maybe Wordsworth was involved in some sort of conspiracy - a really nasty conspiracy with Gwen Di-bley, and Mark knew that he was because when Johnny told him he owed him two-hundred dollars for the medical bill, and fifty for the cooking (and that Johnny wasn't going to wash the dishes), Wordsworth didn't seem to care. He would have had to have had a conspiracy to rely on. He normally got quite passionate when it came to humane things - if he no longer cared, a conspiracy against his friends would be necessary to fool them, especially when they hated him even more now. Mark would have to sort something out about this - he would be required by nature to remedy the situation. He walked over to Wordsworth's table. He sat down. He put his little MacDonald's hat on. He looked critically at the inferior specimen and most malignant tumorically existing odium known to everyone as Wordsworth. Which was a bit of a silly name for someone who didn't talk much. It was difficult loving people especially when there were so many nasty pathetic immoral and hate-deserving people like Wordsworth in the world, who seemed to draw the hatred of others in like a huge fridge magnet. But now, what needed strong consideration was Wordsworth, and the way he had caused problems yet again. Mark looked at him critically, and decided not to get sidetracked. Then he thought about flowers and clouds and meadows and pretty children's faeces. I mean faces. Wordsworth did not look back, even though Mark knew that he knew Mark was there, estudious as ever, criticising his older twin of seventeen years and four milliseconds with wave upon wave of neural condescension. "What would our father say, Wordsworth?" he asked. Wordsworth didn't say anything. Wordsworth never said anything. It was so typically arrogant of him to not remark on his own imperfections, Mark thought, to think that he was somehow evolutionarily at too high a stature to respond to someone as holy as Mark, in all his perfect glory. "What would our father say, Wordsworth?" Mark repeated, for want of reply if nothing else. "He'd say to put a silly hat on" Wordsworth mumbled nonchalantly. Then he began to cry. "He'd say it was a conspiracy. I just want it to be as big as everyone else's." "Don't you worry. Everything'll be alright." "It's just because you're a bit younger than the rest of the people around here. Your conspiracy will grow to be enormous, I bet." Wordsworth sniffled, and wiped bogeys three from his nasal shaft, crushing their monstrous life energy viciously like a totally fascist politician warmongering nazi dolphin-strangling shopping bag floating in the sea with dog piss in it. "You really think so?" he asked Mark. "Yes, I bet. You're only sixteen. And lots of shallow things don't matter, remember. It's whether you've got a silly hat on that counts." Wordsworth sniffled again, and forgave his brother instantly of all the sins he had raged against him. "But this doesn't mean that we're friends" Mark said. "Oh no. I think you're disgusting, and I wouldn't be your friend for a million dollars and seventy-four cents." "Well you're a sillysausage" Wordsworth accused. Mark clenched his teeth, and drew his lips back in frustration. "You'll never get away with that" he said. "I'll see that you're punished. Nobody calls me a silly sausage. You've skinned me of my confidence you bastard. There I was ready to be your friend, and you go calling me a silly sausage. Well I'm telling Johnny." And he left the discussion to inform Johnny of the primordial and destructive nature of his elder brother. And to tie up his shoelace.

"Wordsworth called me a silly sausage" Mark wept to Johnny. *So what?* Johnny thought. He was becoming increasingly tired of his friends who he hated. He wished they would let him retire from the bondage of their company, so he could do his own thing (doing his own thing if you know what I mean). And Mark lay on the floor, gnashing his teeth, and pulling his hair. "Stop gnashing my teeth and pulling my hair you miserable git" Johnny commanded. Mark let go of his teeth and his hair, which Johnny straightened impatiently. He swore to himself that he would wreak havoc on Wordsworth's fragile reality, for this bereavement of Mark's formerly high spirits. But only because it would give him a chance to harm the evil bad guye.

CHAPTER

2

REVELATIONS: THE RECKONING
OF THE CHOSEN ONE

Wow, that last chapter was pretty long!

CHAPTER

3

THE BIT WHERE THERE IS MORE TALK OF CONSPIRACY

There is more talk of conspiracy.

CHAPTER

4

TIIE BIT WHERE THERE IS LESS
TALK OF CONSPIRACY

There is less talk of conspiracy.

THE BIT WHERE THERE IS ONLY A LITTLE TALK OF CONSPIRACY

There is only a little talk of conspiracy.

CHAPTER

6

THE BIT WHERE THERE IS
ANOTHER CHAPTER

There is another chapter.

CHAPTER

7

THE BIT I WAS CONSIDERING TAKING OUT, BUT ACTUALLY IT'S OK

I was considering taking this bit out, but actually it's OK.

CHAPTER
8

THE BIT WHERE THERE IS JUST A VERY SMALL BIT MORE TALK OF CONSPIRACY

There is just a very small bit more talk of conspiracy.

CHAPTER

9

I DIDN'T ACTUALLY DO A CHAPTER 9

I didn't actually do a chapter 9.

CHAPTER

10

THE BIT WHERE IT'S REALLY
REALLY AMAZING

It's really really amazing.

CHAPTER

11

THE BIT WHERE IT'S NOT QUITE AS AMAZING

It's not quite as amazing.

CHAPTER

12

THE BIT WHERE THERE IS AN
ANT CRAWLING ON MY DESK

There's an ant crawling on my desk.

CHAPTER

13

THE BIT WHERE THIS PLACE IS INFESTED

This place is infested.

CHAPTER

14

THE BIT WHERE THERE'S A RUDE WORD

There's a rude word.

CHAPTER

15

HANDLING ERRORS, KNOCK-ONS
AND DROPPING THE BALL

Johnny wanted to be left alone with Wordsworth so he could kill him. "Wow, good guye and bad guye final showdown, that's original" said Andrew, who hadn't become boring in his comments that lacked sarcasm. "I want to be left alone with Wordsworth so I can kill him" Johnny said, and no-one did anything, except pat him on the back and say "don't you worry. Everything'll be alright." Johnny felt a bit silly waking everyone up with his wailing of conspiracies and evil, but it was alright because he could do whatever he liked. After all, he was the main character. And he still is. He wanted them all to sod off. "I want you all to sod off" he demanded, and again nothing happened. He would have to remind them all that he was rich, white, and heterosexual so he had jurisdiction over their actions as they earned less money than his father. "My father's got more money than all of you" he said. Nobody moved, or listened to him, except Mark, who said "Don't you worry. Every-thing'll be alright" and patted him on the back and licked the really sensitive bit behind his ears. Johnny rocked himself gently, going to sleep then waking immediately, and staring with wide, petrified, eyes at everyone, around, him. Mark felt sorry for, him. And got all turned on, horny from role reversal. "Sod off and leave me alone!" Johnny shrieked. He was going to kill Wordsworth. He would put an end to his friend and his annoying knobbly bit, and it was good, because not only would he be ridding the world of stinking Wordsworth scum, he would be getting rid of some stress. Just Imagine it. Wordsworth forming a conspiracy against him. The cheek of it. The sheer nerve of some people. "I'm going to kill you now Wordsworth." Wordsworth said nothing. He was in one of his moods. "I'm going to chop little bits of stuff off you." Again, Wordsworth said nothing. As usual, Wordsworth seemed to think that he was above talking to Johnny, and it got Johnny very angered. "You're involved in a conspiracy." Johnny felt good about the way he had told Wordsworth's evil conspiracy to him. "That's another reason why I'm the good guye and you're the bad guye" he said. "Because I just told your evil conspiracy to you. Yeah. Ha ha." He decided to kill Wordsworth again. "Again, I'm going to kill you now" He said, and slashed Wordsworth across the neck from behind. With the knife. I think I mentioned he had a knife. Well, he has a knife, there I mentioned it. Wordsworth fell forward off his chair, and grasped at his neck. Johnny had not cut deep, he had just wanted to scare Wordsworth and he had. His legs were shaking, he licked his lips, and he was whimpering. It was funny. Johnny had him cornered. He edged closer to Wordsworth, whose hands were spread out against the corners of the wall. He slashed at Wordsworth's left wrist, causing blood to gush forth from it.

Wordsworth stuttered something at Johnny which Johnny didn't understand, then grabbed at his left wrist, as if trying to clot the blood. Johnny cut again, this time further up the arm. Wordsworth did not even struggle. He had turned as white as a white sheet, and was trembling. He was a chicken. Not literally, but, you know, he was scared. Johnny didn't hit the area he wanted, and so he struck again, and this time the sharp knife glided into the arm very well and scraped a bit into the bone - it was a strike Johnny was pleased with, and it deserved a little speech: "That was for being a complete dweeb and giving me such a shitty reputation and for hanging around with me. How long did it take you to realise that I don't like you? You're oh so arrogant. You seem to have a superiority complex as big as mine. And that's bad. Only I'm allowed a supe-riority complex." And he slashed again, going for the deltoid, and managed to cut away a big chunk of muscle from Wordsworth's shoulder that flapped and wiggled around, worming it's small, use-less way out of him in a gesture Johnny found rather amusing. He wondered how big Wordsworth's deltoids were, and he looked at his friend's shoulder closely, but the deltoid was very hard to see, it being smothered in his skin and his shirt. "That was for having one of the aforementioned superiority complexes. And for being such a whoopsy and a useless conversation companion." Wordsworth felt bad, even though he had eighteen intelligence, he was crap at blah blahing to people about stuff he'd been up to. Johnny reached over to where Wordsworth lay whimpering and blubbering in the corner of the room scared. Johnny wondered why people got so scared when faced with death - it was a hell of a lot of trouble having to go on living every day of one's life, and fit in with all the stupid fashions - death in some ways (like Wordsworth's) could be very painful, but Johnny theorised that it would just be like sleeping, except a bit of a rush at the start, due to lack of Oxygen. He wanted to try it. But not yet. When he was old and poor and dying. His hand got even closer to Wordsworth's flopping deltoid. Before anyone could see, he had picked his vile and un-enthused assailant up, and with an almighty girl-disgusting, physical education teacher-impressing, testosterone-spraying, muscle-flexing, chest-showing, armpit-hair-displaying, and awfully masculine shout he had thrown Wordsworth across the room. Johnny's ski trip would have a nice happy ending. He ripped off the rest of Wordsworth's shirt and sliced into one of his nipples. Wordsworth had soft nipples. Nipples were strange, as a lot of blood came from them. This perplexed Johnny because they were so small. Wordsworth's nipples were no exception to this. Wordsworth was bleeding quite a bit now, and Johnny found it quite interesting to watch. He pulled the nipple aside with his knife, and peered into what lay beyond: just more blood and stuff he didn't know the name of. It was weird to think there was so much blood in the human body. "I'm going to throw you out of the castle soon. You're the bad guye remember." He slashed the rest of the nipple off, and it flew across the room aggressively, and splattered into the radio. If politicians knew, they would be proud that the proper and appropriate amount of violence had been restored, and that the weaker, more open-minded and less tough and muscular and caring and loving side had finally been really hurt and suppressed, and that Johnny had solved his problem with the customary and traditional (not to mention *necessary*) violence, for democracy and patriotism to survive. He was also pleased that he had made Guye Armstronge's pages light up with violence so Guye would make more money from the book sales because people just adore violence with blindless enthusiasm. "I cut you for society, Wordsworth" Johnny said. "Oh society, oh how thy leaders adore needless wanton violence, how they would approve of my chopping." "Don't you think it's just going to recreate the same problems if you don't put responsibility for the leader's actions squarely on the shoulders of the people?" Mark shouted from another part of the book. Johnny paused. "Yeah OK well whatever" he said. "So that chop was for politicians, getting in bed – so to speak – with weapons manufacturers and arms dealers, and bad violent people." "Well again, I hope you're not inferring that *only* the upper echelons of society take responsibility for all of the wrongdoing" Mark called from his preachy ranty annoying place. "I mean surely there are people – normal, everyday people – working to build all of those weapons; what would happen if they striked, if they refused?" "Shut up Mark" Johnny said. "I'm chopping up your brother the necromancer bad guye because he looked at me wrong." Mark replied, "So you're taking a cynical position against violence by being violent? How is violence anti-violent?" Johnny wanted the next cut to be for himself, for the satiation of his own bloodlust, not for making any statement about violence in society. "Hey Mark, the next cut's for me!" he shouted. "And be wary" he warned warily. "I'm sure getting a bit weary" Wordsworth wore. "I disagree" Andrew disagreed. "I also disagree" Mark agreed. "Well I'm just greedy" Johnny greed. "Word up" Wordsworth worded. "Oh, my brother, oh society, what hast thou done unto us?" Mark waffled, reading his lines or whatever but I don't think his heart was really in it anymore. Stupid Mark. Johnny poked his knife into the bit of flab below Wordsworth's groin on the inside of his thigh, and twisted it around, much to his delight. He wondered why nobody loved him - if he was like Mark, all open and expressive, everyone would laugh at him and he would then be a new-age loser, and be beaten up. If he was like Wordsworth, all quiet and reclusive, everyone would call him a geek before they even got to know him. "That's for me" he said. "That's because I'm a sick bastard, and I don't know how to control my emotions, and because nobody ever taught me to love." Johnny heaved a sad sigh as he thought about the disjointed relationship he had with his parents. They couldn't even be bothered being in the book with him. They gave him money and rich kid toys instead of love. Johnny suddenly heard a noise from the hall, to which the bunkrooms were adjoined. Someone was about to walk through the doorway after opening the door. He knew he had not a moment nor a quiche to spare. Quickly, he cut bits of himself with the knife, forgetting about the germs - he let the blood from his body run down his rich clothes, making them yellow and stripey green polkadot in hue. He picked Wordsworth up and led him to the centre of the room, and placed the knife in his hand, closing it tightly. He grabbed at Wordsworth's hand, and as the door opened and Mr. Tracheotomy stepped into the room to see that the hut was avalanche and earthquake and fire and hurricane proof, Johnny threw Wordsworth to the ground and fell over himself, and said "Wordsworth's trying to kill himself. He has to be stopped." Mr. Tracheotomy, who was a physical education teacher, wearing only his chest hair, helped Johnny wrestle the nearly dead body of Wordsworth (Johnny only pretended to help - really he was pushing against Wordsworth to make him appear stronger and more crazy and psychotic) to the ground, where Mr. Tracheotomy straddled him, and he and Johnny chopped him all over the body, in an attempt to knock him out and quell his lunacy and his weird activities. Johnny liked Mr. Tracheotomy be-cause he was a good, strong man, who was brisk with efficiency and always knew what he was doing or about to do. Johnny had been in a few of Mr. Tracheotomy's classes over the years, and he had found the physical education side of life a lot more interesting than any other facets at schools, for example teaching English to people who already knew how to speak it, or writing classes where whatever you wrote was INSTANTLEY WRONGE. Johnny also liked physical education classes because the girls would not wear as much clothing as they normally did. Johnny's school was pretty lax about uniforms - students were required by the rule book to wear their full uniform all the time, even in bed when the teachers hopped in for a cuddle, yet few of them bothered to - as long as they got it more or less right they were fine, and Mr. Tracheotomy couldn't have cared less what his classes wore, as long as it didn't constrict their ability to do sit-ups. Mr. Tracheotomy could throw one hell of a punch, Johnny discovered, as his teacher hit Wordsworth in the solar plexus, and the nearly-digested dinner of Ravi Shankar albums and Leon Ulrich books Wordsworth had eaten that night came billowing out of his mouth with the deltoid Johnny had carved out, and all over Mr. Tracheotomy's big ole hairy chest, clinging to it. Johnny quickly stuffed the deltoid back into Wordsworth's mouth where it belonged, while Mr. Tracheotomy was going into a frenzy, with punches and the knife. Johnny thought this was rather amusing to say the least, and he informed Mr. Tracheotomy that Wordsworth was a cheeky one and would stoop to any level to get a joke, and that Mr. Tracheotomy should hit again, this time in the flexypusccicugularities cavitunarildrii. Wordsworth was unconcious after Mr. Tracheotomy's first punch, but Mr. Tracheotomy was not going to be fooled by any weedy necromancer who looked like an insect and thought a computer was more important than push-ups. Mr. Tracheotomy hit again and again, to the triceps, to the the biceps, to the quadraceps, and the fistulaceps and to just about every muscle on Wordsworth's body.

"Where's the left deltoid?" he asked Johnny. Wordsworth lay on the floor, not breathing. "We might have to chop his head off" said Johnny. "To prevent his body from reacting to thoughts his brain has about killing himself." "Yeah wow Johnny wow wow what an amazing genius you are" said Mr. Tracheotomy. "Wanna drink of juice?" Mr. Tracheotomy asked Johnny. "Sure do. This life-saving's thirsty work." "Wanna drink some of Wordsworth's blood?" "No! Now, about this deltoid I didn't get to Punch" Mr. Tracheotomy said, suddenly serious. "It's in his mouth" Johnny told him. "Why is it in his mouth?" "He was trying to eat himself before." "That explains it then. It's the first step in going crazy. Eating yourself. It starts with the deltoids." They walked over to where Wordsworth lay, not breathing. Mr. Tracheotomy kneeled down beside Wordsworth and smashed a few teeth with his huge fist, knocking the deltiod out of his mouth, and somehow getting him breathing again. "Saved him." Mr. Tracheotomy said proudly. "All in a day's work." "Let's call the Mental Hospital" Johnny suggested. "Yeah, good idea. You go and look up their number in the phone book and I'll stop Wordsworth from trying to kill himself again." Johnny went over to the phone, and looked up the mental institution, while Mr. Tracheotomy jumped up and down on Wordsworth's unconcious frail body and chopped off his head, stopping him from hurting anyone. Especially himself. Johnny phoned the looney bin. "Hello, is this the mental institution?" "You bet your best-selling novel about a problem in society." The voice at the other end of the line said. "We've got a mad person here" Johnny said boing boing. "He's recently tried to kill me and himself, he ate one of his deltoids, and he looks like an insect." "Hmmmmm" the recepcionist said. "That sounds like the right symptoms for a mad person. Do you want us to come over right away?" "Yes" Johnny said. "I don't know how long we can hold him." "We'll be over as soon as we can." "Do you think I've got a chance of surviving?" Johnny asked feeling very scared. He breathed a sigh of non-relief. It was extremely epic and had totally taken his breath way away. He was so tired he needed a rest.

Johnny stood at the kitchen sink on the linoleum floor. "Hey man, this fake blood's all sticky and annoying to wash off" Johnny said. "Stupid plastic knife with fake blood-holes." Mark scraped him with a plastic spatula. "Stupid sugary fake blood syrup!" Johnny took his shirt off, pulling the plastic blood-hose out of his sleeve, and unlatching it from the plastic knife. "JOHNNY!" I screamed. "Don't show the readers that it's fake!" Johnny looked around, he was sheepish and guilty. "That violent scene was supposed to be REAL and hard-hitting, you know?" "Sorry Guye" Johnny said, looking at the floor. "Now everyone knows it was all done with a stunt-knife and fake blood. Fuck Johnny, I'm gonna have to edit this. You know I hate editting!" I scratched my head. There was only one thing for it. I stuck my head into the computer, and my mouth went typey-type. Oh, in the ponced-up dictionary of my heart, did I know there was only one thing for it: "Hey can all of you drop a few C-bombs each?" I begged the lads. "Are you sure?" Johnny asked. "Surely swearing *more* isn't going to fix things?" I breathed in and out, nice and slow. I sighed. I gritted my teeth and beared it. I mean I bore it or something, whatever. "Look Johnny: I need a few C-bombs. I can't sacrifice the gritty realism, I need to get it somehow. I have to get the gritty realism demographic sales. Can you and the boys hook me up?" Johnny was stoic. The look on his face told me they would do as I asked. After all, we had come this far. "Isn't that the name of a porno movie?" Wordsworth asked. "Come this far, get it?" "You should know, Wordsworth"

Andrew said. "Stop it lads!" Johnny shouted at their silly time-wasting demographicless banty banter. "Let's give him some C-bombs!" "Oh yeah sure thing" said Mark, "cu " "HAHA THAT WAS A TEST MARK AND YOU FAILED!" I shouted. "Yeah Mark, don't be a corporate sellout" said Andrew. "Yeah Mark you corporate piece of shit" said Johnny. "Damn I *wish* I fitted in!" shouted Mark, bashing his square feet up and down in his round sneakers. "No-one cares about demographics Mark!" we all shouted. After Mark had been roundly beaten and whipped, Johnny went to sleep.

Johnny awoke when they got back to school on a Monday, and he was more tired than he had ever been. He wanted to lie down in his bed and sleep until it was officially summer. He couldn't though. There were a whole group of police people at school who wanted to ask him and Mr. Tracheotomy the same questions again and again and again and again to find out just what had happened to Wordsworth, and so the two of them were stuck in a conference room in their school, bored out of their minds, and wanting to sleep, while the cops kept on coming in and going out of the room and saying "so where did you find this magic lamp?" and "now you're sure that Wordsworth is definitely the bad guye?" Johnny eventually escaped to his dorm, and slept until Wednesday, woke up, had a shower and promptly slept until next Wednesday. Then he got out of the shower. The police had sent Johnny and Mr. Tracheotomy home once their stories had been sorted out again and again. Mr. Tracheotomy's official police report said that he thought Wordsworth was "a bit of a plonker" - Johnny's said "he's mad I tell you. Mad." Wordsworth liked the mental institution because the people there were completely sane. There was a Chinese man there who kept claiming that he saw Gwen Dibley. "I'm a Chinese man who keeps claiming that I see Gwen Dibley!" he would scream during Star Trek, and all the other patients would tell him to shut up and he would be fine until the next time Star Trek was on. There was a German man who was completely sane and just sat in the corner and was totally boring and never did anything. Once Wordsworth asked him why they locked him up. "They locked me up because I'm so silly" the man said sadly with his strong German accent. "I'm a totally sane patient in a mental hospital." "That's a bit silly isn't it?" Wordsworth asked. "That's why they locked me up." For the first time in his miserable life Wordsworth felt welcome somewhere with his fellow mental patients who enjoyed his company, and genuinely liked him. "Get lost" they would say to him. "We may be crazy, but we don't hang out with losers." His trial had been put on hold for a while, so he could go back home and spend some time with his friends who hated him. He would have preferred staying at the mental institution, but at least if he went home he would have a chance to say goodbye to the only *real* friend he had ever had: his computer. Isn't that sweet. "You fuckin nerd" his computer would say to him while it had brutal computer sex over the net. "Get a life." When Mr. Pizazz suggested going back to school, he abruptly refused, unless he could go to a different one. No such talk would be had though. "No such talk will be had though" he informed Wordsworth without any of society's raging emotion. Wordsworth tried to say that there was no way in hell that he was ever going to go back to *that* school ever again, but as usual, his emotions would not allow him the pleasure of complaining. He broke down and cried hot curry zinger sauce tears at the thought of returning to the hell Johnny, Mark and Andrew had made for him, but Mr. Pizazz was ignoring it all. "I'm ignoring it all. Johnny, Mark and Andrew are the best friends you've ever had. I want you to go and apologize to them for being such a nutcase and thank them for all the good times you had with them." Wordsworth could take no more, and he went straight to bed, leaving Mr. Pizazz to his unloving discipline he showed towards everything. No doubt his madness would be all the gossip at school, and Johnny would be exaggerating everything that had happened. Wordsworth was in a real bastard of a situation - he could not even dream of arguing with Johnny as it was far too dangerous. And he awoke the next day to his trial. He dressed somberly, disregarding fashion and casualness - he wore his usual bikini, and faced the music. Then he faced the judge. The judge spoke to him: "You're a dick. So there. Case dismissed." Wordsworth felt good for once in his life. "Get your hands off me" good said. The judge was shocked at Wordsworth's smart attitude, and it took him a poo-and-wee while to regain his composure. "Hurry up and regain your composure" Grid Oblongstrong said to him. "It's nearly the end of the book. It's time for the epic wicked legal thriller climax to get the businessmen-rushing-hurriedly-through-airports demographic." The judge figured that he could not handle such a nasty thing happening to him, and he regained his composure. At least he hadn't been called a silly sausage. "And you're a silly sausage" Wordsworth said to him. Wordsworth had his sentenced lengthened to a whole centimetre. When he was let out, he phoned the hospital. "Can I visit my mother please?" he asked when he was put on to his favourite doctor. "Why do you want to visit her if she's dead?" "I thought she was alive." A great big blob of sadness seemed to fill up Wordsworth's throat. It seemed to take a hold of him, and control him, and make him want to stand on his head. "No that was someone else's mother, sorry. Wrong person.

Did I get your hopes up for a second there? Awfully sorry. Oh, we just removed everything from your father except his feet, because they're the only parts of him which aren't cancerous."

Mr. Woodcock wondered where all the love had gone. "Oh, where was the love?" he wondered, wondering as he wandered, winded breathless. He wanked his wand at the wind. "Oh, love, oh society, society thou dost know love, but only of a plastic type, a short-lived capitalistic advertised sugar-laden customer service artificiality of love... oh how thou hast rambunctious lovers catalysing thy fakery..." No-one knew what Mr. Woodcock was talking about, because no-one was listening to him, because no-one cared. "Oh politicians!" he shouted, doing a pretty rad heelflip-to-nosegrind, one hand reaching up in dramatic flutter to his empassioned brow, "oh politicians politicians, oh, oh oh oooh, in the forward pass of your betrayal, where is thy love? Oh politicans, why dost thou not care about my ollie-fakeys?" Mr. Woodcock wondered where society's love had gone, and he looked for it. He looked in the cupboards and he looked under the stairs. He even looked in the overhead baggage compartment, but there was not love, there was only society's mass of emotional baggage, and it fell all over him, totally ruining his holiday, and the sweet kickflip he would have landed otherwise. The stewardess appeared. "Mr. Woodcock, please don't touch the baggage compartment, we don't want all of society's emotional baggage falling out." "Oh society, oooh society, oh the unprotected penetration of thy class mobility" Mr. Woodcock whimpered. Mr. Tracheotomy, who had recently become head of the Colouring-In Department, and Mr. Woodcock were totally chilling out in the teacher's lounge, back at school. The TV was on. A table. Mr. Woodcock wanted the remote control. Some of Mr. Tracheotomy's family were closer to the remote control than Mr.

Woodcock, who wanted it (I mean he wanted the remote control). "Hey Mr. Tracheotomy kin can you pass me the remote control DO IT NOW DO IT NOW!?" he shouty-asked. Oh, how he wanted, how he desired, how he needed so desperately the remote control, how dissatisfied he was with whatever channel was on, how he yearned... in love so captive... in passion so clanging like a welder just chucking aluminium or whatever bollocks offcuts onto the concrete floor... hard, like an alpha male overcompensating for his insecure daddy and cultural issues... of his workshop and not really giving a fuck about the apprentice who always cleaned up after him, how he wanted to file cases of divorce lawyers against the current channel that was being screamed and screened and squeaked over the airwaves into the gloppy gloop of his brain, how tumultish tumult rocked his desire the fuck all over the mosh pit of his heart, banging into the goths and really hardcore black metal spiky bogans of the Scandinavian wasteland of his visceral bereftness of unfulfilment, deep in the divorce court of his soul where the stenographer of his lust recited the channel-changing yearning to the judge of his brain through the mathematics of his occipital lobe which wanted to make him push his thumb so hard, so turgid, so rigid and erect with scandalous betraying desire to the channel that was on, how he wanted his relationship with that channel to end, how his thumb insertion placement upon the remote control's most intimate place would make him a cheater forever... forever... forever. "OK here bro" said Mr. Tracheotomy, whose long arms actually didn't have any problem reaching the remote and throwing it close to Mr. Woodcock. "Thank you" said Mr. Woodcock. Oh, how he said thank you, how he expressed and vented to his fellow teachy compatriot, how he unleashed a mighty hurricane of gratitude, how his tongue and lips and teeth and buccinators and masseters and voice box and dangling weird epiglotty bit danced together in multiple cavortions of harmonising emotion so urgent and mighty and strong, how he said the words in the language they spoke to make the words 'thank you' spray out of his mouth, how Mr. Woodcock had flung those empassioned, glorious words into the earhole of Mr. Tracheotomy where they straddled his inner ear, tearing off the clothes of his earwax from the supple nubile tender curved femininity of his eardrum, where they totally power-boned his ear drum in missionary and doggy style and reverse cowgirl and heaps of cool positions, and oh, oh oh oooh, how those wordlets had totally sonically jizzed in Mr. Tracheotomy's ear and went bouncey bounce into his brain and made him feel like he was cool and sweet as.

Mark put the oversized wig, silly hat and wacky inventor glasses on the dinosaur fossil that he had spent countless years and hours adjusting, after incredible amounts of painstaking research getting it just right. "It's like pterodactyl correctness gone mad" Andrew said. This occurred not at the ski hut but at the museum, in the Dinosaur Jokes Department of their school, in America. The hut was as quiet as a writer's social life. Nothing was happening. Nothing at all. That's because they had all left the hut, the ski season was over! They were not at the hut. They were not at the mountain. They were back at the school. And it was written – yay, write here was it written so, yay in the most tender romance of harking, that Johnny did squeeze Deborah's shoulders with all his might, "never let go" he said and she whimpered, he pushed her away then pulled her ever closer as she fought, and eventually yielded to his passionate love, as he gazed into her deep blue beers. "Why is this fuckin' beer *blue?*" he asked. "Bro just drink it stop being a pussy you fuckin' faggot!" she said. And even though she was a bit of a bloody drongo, his love still charged her with the perfect precision and accuracy of Mike Brewer's pass to John Kirwan in the 1992 Bledisloe Cup game against Australia which led to a pretty sweet as try scored by Frank Bunce, chur Buncey.

CHAPTER 18: THE BIT ABOUT MR. WOODCOCK'S SEXUAL RELIEF - THE BIT MY MUM SAW ME WRITING AND SAW A RUDE BIT AND TOLD ME SHE HOPED THE WHOLE BOOK WASN'T LIKE THAT AND I SAID OF COURSE NOT IT'S SHOWING SOCIETY'S ILLS AND SHE SAID OK BUT I DON'T KNOW IF SHE TOTALLY BELIEVED ME

MR. WOODCOCK'S SEXUAL RELIEF WAS THE RESPON-SIBILITY OOoops. Forgot to turn the Caps Lock off. Sorry. I'll start that bit again. But you know, all great writers love the old Caps Lock. Probably safer to overuse it than underuse it, right? Of course! Of course of course, I'M ALWAYS RIGHT! "Guye Armstronge couldn't beat me up" Wordsworth whispered to Mark. "He's such a lazy writer he just uses caps lock all the time, he can't even bother doing italics. When I want to emphasize something I talk in ITALICS, I'm not CHEAP AND LAZY like him, I don't use caps lock" Wordsworth said all smug and proud, unaware I had edited his bullshit italics away with the awesomeness of my capsing lock JUST TO PROVE THAT LITTLE BITCH WRONG YEAH BOIII! Mr. Woodcock's sexual relief was the responsibility of – "Nyah, I'm interrupting this bit!"

Wordsworth shouted, as he barged into the maths room. Johnny stood aloft three desks put on top of a whole pile of desks. He raged at the evil bad guye. Wordsworth leapt, fell down upon him, and ran for cover, as Gravity Altitudestrong's pinky finger, soaring so high above the clouds, higher than a teenage love, itching with energy, only *just* missed the delete button! "How about a book-finishing button?" Andrew yawnterrupted. "I won't need it" said Guye, whose delete button had recently been fitted with particle accelerator laser beams that did PLUS EIGHTEEN fire damage. "Plus *eighteen* fire damage, bit unfair?" Andrew complained cynically, throwing the dice angrily across the desk to roll for his random magic item. "Whoever's got you on their side is going to win." "No, I'm not on anyone's side" said Guye Armstronge, "I'm just the Dungeon Master." "Wow you don't sound pretentious at all when you say 'master'" said Andrew, gratitude made obvious by complete negation of sarcasm. "OK so it's me and Wordsworth against you guys" Mr. Woodcock said to Johnny, Andrew and Mark. "Let's get them, Wordsworth."

"Wow, THE ENDING" said Mr. Pizazz. He rubbed his hands, surely he would have a really exciting part in the ending of the greatest epic novel ever written of our time ever ever ever. "Ah, OK hang on a minute" Guye Armstronge said to him, shuffling through all the mounds of rejection letters stuck to his desk by coffee stains and trying to find the plot stuff he'd hastily scrawled on the back of them. "Sorry, I totally forgot about you, I thought I deleted you on like the fourth draft or whatever." "Wow you actually do more than one draft, that's exactly what I would have expected" said Andrew, again with absolutely zero sarcasm. "Which team do you want me to go on?" Mr. Pizazz asked, not smirking a little at what Andrew had said and still looking very professional. "Just go on one of their teams, I don't mind which one" Guye told him. "Yeah, but which team?" "I don't mind, I... I mean... I don't think it really matters." "Yeah it's just the massive finale of the book, it's only the ending, it doesn't matter, it's not really important in any way" said Andrew, who definitely could not be sarcastic even if he tried. "Yeah well" Guye Armstronge said to Andrew, "Mr. Pizazz is the principal so I'm not totally sure what team he should go on." "SKATE OR DIE, BRAH!" Mr. Woodcock shouted. "We're in love and I'm in Wordsworth's team" he said, pulling a pretty sweet kickflip. "Nah, dude, gay" said Wordsworth. "I'd rather go on my own, I'm a necromancer. I've got an army of undead at my every whim −" "But Wordsworth you never said that you summoned any undead yet so there's no-one there so maybe he *should* go on your team" said Johnny. "No I always have them Johnny" Wordsworth said. "They're like automatically being raised from the dead every turn. "Well I'll be on your team and I'll calculate how many there are" said Mr. Woodcock and slurped Wordsworth's ear a bit which he thought turned Wordsworth on but which was really a bit gross and made Wordsworth a bit annoyed and everyone thought he was a pedo and maybe a bit sick, but it was near the end so they didn't care. "It's like a massive undead army, it's like a tidal wave of undead, bro, it's like there's too many to count." "No, *bullshit* Wordsworth" said Mark, "Raise Dead spell only summons one skeleton for d6+1 turns, I remember you told me that one time, and you were worried about you had a small army, remember? Remember when you told me?" "Yeah" said Wordsworth, "but a turn is like ages so it doesn't matter, and I would have summoned heaps by now, so like, just pretend there's hundreds and thousands of skeletons and undead vampires and stuff everywhere!" "But there's no graveyards around here, how can you summon them if there's no dead bodies?" Mark asked. Wordsworth pretended to not hear it as he started rolling for the amount of hit dice for his Black Dragon, which was a bit bullshit because he hadn't even summoned it yet. "Wordsworth? How can you have undeads without any graveyards, we never went to a graveyard?" "Well, just... just pretend we did and *anyway I'm such an awesome necromancer I don't even NEED a graveyard.*" "Which team do you want me on?" Mr. Pizazz asked again. "Yeah bro I don't care" said Wordsworth, who I felt was totally trying to take over the ending of the book or something. "Just go on their team." "Just go on anyone's team!" I shouted a little bit louder than Wordsworth to show that I was still in charge of everything in the whole world. "I don't care which team you go on!" "But which team is the best team for me to go on?" "Bro you're supposed to be all decisive and know what to do! Can you stop worrying and just make it cool?" "Just go on their team" said Wordsworth, but a bit quieter, he knew that his mummies would probably fail their save vs. fire and die really quickly against my +18 fire damage delete button. And it did electrical damage and acid damage too. "Well I'm on Wordsworth's team with the vampires, I hope you guys don't have silver weapons" said Mr. Woodcock. "Wow, vampires" said Andrew. "That's not a giant cliché. Knowing Guye Armstronge they'll probably all start shagging and making out and getting on each other's third base in the first round of battle so he gets the disillusioned gothic young people demographic." "Well they're not romantic teenage vampires" said Wordsworth. "They're like, all blood-drenched, and they're level twenty and −" "they can't be level twenty, that's so unfair" said Mark. "It won't matter if they're all making out and in relationships with each other and infighting so Guye Armstronge gets the goth demographic" Andrew said without sounding arrogant in any way at all. "Hey Andrew I don't CARE about the goth demographic" said Guye Armstronge, but Andrew was sure he peeked out of the computer and saw Guye open a MS Excel document and type 'goth demographic' into it while he looked a bit frustrated that he hadn't thought of it until the very end of the book. "These vampires aren't teen vampires they're ancient, really old, vampire *Lords*" said Wordsworth. "They're really old and powerful, that's why they're level twenty and there won't be any making out or relationships." Johnny looked bored, and Mark looked a bit interested, a bit excited maybe, like turned on by a bunch of old men like as if they were his sugar-daddies. "Hey Johnny, can you not look bored" Guye Armstronge asked. "Sorry Guye, I slipped out of character" Johnny apologized. "I don't care about your stupid gay vampires Wordsworth cos me and Andrew have an atomic bomb." "Ah, it's fantasy" said Wordsworth, "so you can't have a bomb, cos it's in the past." "We time travelled it in or whatever, with, like magic or some bullshit" said Johnny. "So I don't even need to roll dice or anything, fuck your gay dice bro, you're all dead Wordsworth, all your team, your skeletons and whatever. Now let's go and watch the rugby."

They stormed the castle. Wordsworth shouted from the spire in a big loud voice "OK *first* initiative roll phase, *then* choose weapons phase, *then* magic phase, *then* attack phase, in *that* order, OK? No exceptions!" "Ah... nerd alert, nerd alert" said Andrew and Johnny together as they played some rugby and drank beers. "Hang on Wordsworth I'm not even on a team yet" said Mr. Pizazz.

"OK I'm summoning a Black Dragon everybody, you guys are *so* dead" Wordsworth shouted. "OK I'll be on your team Wordsworth" said Mr. Pizazz. "NO I DON'T WANT ANYONE IN MY TEAM I'M A NECROMANCER!" "Sorry Wordsworth" said Mr. Pizazz, "I'm in your team in a senior management role, possibly even a Chief Executive. I'm appointing your highest level lich to take all the responsibilities of the customer service department, this will streamline efficiency." "Necromancers don't care about money and capitalism!" Wordsworth complained. "Well in that case let me say it plainly" Mr. Pizazz plained. "Complaints have to go through the complaints department, we can't have disagreements between senior management – remember, I'm *assuming* you're in a senior management role, but I will demote you into a more simple admin role if there's any antagonism – now: the company website isn't up and running yet, so you'll have to wait a few days for the I.T. department to get that sorted, *then* you'll be able to complain. *Don't* reply to the autoreply email though. Now looking at the number of skeletons here, hmmm, we're looking at a ratio of mummies to skeletons of about three to twenty, so if you could just summon –" "HANG ON I'M THE BAD GUYE NO-ONE TELLS ME WHAT TO SUMMON!" Wordsworth screamed. "I'm the fucking Undead Lord!" "OK fuck you guys I'm going to the pub" said Mr. Pizazz. It was Johnny's blah blah turn. "Hey Wordsworth. Wordsworth. Hey Wordsworth" said Johnny with a big fat obese grin on his face. "If you're a necromancer why are you wearing a bikini? Shouldn't you be in robes or something a bit more serious?" Guye Armstronge threw his keyboard down on his desk, but not too hard because he didn't want to break it and have to nag his mum to buy him a new one. He screamed into the night! "OH GOD WORDSWORTH YOU FUCKIN' BOOK-RUINER!" "It's a good thing you didn't throw your keyboard down too hard because it wouldn't have been cushioned by piles of rejection letters" Andrew unsarcastically said to Guye. "WORDSWORTH PUT YOUR *FUCKIN'* ROBES ON MATE ALREADY!" Then Johnny, using Guye Armstronge's almighty backspace key, obliterated Wordsworth's castle door from existence. "Aaaaah, it doesn't count Johnny" Wordsworth said, "you have to select it with the mouse and shift key first and you never said that so it doesn't count, it's still there." "That's bullshit Wordsworth, you know what I mean! The castle door's gone, now me and Andrew are attacking." "And we're drinking all our potions" Andrew added. "Well I'm gonna cancel out your potions by casting some really negative spells" Wordsworth subtracted.

It took Wordsworth a few turns to summon his Black Dragon. He uttered incredible words of strange power and mystique. His magnificent dragon appeared. It had a huge afro, sunglasses, dark healthy skin and proud, large lips. Its trousers hung lazily around its lower waist, sagging, and it wore Air Jordans and a backwards Starter cap. "Yeah, here to redeem y'all suckers from the man, man" it said, bouncing a basketball. "Oh damn!" shouted Wordsworth, torn and forlorn. "It's the wrong kind of black!" Mark dropped the cake he was eating all over the floor, and screamed. "What do you mean 'the wrong kind of black' Wordsworth? You bloody racist!" "Yeah Wordsworth, there isn't a 'right kind of black'!" I shouted at him through the computer screen. "You book-ruining racist!" "Yeah whatever I'm not a racist but I meant black like undead dragon, like a zombie dragon!" "Wordsworth stop being so RACIST!" Mark shouted – oh I shouted it as well, I hate racism. "Hey man, you jive turkey fool!" the black dragon shouted, spinning around and planting a side thrust kick into Wordsworth's stomach. Wordsworth fell off the castle and into the moat, where he went splat, and when he walked back up into the castle everyone went ha ha you dick bro cos he was all wet and gross and dirty. Oh, and none of their novels ever did get published. Or if they did it took ages, like way after this book ended and no-one cared, and only their mums and close friends read them and it didn't really help society, oh society oooh. "Oh wow, so art *does* imitate life" unsarcastic Andrew said. They all got ready to chop Wordsworth up into little bits. "STOP!" Mark shouted. "Can't we solve our problems peacefully? I don't like the way we have to have a battle; I mean why should war be the final solution?" "Yeah that's actually a really good point" said Guye Armstronge. "I'm really glad I made you think it and say it." And they sorted out all their problems peacefully, after they brutally murdered everyone they didn't like.

THE END